When the Killing Starts

When the Killing Starts

A REID BENNETT MYSTERY

Ted Wood

CHARLES
SCRIBNER'S
SONS

NEW YORK

Charles Scribner's Sons
Macmillan Publishing Company
866 Third Avenue, New York, NY 10022
Collier Macmillan Canada, Inc.

This is a work of fiction. Names, characters, places,
and incidents either are the product of the author's
imagination or are used fictitiously. Any resem-
blance to actual events or persons, living or dead, is
entirely coincidental.

Library of Congress Cataloging-in-Publication Data
Wood, Ted.
  When the killing starts : a Reid Bennett mystery /
  Ted Wood.
      p.   cm.
  ISBN 0-684-18331-5
  I. Title.
PR9199.3.W57W4   1989
813'.54—dc19   88-18441   CIP

      10 9 8 7 6 5 4 3 2 1

Printed in the United States of America

For my sister, Ann Hughes,
"She settled for the looks."

When the Killing Starts

ONE

◆

We were celebrating. At least I was trying to. Freda's good news had come too soon for me. We'd been back together a couple of weeks after a year and a half apart, and now she was heading out of town for a month.

"Here's to success," I said, anyway, smiling and lifting my pint of English ale.

"I'll drink to that," she said, and lifted her own pint. I noticed, as any beer drinker would, that it was the same deep chestnut color as her hair. That's not poetic, but it's accurate. She's a looker, and right now she looked even more traffic stopping than usual. She's tall and slim without being skinny, nicely shaped, good complexion, bright blue Viking eyes. I had to wonder why she hadn't got the lead in the movie instead of the second spot.

She took a healthy glug out of her beer and put the glass down. "There're no skin shots," she said. "I asked them right off. A month ago I might have gone for a little modest flesh on camera, but not now."

"Well, that's a relief for an abandoned boyfriend. There're enough guys grooving on your bod already."

"You're a chauv," she said cheerfully. "But you don't have to worry. It's an aspect of the job that's never appealed."

1

"I'm glad to hear it. It seems that every movie I've seen lately has the clothes off the actresses before they've finished printing out who the cameraman and director are."

She laughed and reached over and squeezed my arm. "You're going to have to start calling them the credits," she said. "Anyway, there's no need to worry your tiny Puritan mind. I'm covered to the chin all the way through."

"And I guess that's why they didn't give you the lead."

"That plus they wanted a name. They've hired Rita Wallace for that part. She gets to roll about in the altogether with the male lead. Not that she's in any jeopardy. From what I hear, he doesn't like girls very much."

"And you're the second lead."

"Right. I'm the star's roomie. I get to give her good advice and cry when she goes off to marry Roger at the end. Hell, I'm playing a schoolmarm; that should put your mind at ease."

"It is at ease," I lied. We were getting on fine. Part of our reunion had happened up in Murphy's Harbour, the resort town where I'm the Law, all of it. Freda—she prefers to be called Fred—had come visiting and wound up helping me solve a homicide. Now we were back in Toronto for a month, checking out whether the fireworks we'd found were permanent. I was also going over my plans for the future. I've been the police chief at Murphy's Harbour for a couple of years, maybe it was time to move on. Only I wasn't sure where. The only skills I have are police work and an ability to put people down so they stay down when things get rugged. That doesn't open up many choices of career path. I hadn't yet made up my mind about quitting.

Fred leaned over and kissed me, a real kiss, not the kind she would have doled out if she was serious about acting.

We disengaged, and she looked at me. "I'm sorry this came up, Reid. You're a good guy for not making a fuss about it. It may be the last part I take, and I'd like to end whatever career I've got with a bang, not a whimper."

"End, hell," I said cheerfully. "Your next stop is Hollywood."

"I'm not sure I'd go," she said. "I like what I've got here."

"Me, too." I gave her arm a squeeze. She was right down under my skin.

Fred looked at me almost sadly. "Why don't you come with me? It's a nothing location, we're living in trailers, but there's lots of room in mine."

"No, I'd cramp your style. You'll do better work if I'm not hanging around looking jealous." It was my excuse but not my real reason. I had no intention of trailing along behind her, the joke boyfriend while all the cameramen and technicians tried not to say how much they wanted to get her and the other women in the cast into bed. I've never been around a film crew, but they figured to be like all the other groups of men I've worked with.

"As long as you're not jealous," she said softly. "I'm a one-man woman, Reid. I don't want you to get away, and I'm not going to do anything that might make that happen."

"Nor am I," I said, and she winked at me. "Come on, finish your beer, we still have all night to say good-bye."

"Parting is such sweet sorrow," I said, and she laughed.

"I'm the thespian in this team, Bennett, don't get carried away."

We raised our pints to one another, and then the shouting started, four feet behind her, at the bar. I glanced up. A young guy, around twenty, was arguing with the barmaid, and gradually his language slipped off the edge and became foul. Fred winced. "Nice guy," she said.

He must have heard her. He whirled and loomed over her, one hand on the back of her chair. "You say something, lady?"

3

I stood up. "Get lost."

He straightened up. He was my height, just over six feet and solid, muscle-builder's muscles, by the look of them, bulging prettily under his T-shirt with "Life's a bitch and then you die" printed on it.

"You talking to me?" The standard bar question.

"Shut up and leave," I told him softly.

"Or what? What the fuck you gonna do about it?"

I smiled at him, into his eyes and down about three feet into his soul. "You really don't want to find out, son."

His mouth dropped open to speak, and then he crumbled. "Fuck you," he said, and turned away. "Fuck all of you," he shouted. But he left without looking back.

Fred was shaky. She tried a laugh, but it came out troubled. "You do neat work, Reid."

I shrugged. "I don't like loudmouths. Come on, let's climb on my white horse and head back to your place."

"Good idea." She stood up and took my hand, and we walked out. I went ahead of her through the door. It wasn't gallant, but I wasn't sure that the guy from the bar wouldn't be waiting out there, mustering his courage for a second attempt. He wasn't, and we walked back to her apartment building and rode up to the eighth floor.

"Now," she said softly, "it's about that long good-bye."

By three the next afternoon we were all good-byed out, and Fred was packed to go. "Why don't you come with me?" she asked again.

"I'd be in the way," I said. "I'd like to be with you, but not in the middle of a crowd scene."

"It will be a zoo," she admitted. "But there's always the nights."

"Get lots of sleep. It's good for the complexion."

She took the suitcase out of my hand and set it down. "You're an obstinate SOB, Bennett. But if you won't come with me, let's say good-bye here," she said softly. "In private." I held her, and we did the thing properly.

4

Then she said, "Don't worry about me, Reid. I'm your girl."

"Never thought otherwise," I said, but it didn't convince her.

"Don't. Ever," she said, and pressed her fingertips to my lips. Then she bent for the suitcase, but I beat her to it.

"Porter service is part of the deal."

"Chauv." She grinned and picked up her carryon bag. The phone rang. She let it ring twice, smiling to show me how clever she was being, then answered, listened, and said, "Yes, may I tell him who's calling?"

She covered the mouthpiece as she passed me the phone. "Says her name is Norma Michaels."

I frowned. The name meant nothing to me. Then I took the phone. "Hello, Reid Bennett speaking."

"Hello." She sounded fortyish. "You don't know me."

"No, ma'am. I don't think I do."

"You don't," she said anxiously. "But I got your name from Simon Fulwell. You know him?"

"Yes. I know Simon." Fulwell was in security. I'd met him up at Murphy's Harbour when a man from his company's New York office had been killed.

"Mr. Fulwell works, at least his company works, for my husband. I wanted someone to carry out an assignment for me, so I called him, and he recommended you."

"I see. What kind of assignment?"

"Well, it's a long story," she began, and I cut her off.

"Then I'm sorry, it'll have to wait a little. I'm just driving to the airport."

"You're not leaving?" Her voice was panicky.

"No, seeing someone off. Can I call you later?"

"Yes, of course. Or I could come and see you. When would be convenient?"

I thought about that for a moment. I'm not much for entertaining. I never know whether to lay out chips and onion dip. Besides, I didn't know this woman, and I

5

didn't want the doorman at the apartment thinking I was moving in a replacement for Fred. "I've got a better idea," I said. "I'll meet you at the Duke of Marlborough, north of Eglinton on Yonge. Say, five o'clock."

"That will be fine," she said. "How will I recognize you?"

"I'm wearing a green check shirt and gray slacks. Thirty-seven, dark, six one, one eighty."

"You'll stand out, I'm sure," she said ambiguously.

"Thank you."

"You're welcome," I said, and hung up.

Fred frowned. "If I hadn't answered the phone myself, I'd think you were setting up a blind date."

"Some woman looking for help. A friend of mine put her on to me." I thought about that and frowned. "I guess he must have called my sister and she gave him this number."

"Sure." Fred grinned. "I still think you're lining up my replacement."

"Impossible," I told her. "Anyway, I guess we should get going." I bent and took the suitcase. Sam, my German shepherd, stood up when he saw we were leaving, and Fred said, "Let him come with us, he'll be glad to see me go. He can have you to himself again."

The whole cast was flying out together, to Regina and then on to a small town on the prairies somewhere. There were a couple of reporters around, following the star, one of those over-thin blondes you see on talk shows on TV. She was the known personality, but the photographers concentrated on Fred, whose name was still in the news over the homicide case she'd helped me solve. They also took a shot of her with me, hoping to get some angle, I guessed, to spin out the news value they could wring from Fred, the actress turned detective.

The star, Rita Wallace, was too professional to act bitchy for the press, but I was treated to a little demonstration of upstaging as she suddenly found that I was the most fascinating person she had ever met and poured charm all over me like coconut oil. She managed to squeeze Fred out of the picture completely, but over her shoulder I saw Fred wink at me. Then they went, Fred giving me just the quickest of kisses. "A good job we spent the morning saying good-bye," she whispered. "Call you tomorrow, around seven."

"Sure," I told her. "Break a leg. Preferably Rita's."

She laughed and went, the last one through the security gate. I waved once and then left.

It was Saturday afternoon, and there was a fair amount of idle summertime traffic, but I made it back to the Duke of Marlborough by ten to five. I left Sam in the car, with all the windows down, and went into the pub, ordered a pint, and stood at the bar, looking around for someone who answered the description I'd formed in my mind.

The place was quiet: a few yuppie couples back from shopping, relaxing before heading off to their apartments to cook squid; one or two older men who looked as if they worked in advertising agencies, dressed expensive casual, their hair too long, their mustaches a little too ferocious. And then I saw a likely woman in a booth on her own. She looked rich. Her hair was a sleek helmet, and she had the kind of casual cotton blouse on that they advertise in magazines Fred took. She was sitting in a booth with something pink in a glass in front of her. It looked as if she hadn't touched it. She stood up and made to come out of the booth, but I beat her to it, ambling over, carrying my pint.

"Mrs. Michaels?"

"Yes. You're Mr. Bennett?" I nodded, and she stuck out a hand with a big yellow-stone ring on it. Her hand was cool, the overall impression I had of her. Forty-five, I reckoned, and on the way to her third face-lift.

"Pleased to meet you," I said.

She waved at the seat opposite, and I sat, looking at her and waiting for the next move.

"Thank you for seeing me. I understand you're on vacation." She reminded me of an executive with a new employee, gracious but distant.

"Yes," I said.

"Mr. Fulwell told me you were in town with your . . ." She paused, seeking out the least obnoxious way of describing someone else's lover.

"I think 'significant other' is the expression they use today."

She managed a tiny laugh. From the mouth only, saving the wear and tear around her eyes. "I suppose it is," she said. "Has she gone away?"

"She's an actress. She's on location on a movie, out west."

"How exciting," she said, trying not to be condescending. Not my type of woman, no spontaneity.

"She's pleased." I sipped my beer. "You said something about an assignment."

"I hardly know where to start," she said. "I mean, you don't know me or anything about me. This was just an idea I had. I was desperate, but now I feel a little foolish about taking up your time."

"I've got a month before I go back to my job."

She did the same automatic smile, a finishing-school smile. I imagined the nuns had given her six out of ten for it.

I sat and waited, and she went on, slowly. "It's about my son." She stopped again, and I waited. This was hard for her; that was all I'd picked out of the impression so far. This was work.

"He's done something foolish," she said.

I held up one hand. "I guess Simon, Fulwell, that is, told you I'm a copper, so if your son's done anything illegal, you should be talking to a lawyer, not to me."

She shook her head. Her hair moved all of a piece. It was fascinating to watch. "No, not illegal. Just foolish. Very foolish. Very dangerous." She took a sudden quick

8

gulp of her drink and rushed on. "He's joined a force of mercenaries."

I almost laughed out loud. "Mercenaries? In Canada?"

She didn't laugh. "Yes," she said softly. "I didn't know there were any groups like that in this country, but he found one, and he joined it."

There were a lot of questions to ask, but I started with the easy ones. "How old is he?"

"Twenty. But a very immature twenty." She sipped her drink again and waved one hand dismissively. "We're quite wealthy, and Jason is, well, he's spoiled, I suppose. He went to university for a year, and then, when he found it took work, he dropped out and he's been, let's say, trying to find himself ever since. That's almost a year."

I gave her a policeman's response. "You realize that he's of age. Once he's over sixteen in this province, he can do what he likes as long as it's legal. What you say he's done is dumb, but not necessarily illegal."

"Yes, I know that," she said quietly. "I went to the police when I got his note, but they told me what you just said. As long as he isn't involved with some terrorist group, there's nothing they can do for me, or for him."

"Does this group he joined have a name?"

"They call themselves Freedom for Hire." Her voice gave the group all its capital letters. "They're run by a man who is, or says he is, a former paratrooper from the British army."

"You're telling me your son put all of this into a farewell letter?" I was frowning at the thought. A twenty-year-old dropout wouldn't go into that kind of detail. Any note he would leave would probably consist of "Screw you."

"No." She shook her head dismissively. "No, but the day he left, the day before yesterday, he came in very late, about two in the morning. I was up at the time, and we had a discussion." She stopped herself and considered the statement. "Well, more of a row, really. He told me he'd been out drinking with some men, real men. They had talked to him about going and training with them, then heading off for somewhere warm to . . . to kick ass. Sorry about the language, but that's what he said."

That's what he would have said. Beer and machismo talking. I'd heard it before, done my share of it, for that matter, as a nineteen-year-old marine on the way to Vietnam. That was before we met the Vietcong. After that, we had stopped making promises we weren't always able to keep.

"Any idea where all this kicking is going to take place?"

"Somewhere warm was all he said." She blinked and swatted at her eyes with the back of her hand. "It could mean Central America, Africa, anywhere. From the way he was talking, he thought he would be fighting ignorant tribesmen or something. But those nations all have professional armies. He's going to get killed."

I sipped my beer and thought for a moment. "Not being personal, Mrs. Michaels, but what does his father say?"

"His father is out of the country. In Geneva at the moment, on business. But it wouldn't have made any difference; he and Jason don't get on."

That was part of the answer I needed. We were talking about a sore-assed dropout. It explained the breadth of his gesture, if nothing else.

"Have you told your husband what's happened?"

"I called him yesterday. Jason had left the night before; just threw some clothes in a bag and went, left his car in the garage. My husband told me to hire a private detective to trace Jason and persuade him not to go along with this scheme." She was in control again, holding her glass with both hands, staring into it as if it were a crystal ball.

"And have you done that?"

"Of course. I tried, immediately I hung up. I retained a Mr. Broadhurst. His was the first name I came to in the yellow pages. He's a man in his late fifties, I'd say. I just don't think he's capable of following this up the way it should be followed up."

"How so?" I knew what she meant. I just wanted her to spell it out for the record.

She raised one hand and flapped it, a teenager's trick. Something else she'd picked up twenty-five years ago in finishing school, but not from the staff. "I believe these men are dangerous. Potentially, anyway. I don't think Mr. Broadhurst would be forceful enough to persuade them to relinquish their hold, whatever it is, on Jason."

I thought about it for a minute. It was less painful than thinking about a month without Fred in my life. "You said he was going to get trained first. Any idea where?" I knew that there are camps set up in places in the Everglades or the Appalachians where an army could work out without attracting notice. And if this group really was Canadian, there were millions of square miles where they could train without anybody knowing they were there.

"I'm not sure. I don't think he was, either," she said with another synthetic smile. "The only thing was, he was acting so contemptuously about Canada that I got the impression they would be training here. He said that this was a dumb country and people could get away with anything here."

I didn't say anything. We have the liberties and the geography to make that statement true, except for the dumb part. I didn't like the sound of young Michaels.

"Two questions," I said at last. "First, are you sure he's done what he said, or is he just trying to scare you? Second, did your detective make any progress in tracing them?

11

"Yes. And no. Yes, he left a note, but no, Mr. Broadhurst didn't have any success. At least he hadn't by four o'clock today."

"And is he still looking?"

She looked me square in the face. Her eyes were gray, almost colorless. Since knowing Fred, I'd learned something about theatrical makeup, and I could see that she went heavy on the mascara, trying to take away the chill in her eyes. "He's getting three hundred dollars a day. Yes, he's still looking. But I don't think that's enough."

"What would you expect me to do that was different?"

She cleared her throat. "I was hoping you'd apply police techniques to the search. And if you found the men, you would talk to them. From what Mr. Fulwell told me, when you talk, people listen."

Fat chance. Her son wouldn't. He would dismiss me as a washed-up over-thirty copper. He wouldn't know I'd traveled the same road, only legitimately, leaving Canada to join the U.S. Marines. There was a lot of it going on back then, in the late sixties. It was almost fashionable for an angry kid from an ugly mining town in the bush.

"I don't think they will, but what makes you think I'll drop everything and do it? I'm on vacation."

"I can pay you," she said, and although she was still nervous, she was regaining her confidence. Paying was something she was good at. "His safety is very important to me, to his whole family, Mr. Bennett. I could pay you twenty-five thousand dollars."

"That sounds like a lot of money for making a few phone calls and talking to your son. What else did you think this job would entail?" I'm a little old to believe in Santa Claus.

She gave me another of her no-nonsense looks. "I imagine these are hard men. You could run into some arguments or something, perhaps worse."

Perhaps a lot worse, I thought. Perhaps I'd find myself arguing with a bunch of tough ex-SAS men from Britain, and a few automatic weapons as well. I would need a lot more than a golden tongue to get out of that one without having somebody hand me my head.

I sat and considered the offer. Twenty-five thousand was a lot of money, almost as much as Fred stood to make from her movie part. That was its biggest attraction. I didn't want to be the poor partner in our relationship. If I could salt a few dollars away, it would prop up my poor bruised ego. I'm chauvinist when it comes to having my girl earn more than me.

"And if I say I'll do it, when do you plan to pay me?"

A man would have said, "Right now," and reached into his pocket. She said, "Would you?" and the tears glinted in those icy eyes.

I said nothing for a moment, still thinking. The job didn't appeal to me. It didn't ring true, and part of me resisted being in debt to this woman. The money meant nothing to her, but once she had paid it out, she would figure she owned me. "I might," I said at last.

She reached out her hand impulsively. It was her left hand, and I caught sight of her wedding ring, a nugget of gold set with big diamonds. She had money and didn't mind people knowing it. "Please say you will." She whispered it. "This means so much to me. Jason is very important to me."

"All right. I'll try," I said.

She reached into her purse. It was on the seat next to her, a battered-looking leather thing that had probably come from Italy and cost a thousand dollars. She dug into it for a moment and came out with a check.

"You had a check already written out?"

"Yes," she said, surprised I was asking. Very few people ever said no to her.

"You seem like a woman who's used to getting her own way."

She paused with the check in her hand. Then she tried a little laugh, only it came out sour. "Is that a judgment, Mr. Bennett?"

"An observation. Most people would have waited before putting those kinds of figures on paper."

She shook her head. "Money is just that," she said. "Just figures on pieces of paper. I want my son back. I'd do anything to have that happen." She paused again and looked at me levelly. "Anything," she repeated.

"The money will be sufficient," I said, and dots of white appeared on either side of her nose. She was angry, but she handed me the check. I read it over. Everything was in order. She'd put the proper number of zeros on it, my name was spelled with two Ts.

"Thank you. Consider me hired," I said. "Now let me ask some questions."

We sat and went over everything I could think of. Who were Jason's friends? Where had he gone to school? Had he found himself a steady girlfriend? I was hoping that somewhere in the plush fabric of his life there might be a thread that would lead to where he was, someone he had boasted to, something.

The picture that emerged was of a spoiled, rich loner. No friends of any consequence, girls or boys. No real interests. If he had liked to play trombone or shoot pool or even listen to one kind of music, it might have led me somewhere useful, but there was nothing like that. He had hung around the house most of the time, lying in bed until afternoon, watching TV. At night he had drifted out, she didn't know where. He sounded like an ideal candidate for an outfit like Freedom for Hire, or the Moonies.

"Any idea what your detective has done so far?" I asked.

She shook her head. "No, he only said he had been trying to find the group. I'm not sure what that entails."

Neither was I. There are some ethical private detectives, but I have a policeman's suspicion of them all. He may have decided to spin out his three yards a day by taking his time, moving so slowly that the boy never did turn up.

"Have you offered him any kind of bonus for finding your son?"

"I was going to, but then I got impatient with his lack of progress and decided to find someone else. That's when I found out about you."

"All right. Now I'm on the case. Do you have a photograph?"

She dug into her purse and brought out a three-by-four-inch color shot. It showed a dark, lean kid whose face looked bland until you realized he had his mother's eyes. They didn't fit with his dark hair, which was overlong and pulled back behind the ears like a foreign movie actor's. He was sitting in the stern of a yacht, a big one. Poor little rich boy.

"How tall is he?"

"Quite tall, five foot ten," she said. "Of course, his father is tall, the same height as you, I'd say."

"And he hasn't changed since this was taken? Not gone punk and died his hair orange, anything like that?"

"No, he's cut it a little shorter, it just covers his ears, but that's about it." She was embarrassed at having to discuss the boy with me at all, angry that he wasn't quarterbacking the university football team or curing cancer or any of those wonderful things we expect the next generation to do for us.

I finished my beer, and she pointed to the glass. "Could I get you another?"

"No, thanks. I've got some thinking to do. Maybe next time. Who knows, we might even have something to celebrate."

"I hope so," she said, and her eyes misted again. It was hard to read her. Sometimes the woman broke through the wealth and power.

I leaned back and said, "I've got a few contacts who

15

might be able to find out more about this group of his. I'll do some asking around. Can you give me the phone number of Mr. Broadhurst so I can check with him, and your own? I'll call if I learn anything."

She nodded. "Here's Mr. Broadhurst's card. My own number is unlisted. Will you write it down on the back of the card?"

"Sure. Can I borrow your pen, please?"

She handed over a gold pen, and I wrote her number on the back of Broadhurst's card, which read "Insight investigations. Discreet inquiries." I imagined his income came mostly from jealous husbands. Then I stood up, putting the card into my billfold. "I don't suppose I'll be calling before Monday. It's too late to get much official information today. The guys I want to talk to work office hours. But I'll do what I can."

She stood up with me, picking up her purse and holding it in both hands as if it were heavy. "I hope you'll be able to do something sooner than Monday, Mr. Bennett. It could be too late. He could be gone out of town by then."

"Believe me, I'll try my hardest," I said. "You're paying me a lot of money."

"It's worth it to me," she said. "And, of course, if you run into any expenses, I'll be glad to pay them.

"Thank you. I'll let you know." I nodded to her, and she did another of her tight little smiles.

"Please try," she said. "I'm counting on you."

TWO

♦

I don't like apartments at the best of times. Especially in big buildings. They make me feel like a folder in a file cabinet. For the first time since coming down to Toronto, I missed the house I rented at Murphy's Harbour. Not that I stayed indoors much, anyway. On a day like this, up there I would have gotten into my canoe and headed out with Sam in the bows and my fishing rod between my knees, trolling the deep weed beds for pickerel. It's the world's best way of getting your brain into neutral so that good ideas can float in without hindrance. Stuck in Fred's Toronto apartment, I did the next best thing, pulling a chair out onto the balcony, opening a Labatt's Blue, and sitting looking down on the treetops of the quiet streets below me.

Fred has a portable phone, so I took it with me and called the detective agency. I reached the answering service, and a woman told me she would give Mr. Broadhurst my message. Fine. So I wouldn't be able to save any steps. I'd have to go the whole distance on my own steam. Question: How?

The next thing I did was to start making like a policeman. Our national police force, the RCMP, has split off a security force, mostly ex-Mounties but some new men, including a detective I knew faintly when I was a detective myself with the Metro Toronto police. I dug out the little phone book I usually kept in my desk at Murphy's Harbour and rang his office number.

"Inspector Lenchak here," he said. Bingo. Fate was smiling.

He sounded laid back. I guessed the long-term pressures of keeping Canada safe from subversion were lighter than the old grind of robberies and homicides he'd worked on in the Metro department. I introduced myself, and he said, "Hey, Reid, nice to hear from you. You're a big deal in the papers."

"Great," I said. "Maybe I can get my old job back in Fifty-two Division."

"You wouldn't like it," he promised. "All those old slums have been painted pink and filled up with yuppies. The only excitement you ever get is domestics, some trendy whacking his boyfriend with a squash racket."

We laughed and reminisced, dredging up the few cases in which we'd both been involved. Then I put my question to him. "In your new job, do you keep tabs on mercenary outfits?"

"Sure," he said. "Thinking of heading down to Nicaragua or somewhere for some fun in the sun with a gun?"

"Nah, but I'm trying to do a favor for some woman. Apparently her kid's joined up with some bunch of Limeys call themselves Freedom for Hire. That ring any bells?"

"Y'ask me, that's a scam," he said. "Yeah, they popped up about a year ago. Their spiel is they train you, then send you on an assignment. Only thing is, they take the price of your training out of your pay, which comes to them, anyway, not to you. Kind of like being in hock to the Mob. You never get out of debt, the way I hear it. Only you don't know until you come back from getting your ass shot off and find you still owe them money. They pay your airfare and maybe give you a week's training. Then they keep your ten grand or whatever. Big profit margin."

"And it's running out of Toronto?"

"Not exactly. We're just one of their fishing holes. We don't like it, you can guess, but there isn't anything illegal, as you know. They just assemble a bunch of misfits and ship them out. Personally, I think it sucks, but since when did a copper have any say in the way things are run?"

We agreed on that one, but I had other questions to ask. "Any idea where I can find them?"

"We don't have an address. The guy in charge, he usually calls himself the Colonel, by the way, his name is George Dunphy. He was a sergeant with the British paras one time. A sergeant, not a colonel. They court-martialed him for brutality to a guy in his outfit. I don't have the details, only that he got a year in the brig, or whatever they call it over there, then he was dishonorably discharged."

"Sounds like a rounder," I said.

"For sure. We saw a psychological profile on him. He's a head case. Sadistic, ugly. But he's also cute as hell. Never takes a permanent address. When he's in town, which he is maybe every two months, he moves to a different hotel every day, no forwarding address. Checks in at night so we can't search his room while he's out or anything sneaky. Carries his gear with him."

"A moving target. The Brits train their guys well. Tell me, does he have any kind of circuit, any pattern?"

"It's not a circuit," Lenchak said. "He hits the bars, loser's bars mostly. You won't find him at any place there's a wealthy clientele. At least not until he's found a pigeon. Then he usually wines and dines the guy, taking him to better places than he's used to, you know how it goes."

"I see the picture. Yeah. So if I wanted to contact him, I should start making a circuit of the rough spots, down around Queen and Sherbourne, and out Queen West."

"That's it." Lenchak laughed. "I figure you'd better start at the redneck places. Anywhere they play country music is a good bet."

"Don't be hard on us rednecks; I like country. Anyway, what's this guy look like?"

"Not big, around five nine, one seventy, but it's all muscle. He moves like a soldier. And he usually wears a leather coat. He's thirty-eight this year, short fair hair, blue eyes, little brush of a mustache. Like when he calls himself Colonel, guys believe him."

"Should stand out in a redneck bar, among all the ponytails," I said. "But his recruiting sounds a bit hit-and-miss. Don't these outfits usually advertise in *Soldier of Fortune*?"

"No, those ads were outlawed some time back. But what Dunphy does is hit the help-wanted ads in the Toronto papers. "Wanted: strong, capable young men who want to earn big money. Strictly legal."

"And there's a box number, what?"

"No, a phone number. It's different every time. We've checked it; it's always a pay phone in a bar. He has different guys answering it; he calls them and picks up names and arranges the contacts."

"Have you shaken any of these guys down?"

"Losers, all of them. One's a guy in a wheelchair, another is a veteran of the big war, around sixty-five, heavy boozer. He's always half-corked, doesn't know anything. Says the colonel comes in early in the evening and buys his beer all night to take the phone."

He didn't have any more to add, so I thanked him and hung up. A scam, he'd said. The name of the outfit suggested that. It was the kind of thing you'd expect a TV series to be called, something to appeal to the average misfit sitting in front of the set with his cigarettes and his dreams. He would need to be pretty unsophisticated to bite, but that isn't a requirement that will exclude many young men. No, it looked to me as if Lenchak was right; young Michaels had gotten himself into deep trouble.

I wondered what their training would consist of. Not much, probably. A few lectures on field stripping weapons, firing, learning how to use captured weapons. Some nod in the direction of fitness, just enough to make the guy feel he was being subjected to discipline, not enough to do him any good.

That was what reminded me that it had been two days since my last run. Living with a woman after years spent mostly on my own had cut into the workout ritual I've built for myself. I dug out my running gear and headed out with Sam at my heels.

It was hot on the street, the slow, soaked-in heat of late afternoon when the sidewalks smolder with stored warmth. Beautiful weather to be on vacation with your girl. Ah, well. Fall for an actress, plan to spend a lot of time on your own.

I didn't push too hard but kept it down to three miles in twenty-five minutes. Sam enjoyed it. City life didn't suit him. He was happy to be moving, clicking along behind me as if we were tied together.

I got back and showered and then fed Sam and made myself some supper. Fred had been doing most of the catering, running a lot to salads and things in woks. I was relieved to find she had a can of Fray Bentos bully beef in the cupboard, and I parboiled some potatoes and fried up a solid meal of corned-beef hash, heavy on the onions. Why not?

Broadhurst hadn't returned my call when I finished eating, so I went out to start searching, taking Sam with me. Toronto's a law-abiding city, but I was on an ugly hunt, and I might need some backup. If Sam was within whistling distance, he'd provide it.

He settled comfortably on the front seat, and I opened all the windows and left the car outside one bar after another on my circuit. In every place I did the same thing, first checking for the colonel, who was never there that I could see, then looking around for anyone who might be his answering service. It was like following a very slight trail over very stony ground, but it was all I could do. I'd checked the newspaper, and there were no ads that might have been placed by Freedom for Hire. I'd even dug through back issues of the *Sun* for the past two days, as far back as I could find on a Saturday evening, when both the library and the *Sun* office were closed. Nothing in any paper to guide me, so I kept slugging around, leaving a single draft beer going flat on all the bars. Even one beer in each would have slowed me down too much for my own safety if I did run into the Freedom for Hire boys.

It must have been a little after ten when I finished the first circuit of all the likely places. On Queen Street West there's a country bar called the Chuckwagon, well enough known in the country-music crowd that the Saturday nighters were mostly in western gear, blue jeans—national dress for the under thirties, anyway—but with check shirts and Stetsons. The music was deafening, but it was Waylon Jennings, so at least it was telling a story.

I got myself a beer and looked around. No sign of the colonel. That would have been too easy. I looked for his phone jockey, someone old or out of place in this young crowd. Nobody answered that description, either. But there was one guy on his own who interested me. He wasn't on the make, which put him in a class by himself in there. He was nursing a beer and doing his best to look at a magazine in the limited light that was available. Killing time, glancing up now and then, trying not to look obvious.

I left my beer on the bar and sauntered past his table as if I were heading for the john. His head was down, and he was studying a picture of a guy in combat fatigues holding an automatic weapon. It had the curved magazine of the AK 47. He looked up and caught my eye and closed the magazine. *Soldier of Fortune.*

He stared at me, coldly. Getting himself psyched up to show how tough he was. He was already working at it, high-crowned baseball cap dead center, crisp haircut, clenched jaw. A recruit waiting for his army.

I nodded at him. "That's a good magazine."

He kept up his stare, not sure I wasn't sending him up. "How would you know?"

"Used to read it all the time," I said, and then set the hook. "When I first got back from 'Nam."

"You were there?" His face changed. "No shit, were you?"

"U.S. Marines. Two years." Fred would have been proud of me. I didn't follow up right away. I nodded again and went on to the washroom. It was busy, and I had to wait, watching a young guy slamming the contraceptive machine with the heel of his hand because it had eaten his quarters and left him unprotected. He was taking some heavy joshing from his buddies about his possible sexual preferences.

I walked back out past *Soldier of Fortune*. He was waiting. "Hey, got a minute?" His voice was as gruff as he could shade it without picking a fight. Anxious to talk but not at the cost of losing face, I figured.

" 'S on your mind?" I smiled to show I was playing nice.

"You a vet, really?"

"No big deal, there were a million guys there. Most of us came back."

"Yeah, but you're Canadian, eh? Like I figured you had to be American."

I leaned my knuckles down on the table so we could talk without bellowing over George Jones and Tammy Wynette. "There were lots of Canadians there, thousands of us. I was marines."

His jaw had come unclenched. He looked as close to pleading as he could allow himself to get. "Were you in the boonies?"

"Most of the time."

"Listen." He looked around, at the bar, where I'd left

my beer. "You with somebody, or can I buy you a beer, shoot the shit?"

"Kinda boring," I minimized.

He said it. He honestly did, like a school kid. "That's easy for you to say."

I grinned and dropped into the chair opposite, waving at the waiter, who was plowing through the crowd with his aluminum tray at arm's length over his head. I hoped somebody didn't tickle him.

He stopped at our table and dropped four draft. The *Soldier of Fortune* would have outdrawn Billy the Kid to get his cash on the table. He tipped a quarter. The waiter sniffed and left.

He pushed a glass toward me. "Down the hatch," he said almost jovially.

"Here's looking up your address." Freda, if you could only see your boyfriend now!

I can see why women are reluctant to let a guy pay for their drinks. It gives him a share of your life. Even if you gulped it down, you couldn't leave without giving him what he considered his money's worth of time. Maybe more for a woman. He flung the questions at me like incoming fire. I could soon tell that he was a reader; he knew the history of the war better than I did. But I guess a ringside seat gives you perspective that the fighter in the ring never gets. I sat and answered questions for twenty minutes, nursing that first beer while he finished his two, and started my second, waving to the waiter, who had developed short sight as far as our table was concerned.

"Where were you wounded?" he was asking when I held up my hands to stop the questions, doing it slowly enough that he could see the white slash across the underside of the left arm, where my radius bone came up for air.

"No more questions, okay," I said, but he was peering at the wrist.

"Hell, that looks like it was painful."

"It was." I took another little nibble at my beer. "But tell me, if you're this interested, why don't you join the marines yourself? They're still looking for recruits." It was like fishing. I let the line go slack here by adding, "And right now there's no chance of getting shot at."

He straightened up again. "Yeah. You unnerstan' I'm not gung ho or nothin', but I don't wanna sit around polishin' brass. I wanna see some combat."

I gave the fishing line a tiny tug. "Well, you ask me, the marines is your best bet."

At last it was his turn to act superior instead of humble, and he clenched his jaw again, managing to smile as he did so. He looked as if he had heartburn. "Oh, no," he said. "Oh, no, it ain't."

I laughed. "There wasn't any war on last time I saw the papers."

"Plenny of 'em," he said. "You gotta know where to look."

"Yeah?" The old soldier kidding.

"Yeah." He was bursting to tell me now. "Like you won't let this go any further, okay?"

"Hell, I don't even know your name," I said.

"Baks," he said, and stuck his hand out. "John Baks. I'm from Huntsville."

It's a small town up in the bush, nothing much there but a sawmill and a Canadian tire store. I said, "Oh, sure, I know Huntsville."

"They oughta call it Dullsville," he said.

I laughed again, Uncle Tomming.

He smiled, then clenched his jaw. It must be tired by now, I figured. "Two hundred a week, working at the feed store. Not for this sucker. I'm heading for big money."

"Gonna rob a bank?"

He shook his head and leaned forward, almost whispering, although he could have shouted under the bass voice of Johnny Cash with "Sunday Morning Coming Down." "No. I'm meeting a guy here tonight, gonna head south, see some action, earn some real money."

"Doing what?" I stared at him suspiciously, dumb.

"That's classified," he said happily. He sat hugging his snug little secret, smiling his tight-assed smile.

"Well, what kind of money? How much?" I put enough disbelief into my voice that he had to prove his superiority. He bit.

"Two grand a month, plus uniforms, plus food." He did the little trick with his eyes, lowering his head a fraction and sagging the chin for a moment. It only ever makes sense as a send-up, but guys like Baks do it all the time, for real.

I acted impressed, anyway. "Who'd you have to kill?"

He snorted with laughter and buried his nose in his beer glass.

"I ain't met the guys yet," he said.

I scratched my chin and looked at him slyly. "Listen, sounds interesting. You think you can put a word in for me?"

He liked that. He sat up even straighter and looked me up and down. "Hell, you must be thirty-five."

"Thirty-seven, but who's counting. I could do with a few paydays like that. Get my ex-wife the hell off my back."

He shrugged. I could see he was torn. On the one hand, he wanted his swell new career to himself, but on the other, it would be reassuring to have a veteran alongside him if the other guys started returning fire. Prudence won. "I'll ask him," he said. "That's all's I can do, y'unnerstand. I'll ask him. What say your name was?"

"Michaels. Tommy Michaels." I grinned happily. "Yeah, I'd like to talk to this guy. Maybe he was there as well. In 'Nam, I mean."

"Doubt it." Baks shook his head, a tight little drill movement. "He's English."

26

"You met him already?"

"No. Spoke to him, though. He told me to meet him here. Said to carry *S.O.F.*, be here ten-thirty."

"Must be close to that now."

"Twenny-seven after." He confirmed it on one of those watches you can take to the ocean floor.

"Time for another beer," I said, and waved the waiter over. This time he came, hoping I was the tipper of the table.

I paid for the beers and picked one up. It was exactly ten-thirty. And on the dot of the half hour two men came into the bar. One of them was Dunphy. Exactly as my contact had described him, not tall but capable looking, cropped hair, bristling English-style army officer's mustache. The other one was bigger and looser. Without hearing him speak, I guessed he was American, a southerner. He had that plantation owner's sneer you see on the faces of a lot of tall crackers. He would be the court jester, I judged, making bitter little jokes that meant pain for other people. If young Jason Michaels had been alert, he should have veered off when he saw this character.

Dunphy stood in the doorway, looking around, not moving anything except his head, standing rigidly, a studied pose that said, Look how military I am. Wouldn't you like to be as tough as this?

It worked. Baks was on his feet as if this were a boot-camp room inspection, holding up his copy of *S.O.F.* the way a knight would hold his coat of arms. Dunphy's partner saw him and bent forward slightly to say something that made Dunphy's mustache twitch with amusement. Then they came over, walking right across the middle of the dance floor, ignoring the couples who were swaying together to the record.

Dunphy stopped at our table and nodded at Baks. "You're John Baks."

"Yessir," Baks said, standing very straight.

Dunphy looked over his shoulder at the other guy. "What do you think, Mr. Wallace?"

"I b'lieve it might be possible to make a soldier outa this man," Wallace said. His voice was airy, as if he were having trouble hiding his contempt. He would be the instructor, I judged, making sure that everyone got as muddy and humiliated as he could contrive while he stood around in immaculate fatigues. A bully.

"We should sit and talk for a few minutes, somewhere private," Dunphy said.

"Yeah, right. Shall we go?" Baks wasn't going to risk making either of them mad by bringing up my name. I think he would even have left his magazine behind if they'd wanted him to.

"You're the colonel," I said, and Dunphy glanced at me in surprise. He didn't answer. Instead, it was Wallace.

"An' what's your name, boy?"

"Who're you calling boy?"

Baks had gone catatonic. He could see his dream getting blown away. I was making these wonderful people angry.

Dunphy said, "You have a big mouth, friend."

"Listen, Colonel, I don't have any fight with you. But no cracker gets to call me boy."

"Tough guy, huh?" Wallace asked me.

"Tough enough. I was kicking ass in 'Nam while you were in grade school pushing nigger outhouses over." I could remember the fight that comment had started in a southern bar where some redneck had confronted a buddy and me. My buddy had been a cracker, like the one in front of me now, only mellowed out by combat. We had fought a roomful of rednecks before the MPs came and saved our necks.

"I don't b'lieve you're that tough, mister," Wallace said.

"Let's head on outside and find out," I said.

" 'S wrong with here?"

28

Dunphy finally spoke. "Gentlemen. I'm sure you're both very tough, but why waste time proving it on one another. Mr. Wallace, perhaps our friend here is looking for a chance to show us what he can do in our employ." Dunphy had worked on his accent. He sounded like an officer, a trick most British enlisted men never master.

"Thanks, Colonel." I nodded approvingly. "I heard you might have some interesting work. I also heard you were a fair man. Nobody told me about this guy. Is he part of your outfit?"

"Yes," Dunphy said shortly. "Tell me what's on your mind, Mr. . . ." He paused, waiting for me to supply the name. Baks did it for him.

"This is Mr. Michaels," he said, and Dunphy turned to Wallace and frowned.

Wallace must have been a mind reader. He responded at once, without blinking, stepping forward and slamming a punch at my head. Only I beat him to it. People don't ambush me, not since 'Nam. I was to one side of the punch when it got there, grabbing his wrist with my left hand and crunching my balled-up right fist into the back of his neck like a hammer. He grunted and collapsed across the table, spilling beer in all directions.

I turned to face Dunphy, crouching. "What was that all about?"

He ignored me. "Pick him up," he told Baks. "We can talk outside."

THREE

◆

The bouncer was coming toward us, shoving through the dancers on the tiny floor like a battlewagon through a yacht regatta. He was big and ugly enough to be a dropout from a biker gang. I wondered what Dunphy would do. He showed me instantly. His billfold was in his hand before the man reached us. His voice was confident as he spoke. "I'm sorry about the mess. Our friend here has had a drop too much of your good beer. We're leaving. I hope this will take care of any damage."

The biker took the twenty and put it in his shirt pocket. "Looks to me like he needs some air," he said.

Dunphy obliged him with a neat little chuckle and turned away to where his new recruit was draping Wallace's arm over his shoulder and getting ready to carry him out. I stood back, not offering to help. To the victor the spoils.

Dunphy led the way to the door, and I came right behind him, leaving the kid staggering under Wallace's weight. The inner door was shut, but it was glass, and I could see there was nobody waiting outside to throw any punches. The street door was open. Dunphy stepped through it and paused to glance back at the other two. He ignored me. I checked around. There was nobody on the street but the usual Saturday night strollers. Wallace had been his only backup.

I waited until the kid had made the door and paused, grunting with his efforts, propping Wallace against the wall and leaning against him. Then Dunphy turned to me. "You're very good, old chum," he said.

"Good enough, a lot of the time."

"Tell me, were you hoping to find employment with my organization or what?"

"I wouldn't want to fight alongside Wallace," I said. "But that's not why I came looking for you, anyway."

"Oh, and what was your reason, Mr., er, Michaels, you said, didn't you?"

"Yeah, Tommy Michaels. My brother asked me to see you. Said his dumb kid had joined up with you. The kid's underage; we want him back."

Dunphy straightened himself up, a sure sign he was going to start lying. "I've no idea what you're talking about."

"Fine. Then I'll call a cop and we'll head down to the station and you can talk to somebody who can make you remember a little better."

"It wouldn't change anything," he said in the same tone he had used on the bouncer. "I've told you, I've never heard of anyone called Michaels, except yourself, of course. However, you do impress me, and I could offer you a very rewarding assignment if you chose." He didn't let me answer but went on. "I assume, from the way you acted, that you've seen service. Canadian forces, was it?"

"He was in the United States Marines, in Vietnam," Baks said.

Wallace was starting to recover, rubbing his neck and groaning. I worked out how far away Sam was. Thirty yards, on this side of the street. He could be fighting alongside me inside ten seconds if necessary.

"How interesting," Dunphy was saying. "You saw

some actual fighting, I judge. You're a trained jungle fighter."

"We're talking about Jason, a kid with the IQ of a cord of firewood," I said. Wallace was straightening up, measuring his chances of taking another lunge at me. If Dunphy tried at the same time, it could be trouble.

"You. On the deck," I said, pointing at Wallace.

"Really, Mr. Michaels. There's no need for that," Dunphy protested.

"Down. Or I put you down," I said, and Wallace slowly and angrily slid down the wall until he was squatting on his haunches.

"Flat on the deck," I said. He looked murderous, but he complied.

"Right. Now do you tell me where the kid is, or do I call a cop and get this cockamamy outfit of yours busted?" It was my last and only possible threat. If he said no, I would have to fight him, and I wasn't sure I could win. A British para is tough, and this guy was built for fighting.

"Look," he said at last, "you're a very forceful chap, and so I'm going to let you in on a little secret. Yes, I did meet the boy. He had seen one of my advertisements, and he came to see me. I took one look at him and knew he was useless. Too soft, too pampered. You should know that. However, I did take pity on him, and so I gave him some money. Two hundred of your funny dollars, to be exact. He thanked me and said he was going to Vancouver, anywhere to get away from his dreary father."

"The hell you did. You wouldn't have given him the time of day. You hired him. Where is he?"

Dunphy raised both hands. It's a good move. It looks peaceful, placating, but it gives you an advantage. You can punch with one hand before the sucker you're talking to realizes you're ready.

I stepped back. "Swing at me and I'll wrap you around that fire hydrant," I warned him. "Where's the kid? Quit stalling."

"For the last time, I don't know. You can have me arrested and beat me with rubber hoses, but I can't tell you anything else. It's the truth."

I said nothing, and he lowered his hands. "Look, Michaels, if that's who you really are, I appreciate why you're here. But you understand, don't you? You volunteered to go and fight, just for a change in your life-style. For all I know, this boy has done the same thing, bought himself a ticket somewhere and joined the army there. I hope so, for his sake. He needs discipline. But I didn't take him."

This was getting me nowhere. I looked around to see if there was a police car cruising somewhere close. There wasn't. There never is when you need one, even if you're a copper.

"Getting anxious, Mr. Michaels?" Dunphy asked. "Hoping for some backup, were you? Maybe some of your fellow policemen?"

I glanced at him sharply. He grinned, a smirky little gesture that made his mustache bristle in the light from the front of the bar. "Oh, don't look surprised. I know you're a policeman. You've got the haircut, you've got the authority. You've got all of it, except the one thing you need, a reason to arrest me."

"Abduction will do," I said, and he smirked again.

"Really, against three of us? I can see you're not wearing a gun, unless you have one in your sock, and even that doesn't look possible to me," he said, and threw himself at me.

I kicked out, automatically, catching him high on the thigh, not slowing him; then he was on me, clawing for my eyes. "Get him!" he snapped, and Wallace was on his feet in a moment, moving fast, coming at me. I had time to shout, "Fight!" and to see Wallace laughing, thinking I was trying to get the crowd on my side, knowing from experience that they would watch, not help. And then Sam was with me, snarling, grabbing Wallace by the arm.

I didn't have time to watch whether he was pulling a knife. Sam could take care of that, anyway. I was fighting for my eyes. Dunphy's thumb was squirming at my temple, his face just inches from mine, his body pressed so close I couldn't knee him or punch. Instead, I spat in his face, and he recoiled far enough that I got an arm free and smashed him across the nose with my elbow. He grunted and let go, and I kicked him in the knee, hard. He yowled and folded but straightened up at once and grabbed for me again.

Then Baks came out of his dream and joined in, grabbing me from behind. I used him as a brace to swing both feet off the ground and smash them into Dunphy's chest. He rolled backward but was up again instantly as I scraped my heel down Baks's shin, making him yell and let go. I turned for a moment and smashed him square in the nose. Not scientific but a good reflex. He staggered away, covering his face, and I turned back, but Dunphy had gone. He was sprinting for the car parked at the curb.

Before I could reach it, he was inside, jumping away from the curb and pulling away. His lights were off, so I couldn't get the license. I swore, then turned back. I still had Wallace.

By now I also had a crowd to deal with, patrons from the bar, spilling out onto the sidewalk for the free show. They were a rough bunch, even the women, and I was alone except for Sam. One of the men was bending to pick up a knife. I roared at him. "Don't touch that, it's evidence."

He stopped, still bent over, glancing over his shoulder at me. I dipped past him and grabbed the knife. "Police matter," I told him. It didn't win me any friends.

"This guy's a narc," he shouted, and suddenly I was the bad guy. But Sam could take care of that. I checked him. He was covering Wallace, who had realized he was beaten and was sitting against the wall, rubbing his bruised wrists. Sam was crouching in front of him, barking, slavering. Good. That was one problem taken care of.

But the crowd was getting angry. It happens everywhere, even in Toronto, once you get out of office hours. A bunch of truckers with a gutful of beer and something to prove. If they decided I was the enemy, I had trouble. I watched them. They were shouting and shoving through to the front to get a look at me, but so far none of them had taken the first move, suggesting they rescue the downtrodden. I hoped the police would hurry.

Baks was up the street about three doorways, sponging the blood from his face with a sodden red handkerchief. I hoped he stayed there. Bleeders raise more sympathy than unmarked people like Wallace.

The Toronto police were quick. Someone must have phoned in, and they were there in another minute, two neat young guys with look-alike mustaches. They pulled up in the roadway and piled out, carrying their big sticks. I judged they'd been called to fights at the Chuckwagon before this.

One of them came right up to me while the other one cooled out the crowd. I liked the way he worked. "Okay, folks, show's over. Go have another beer."

My guy said, "What's going on?"

"I'm a visiting police chief. The guy on the deck came at me with this, and my dog disarmed him."

He took the knife from me and looked at it. It was one of those narrow-bladed jobs that they used to call Tennessee toothpicks. "Not friendly," he said. "Can you call your dog off?"

"Sure. Easy, Sam."

Sam relaxed and fell back a step, alongside me. I patted his head. It did more than the policemen had done to cool out the crowd. They slapped one another on the back and pointed at him. Controlled force like his impresses the hell out of people with dull life-styles.

35

"I want to charge this man with assault with a deadly weapon and weapon dangerous to the public peace. Also, he's involved in an abduction."

"You got it." The cop brightened. Three good arrest charges on a night when he would have been telling drunks to take a cab instead of driving home. He went over to Wallace, standing to one side of him, where he wouldn't get kicked. "Okay, sir. If you'd stand up, please, I'd like to talk to you."

Wallace stood up, not looking at the cop, staring at me through eyes that promised trouble if we ever met again. The cop said, "If you'd come with me to the car, sir."

"What for?" I guessed he'd been in jackpots before this. He knew his rights, or at least the American version.

"This gentleman has made certain allegations," the cop said. "He's a police officer, and you're under arrest. If you'll come over to the car where it's quieter, I'll tell you your rights."

Wallace didn't argue. He went quietly to the side of the cruiser and stood there while the young cop read him all his rights. Then he got into the cage. I guessed he was expecting Dunphy to ride to his rescue. From the way Dunphy had gone, it didn't seem likely. If Wallace was expendable, he would stay in jail, if the charges stuck. They probably wouldn't. Not in the cold light of court in the morning. I didn't care about that; people have attacked me before. It goes with the job. And the abduction charge was a phony. I just hoped that Wallace would get bitter about his boss and open up about where they had taken young Michaels. This investigation was starting to get to me.

The other cop joined his partner, who waved me to follow, so I called Sam and trailed behind them to the station. It was the new one, next to the Art Gallery of Ontario in the heart of Chinatown. The usual Saturday night uproar was in full swing. Not many drunks, but quite a few citizens clamoring for information, phones ringing, uniformed men and detectives coming and going.

The two cops sat Wallace in a corner. One of them stood with him, while the other one left. "I'll get the brains," he said. The detectives. I hoped it would be someone I knew. I'd never worked out of this division, but you make plenty of contacts in detective work. I might get lucky.

While I waited for him, I called Broadhurst's detective agency. He was in, and he said he would be down right away. Mrs. Michaels had asked him to collaborate with me in any way he could. He wasn't happy, but he knew who was paying his bills.

The duty detective in the station was young, young enough to be wearing his jacket despite the heat, which felt as if the air conditioning had given up a couple of days earlier. By the time he reached us, the uniformed man had filled him in. He came over, frowning, and spoke to me. "Could I have a word with you, sir?"

"Sure." I told Sam to stay and walked over to the corner of the counter, out of earshot of Wallace, who was sitting rubbing his wrists.

"You're a police officer?"

"Reid Bennett. I'm the chief up at Murphy's Harbour, in Toronto on vacation."

"You have some ID?"

I showed him, and he glanced at it. "Good. Tell me, what were you doing down at the Chuckwagon. You always hang out around those kinda places?" Young cops are very judgmental.

"No. Look, it's going to save your time if I tell you what's going down. The assault doesn't matter. It happens. Shall we do it my way, or you want to ask all the questions?"

He looked up at me sharply. I was throwing him. He was the detective, I was the victim. I should be answering questions. Only that would take us down some unnecessary byways.

He didn't answer, so I started. "This guy works for a mercenary outfit called Freedom for Hire. I checked them with the Intelligence Service, talked to an ex-Toronto detective there. He runs with a man called Dunphy, who signs up volunteers and ships them out to places like Nicaragua, wherever."

"That's not illegal," he said. He knew his law, anyway.

"Not quite. But anyway, I was approached by the mother of a kid who just joined them. My job is to get him back. All I want to know from this guy is where they've got the kid. After that I'll drop the charges and we can all go home."

"That's not a police matter," he said.

"No, it's not." I was patient. "But trying to fillet me with that goddamn knife of his is a police matter. What I'm suggesting is that you talk to him, see if you can get him to talk. Then he can walk, as far as I'm concerned, and save you all that paperwork."

"So you want us to do your job for you?"

"I want help in keeping the peace. That's why I was glad to see the blue suits turn up. These Freedom people are bad news. The kid could get blown away. He's a citizen, I'm a citizen. This guy here isn't. He's a Georgia cracker looking to kick anybody's ass he can reach."

"I'll give him five minutes," he said. A sawoff.

"Should be enough. Want me along?"

"No. What's this kid's name who's missing?"

"Jason Michaels. He's twenty but kind of backward, dumb. Not fit to be looking after himself." That wasn't true, but it gave the detective something to believe in. Everybody needs a cause.

"Go and sit down," he said.

I went to a chair, well away from Wallace, and shrilled a low whistle at Sam. He came over and sat, and I patted his head and watched the detective work.

38

I couldn't hear what he was saying, but I could tell from the look on Wallace's face that he wasn't buying. He just sat and listened, not moving a muscle. He was angry, scared enough of the law that he wouldn't make a fuss, but he sure wasn't going to do any favors. He probably knew he would be let out on bail. A law-abiding citizen wouldn't, but a professional rebel would. He knew he could sit tight and wait for a bail hearing; then he would vanish.

After a while he spoke, opening and shutting his mouth without moving anything else. The sure sign he wasn't giving us anything. The detective spoke again, then called me. I told Sam to stay and walked over, moving easily so Wallace would know I was a policeman, not an embarrassed visitor to the station.

The detective said, "Your friend here says he never heard of Jason Michaels."

I nodded and spoke to Wallace. "When did you get here?"

He thought about it, wondering how far to go obstructing me.

"Yesterday," he said at last. He was going to play the "I'd like to help, but" game.

"With Dunphy?"

"No." He'd been trained well. Number, rank, and name was all he would give up. Only he didn't have a number anymore.

"Where did you meet up with him?"

"How'd ya mean?"

"You're his instructor. I heard you say so. You're in this with him. I want to know where you met him yesterday."

"Just bumped into him in a bar someplace. He offered me a job. I said, 'Sure.' " He shrugged.

"Where did you come from?"

The detective was getting restless. This wasn't his case. If it had been, he might have been asking the same questions. Right now he wanted Wallace out of his life so he could get back to working through the cases on his desk. I ignored him. So did Wallace.

"New York," he said easily. "Yeah, New York. I heard this was a nice friendly town, so I came up here to kick back for a spell. Then I met Dunphy and hung out with him."

"You met him when?"

"This evening, 'bout an hour before we came into that bar where you an' that kid was hangin' out."

"What kid?" the detective asked me. I turned and gave him a "hold it" look.

Wallace answered the question for him. "Some buddy o' his. Suckin' around this guy on account'f this guy's been in the Younited States Marines." He chuckled. "Kids."

The detective was buying it, starting to see me as some kind of cowboy who worked on impressing civilians. I could tell by the way his stance changed. He leaned back on the counter as if to say, Go ahead, smart guy, let's see you do better.

I cut the losses. "Okay, Wallace, if that's your name. You've been charged with assault with a deadly weapon, weapon dangerous to the public peace. Let's see you laugh yourself out of court in the morning." He chuckled again. Bravado. He didn't want to go inside, but he'd be damned if he'd let it show.

I turned to the detective. "I'll give you a statement. Lock him up, please. And then I want to speak to your inspector."

"Help yourself." The detective waved me toward the desk officer.

I nodded and walked over to the uniformed man who was tapping something into a computer terminal. He looked up, and I took out my ID. He stood up and took it, then said, "Yes, Chief, what can I do for you?"

"I'd like to talk to the duty inspector, please."

40

He went into the inspector's office, and a minute later I was in there. And once again it was a man I didn't know.

He didn't shake hands. He was sitting at his desk, working on some paper or other. He looked up. "You're Chief Bennett."

"Yes, thank you for seeing me, Inspector."

He closed his file folder and frowned at me. "You used to be with the department here, didn't you?"

"Yeah, until two years ago. I was a detective in Fifty-two Division."

He nodded. "Rings a bell. You offed a couple of bikers, or something like that, got arrested, right."

"Right. For manslaughter. Was acquitted but left the job when the papers wouldn't let go of it."

Now he stood up and stuck out his hand. "Crawford."

We shook. "Reid Bennett. I've just handled a case up in my patch that involved some more bikers. I'm in town on vacation, and a woman asked me to look into a mercenary outfit that's signed up her son."

"How can we help?" He waved to the chair in front of his desk, and I sat.

"Thanks. Well, I found the guy in charge. Limey, name of Dunphy. According to a guy I know in the Intelligence Service, he runs an outfit called Freedom for Hire. I went looking for him, found him, and then the guy outside, who works for him, came after me with a knife. So, he's charged with weapon dangerous, but Dunphy took off in the scuffle. I want to try and track him."

"What's your plan?"

"According to my source, he doesn't hole up any-where permanent, keeps moving every night. So I won't find him through a hotel registration, but he had a car, an '87 Chev. Beretta. There's a chance I could track him through the hire-car companies. I'd like to use an office, or a phone, anyway, for a while, see if I can get a handle on him."

41

"That's no problem. You can use the detective office."
He leaned back in his chair. "Of course, it may not help.
If he thinks he's blown, he'll dump the car, or he may
have used a phony ID."

"Yeah, I know, but it's all I've got to go on. I've been
trying to shake something out of Wallace; that's the guy
with the knife. Only he's playing dumb."

"He would." Crawford nodded. "I'll get one of the
other guys to talk to him. Looked to me as if Hennessey
was out there. He's still kinda green. Maybe we'll get
somewhere with an experienced man." He frowned at
me. "I can't promise anything. You know that."

"Appreciate the courtesy, Inspector Crawford. If there's
anything I can do for you up at Murphy's Harbour, like
maybe show you where the pickerel are. Something
unofficial."

He grinned. "Thanks, anyway, I'm a golfer. Tell the
duty officer to take you up to the detective office."

"Thanks, Inspector."

I went back out, and the young PC pointed up the
stairs to the left. I called Sam and went up there. It was
the typical detective office. Tables shoved together in
the middle of a big room, a couple of old manual type-
writers, phones, file cabinets, departmental memos on
the walls. It brought back memories of nights like this
two years ago when I'd worked a mile from this place,
twelve–fourteen-hour days tidying up the mess that passes
for life in the fast lane even in a law-abiding city like
Toronto.

I found the phone book, dug out the hire-car section of
the yellow pages, and started calling. Between them
they had seventeen dark-colored Berettas on lease. None
of them was on loan to anybody called Dunphy or Wallace. Three of them were out to women drivers. In the
other cases, the clerk who answered had not been on
duty when the car was released. They had no idea who
had taken them out, but none of the records showed a
Dunphy or a Wallace.

I was still working when a short middle-aged man came into the office. He was wearing a dark gray suit and a fine sheen of perspiration. He mopped his face with a handkerchief and waited for me to finish the call I was making.

"You're Reid Bennett?"

I stood up. "Right, you're the private detective?"

He put his handkerchief away and stuck out his hand, smiling ingratiatingly. "Sam Broadhurst. Yes."

"Okay. Mrs. Michaels asked me to help you look for her kid. I've found the people who signed him up. One of them is downstairs under arrest. When I'm through here, I'm going to latch on to him when he's released on bail, try to track down the boy."

"You may be too late," Broadhurst said nervously. "As I was coming in, I saw the justice of the peace leaving. I think the bail hearing's over. And the door of the hearing room was open. It's empty. I'd say he was gone."

FOUR

◆

Broadhurst was right. The hearing had happened, and my man was gone. I swore. Hennessey should have called me when the hearing occurred. I wasn't sure whether his failure to do so was an oversight or deliberate punishment for doing police work on his turf. It made no difference either way. Wallace had slipped through the cracks. My work had been for nothing. Only now the mercenaries knew me and would avoid me even more carefully.

I did the only thing possible. I reclaimed Wallace's knife and gave it to Sam to sniff. He led me out onto the street and along a half block before coming to a dead end at the edge of the roadway. Wallace had gone off in a car, a cab probably.

Broadhurst suggested that he contact all the cab companies to see if any of the drivers had picked Wallace up. There wasn't anything better to do, so I turned him loose. I didn't hold out any hope. A man like Wallace would change cabs at least once before reaching his destination. Most likely he would switch to the subway for the last lap. I'd lost him.

I returned the knife to the detectives, got into my own car, and drove Sam over to the hotel Wallace had given as his Toronto address. Too late, of course. He had checked out that morning. The clerk let me see his room, but it was empty. He hadn't left any indication of where he was heading. Smart, just like Dunphy.

By now it was midnight, and I drove back up Yonge Street to Fred's apartment. The strip was busy, as always. At its worst it's like the least scrungy part of Forty-second Street in New York. There are all kinds of girlie shows, but the Toronto Morality Squad keeps an eye on things, and the pictures of the girls displayed outside are eight-by-ten glossies, not posters. But the people are the same creepy bunch you get in districts like this everywhere, pimps, punkers, a few hookers, and a crowd of shiny-faced tourists. I kept my eyes open for Wallace but didn't see him. It was a long shot, anyway. He'd probably rejoined Dunphy and they were making plans to leave town.

I got back to Fred's place at midnight and parked on the street, putting a Murphy's Harbour police summons card in the windshield. So far it had kept me clear of parking tickets.

I walked around the block in the midnight warmth, giving Sam a chance to stretch his legs before we went up to our cell. A few people were sitting on the front stoops of their houses, talking softly, laughing. I heard the clink of glasses and at one point whiffed the familiar smell of grass. Maybe it helped the smokers forget the concrete around them, let them imagine they were out somewhere peaceful, like Murphy's Harbour.

The apartment was warm, and I didn't fancy sleeping alone in Fred's bed, so I took the cushions off the couch and a blanket outside onto the balcony. From there I could see the sky, and in the quiet that slowly settled over the city it was possible to forget where I was.

I woke early and dressed for a run. Sam came with me, and we clipped through the sleeping streets for most of an hour. Then I showered and reheated what was left of my hash, frying up a couple of eggs to go on top and making a pot of good coffee. I was drinking my second cup when the phone rang. It was Mrs. Michaels.

"I hope I didn't wake you up, Mr. Bennett," she said.

"No, I've been out for a run."

"Oh," she said. "I was wondering whether you had any luck in your inquiries."

"Yes, I did. In fact, I found the man who signed your son up."

"And what did he say?" Her voice was all business. We might have been discussing her stock portfolio.

"He wasn't very helpful. In fact, I was obliged to fight him and a partner of his. I stopped one of them, but the man I wanted got away." There. It didn't sound so foolish put that way.

"Does that mean you've lost him?" she asked. She wanted value. She'd done her part, handing over the check. Now it was my turn, and I could expect the screws to keep on tightening.

"I'm going out to the airport to check around. I figure he's heading out of town. He'll most likely fly."

There was a silence. I could imagine her gray eyes focusing on some distant object while she thought, wondering what else to do. At last she said, "Did you get in touch with Broadhurst?"

"Yes, he turned up and helped after the fact. I'm taking him with me this morning."

"Is there anything I can do?" The first human thing she'd said to me.

"Yes, Mrs. Michaels. If you hear from Jason, ask to meet him. Tell him you respect his decision but you have something for him."

"I don't think that would work," she said. "He would probably sneer and say he didn't need anything. In fact, I don't know that he will call me at all."

"Well, you know him better than I do, but it's kind of an instinct when you're heading out. You touch base with home, just once, kind of a good-luck charm, something like that."

46

"If he does, I'll call you," she said. "Do you have an answering service or anything?"

"Yes, there's a machine. I'll call in for messages."

"Good." Another silence, and then she said, "Thank you. You seem to be making progress."

"Not fast enough to suit me, but some," I said. "I'll update you on anything that happens today."

"All right. Have you run up any expenses?"

"Nothing heavy so far, thanks. If it runs into anything serious, I'll keep the bills and let you have them next time I see you."

"Good. Please do," she said, and hung up.

The next thing I did was phone Broadhurst, reaching his answering service. However, the operator let me ring through when I told her it was urgent, and I got him out of bed by the sound of it. "Any luck with the cab companies?" I asked him.

"None," he said. "Are you still looking?"

"I'm about to head out to the airport and check the departures, see if I can find anything. How about meeting me there?"

He hesitated a moment. "I haven't eaten yet. When will you be there?"

"Let's say an hour. I'll see you at the eastern end of the Air Canada terminal." He could pick up a doughnut on the way. Work is work.

"Fine," he said without enthusiasm. "See you there."

I hung up the phone and packed the few things I'd brought with me to Toronto. If I learned anything at the airport, I would follow up on it. Sam wagged his tail when he saw me pick up the bag. Behaviorists tell you that dogs don't think, but I'd make an exception in Sam's case. I'd swear he was a mind reader.

Toronto's Lester B. Pearson Airport has two terminals. One of them mostly deals with overseas flights. It's where most of the foreign carriers come in. The other is for Air Canada and some charters. From there you get most of the domestic flights. I decided to check

47

there first. If Michaels was being tossed directly to the lions, he would probably fly out of the other terminal, direct to Dallas or some other crossroads for Central America. On the other hand, if his mother was right about his contempt for Canada, he was probably flying off to some remote location inside the country to learn soldiering before doing it for real.

At this time of year, a month before the first frosts, you can get a pretty good simulation of jungle conditions at a lot of points in Canada, remote points where you could fire all the guns you wanted without being heard. Going by the kid's comment to his mother, I figured that's what was happening. The only way to find out was to make like a copper.

I left Sam in the car, with the windows down, and went into the eastern end of the domestic terminal. Toronto is a city that lives and dies by its map references. Broadhurst was there, still wearing the same suit, eating a doughnut and holding a Styrofoam cup of coffee. "Hi," he said.

"Hi. Thanks for coming over. I thought I'd check the reservations people, see if the guys we need are booked on any flights."

"You think they'd use their own names?"

"No, but it's a starting point. I'll try the central terminal. Maybe you can talk to the people on the ticket counters. You have a photograph of Michaels?"

"Yes," he said. "But not his clothes. Nobody's gonna remember a kid like that from a photograph."

"Give it a whirl. Meantime, you might try describing the other guys I met." I told him what they looked like, and he nodded.

Then I flashed my ID at security and was admitted to the central reservations terminal for Air Canada. It was cool in the air-conditioned office, and the pale clerk who checked the passenger lists for me had a savage cold. He sniffed constantly as he did things his way, starting out

48

by checking that there was no J. Michaels flying out to Montreal or New York or Florida before he got around to the northern flights. And here we struck oil.

"Yes, there's a J. Michaels booked aboard flight 76, to North Bay," the clerk said. He looked up at me and grinned, then sniffed, pulling in a dewdrop of misery that was dangling on the end of his nose.

"Could I see the whole listing, please?"

He pivoted the terminal so I could look over his shoulder. The names were a mixture of French and English, a good cross section of the area around North Bay, which is only a hundred miles from my patch at Murphy's Harbour. I scanned it quickly, noting the J. Michaels. "Any idea how this flight was paid for?"

He checked. "Credit card J. Michaels. Used for three tickets."

"Thank you very much," I said. "When does it leave?"

"Oh, it's gone," he said. "Left at 0850, that's half an hour ago."

I frowned. "Can I use your telephone, please?"

"Help yourself." He pointed, and I sat on the desk and hooked the phone off the cradle.

"Thanks." I dialed out and asked the operator to connect me with the North Bay police. She put me through, and I was talking to Constable Dupuis. Good. I knew him. "Bonjour, Marcel," I said, and then rattled to him in French. He's bilingual but prefers French, and I'm fluent, so I paid him the courtesy. "Flight seventy-six from Toronto is coming in very soon at North Bay. There're three people on it I'd like detained. One is a bail jumper from Toronto, name of Wallace, K. Wallace." I described him. "He's from Georgia, talks like Gomer Pyle. He's on bail for a knife assault, so watch how you handle him. The kid I want is a J. Michaels, twenty, rich, five ten, dark hair. Can you hold them?"

"I'll try, Reid. We've only got one car on duty this

49

morning. Maurice will be out at ten, but he's at mass right now." Maurice Gagnon was their detective sergeant.

"Can you try to get him out there after church? And make sure he's got his gun with him. Wallace can be ugly. In the meantime, can you have the uniformed guy check the airport, detain them? I'm on my way up there on the next flight."

"For sure," he said. Then he chuckled. "We heard you were on vacation with that actress lady."

"I am. But this came up, and she's working on a movie, so I'm at loose ends."

He made a frank French comment, and we both laughed, me dutifully, him with real amusement. Then I added the wild card. "The third guy who may be with them is called Dunphy. He's a dangerous SOB, but hold him if you can. He's wanted for assault." I gave him a description, and he wrote it down.

"Who did he assault?"

"Me," I said, and he laughed and broke into his accented English.

" 'E assault you, an' 'e get away. You slowin' down, Reid. Good t'ing your lady workin' for a while."

"I'm fighting fit this morning. I'll be there as soon as I can."

The clerk had been listening. Like most Air Canada people, he was bilingual. He had gotten so wrapped up in my conversation that he hadn't kept track of his nasal drip. I handed him the tissue box off his desk. He took one and blew his nose. "I heard what you said about getting the next flight. I'm sorry to tell you, Chief, there's nothing else before six o'clock tonight. Get you to North Bay around seven."

"How about the other carriers?"

He shook his head. "No, there're a couple of flights early tomorrow, but nothing before that. I'm sorry. You want a seat?"

"No, thanks. I can make it up there by two if I bend a

50

few laws," I said. "Thanks for the assistance. Please keep it all confidential. This is a police investigation."

"No problem," he said grandly. I left him rooting for more Kleenex.

Broadhurst was eating another doughnut, not making any progress with his photograph. I told him to keep on checking. I was just following a hunch about Michaels. I asked him also to call Mrs. Michaels and fill her in. Then I went back to my car, spent half a minute fussing with Sam, and left.

Traffic was thickening up. Sunday brunchers were heading for one another's houses. Families with kids were taking them out to the conservation areas that hang around the fringes of Toronto like a big jade necklace. Everyone was headed somewhere. Some of the moms and pops were obeying the law too closely for my schedule, so I drove across the 401 then headed north on the 400 Highway, three lanes each way, a freeway that really is free. About twenty miles north of Toronto we finally shook loose from Sunday drivers, and I tucked in behind a Corvette that was humming down the outside lane about twenty miles an hour over the limit. We were both pulled over at a radar trap half an hour later, but the guys let me go when I flashed my ID and told them what the rush was.

The 400 ends at the two-lane highway that runs up past Murphy's Harbour. It was thick with traffic, and I debated whether to stop, but finally I pulled off and into the lot of my little police station. The place was locked. I had left it in the charge of George Horn, an Indian who is a law student at the University of Toronto, home on vacation. He's helped me in a number of cases, and if he weren't off getting more education than he needs for the job, I would nominate him to replace me. If I can convince myself to quit.

He was out back, sitting in the stern of an aluminum johnboat, holding a fishing rod with an old-fashioned casting reel on it, watching a red-and-white bobber far out in the lake. He had one of those remote telephones with him and a minnow pail of bait.

He jumped up when he saw me, rocking the boat as he reached for the oars and pulled in the fifteen paces to shore. "Hi, Reid, what're you doing back here? Don't you trust me?"

"Where would Tonto have been without the Lone Ranger?" I asked him, and he laughed and shook his finger at me.

"Beware, racist, I know the statutes you just broke there. You're messin' with a lawyer here."

"I will live to rue the day. Mind if I open up? I need a couple of things from inside."

"*Su casa* is still *su casa*," he said, and turned as the reel on his fishing rod started paying out line. He picked up the rod and held it, unmoving while the bobber pulled out of sight for two more seconds. Then he struck, and the rod bent. "There's a pike out there, twenty, twenty-five pounds," he said happily. "This is thirty-pound test."

"Keep a tight line. I'll be inside," I said, and took out the station keys.

The first thing I did was phone North Bay. Marcel had good news and bad news. The flight had arrived early, and according to the clerk on the ticket desk, the three men I was looking for were on it. The bad news was that they had walked out and got into a waiting vehicle about two minutes before the police cruiser arrived.

"The clerk didn't get a make on the car, of course?"

"You know 'ow it is, Reid. We was lucky 'e see anyt'ing."

"Well, at least we know that they're in town. That's good." I said. "Thanks, Marcel, I'll be up there in about two hours."

I hung up the phone and thought for a while. Then I decided to bend the law a little. I'm licensed to carry a gun while I'm in the Harbour or on duty elsewhere. Technically, it belongs in the office safe if I'm off duty. But these guys were rough. If I came up against Dunphy again, I wanted some backup. So I unlocked the safe and took out my .38. It's a modest little piece by American police standards. Half their men carry heavier weapons, Magnums sometimes. But in Canada the possession of a gun is usually enough to cool a situation out. A .38 is as good a totem as anything else. The safe also contained the shoulder holster I'd used as a detective in Toronto. I don't like it. You take too long drawing your weapon. But then again, you should be enough on top of things to have the gun out in lots of time.

In this case, I might not be. The Freedom for Hire guys were probably armed with the guns they would use in the bush. Most likely the M-16 I'd used in 'Nam. Or if they were wealthy enough, the new automatic weapons that elite squads use these days. Either way, my .38, with its effective twenty-yard range, wouldn't be enough firepower. So, after some thought, I unlocked the station rifle from its stand. It's a Remington .308, and I'm accurate with it at 400 meters, probably farther than they would teach kids like Jason Michaels to shoot accurately in the time they had him up there, wherever they had taken him.

George Horn came in as I was loading the rifle. He was carrying a pike so big that its tail trailed on the floor as he stood there with his arm crooked against the weight.

"You got yourself a keeper," I said.

He grinned automatically, but his eyes were on the gun. "Yeah," he said, then, "I guess you know it's not hunting season, Reid."

"It may be where I'm going." I finished loading, put the safety on, and picked up the box of shells.

"You on a case?" He straightened his arm, and his fish trailed half its length on the ground. He was looking at me very straight, an athletic, good-looking kid who would have made any marine recruiter snap out of his lethargy. He wanted to come with me but was too proud to ask.

"Not a case exactly. I'm looking for a kid who's run off with a bunch of crazies. It's just a favor to his old man, not a police case at all."

"Then why the weapons?" He was turning into a lawyer right enough. A year ago he would have said guns.

"They're armed. And, like I said, they're a bunch of crazies."

"If that's the truth, why aren't you working through the police? Your jurisdiction only extends over the Harbour."

I laid the gun on the counter, pointing away from both of us. "Well, it's sort of borderline." He didn't say anything, but I could tell from his expression that he wanted more. He deserved more. He'd helped me out a number of times in the past, and he was twenty now, adult and sure of himself, getting good grades in a class filled with bright kids with expensive educations behind them.

"Okay." I gave in at last. "I'll tell you. I'm dealing with a crowd of mercenaries. They've scooped up this kid, and they're up outside North Bay somewhere holed up, teaching him how to fight. They they'll ship him out someplace and he'll get his dumb head blown off by some very capable Cuban-trained revolutionaries."

"What makes you say that? Maybe he'll be on their side." The lawyer emerging again.

"No, that's not how it works. The revolutionaries are fighting for a cause. They despise mercenaries. And with good reason. Most of them are psychos, misfits who can't hack it in civilian life. They're happy to get paid for killing people."

He frowned at me, thinking back to the law libraries in Toronto. "If they're hired here and shipped out, I don't see what laws they're breaking."

54

"Nor me. The only one I can dream up, if they train here, is possession of automatic weapons."

"Yeah." He nodded. "That would stick, but it wouldn't be much of a penalty. They'd lose the guns, get a fine, that's all."

I picked up the rifle, slipped out the magazine and put it in my pocket. Then I worked the action once, to be sure it was unloaded, and crooked it into my left arm. George watched me silently.

I broke the impasse. "This isn't something you should get mixed up in, George. It's only borderline police work. You've got a job to do here and a career to go back to in September."

He sighed. "This job looked good until I'd been doing it for a week. If it wasn't for fishing on my noon hour, I'd go crazy."

"Look, it could get exciting fast if the bikers came back into town. We need you here."

He grinned. "I'll try and remember that. It'll help keep my eyes from closing in the long afternoons."

"Make the most of the leisure. The line of work you're in means seven-day weeks, twelve–fourteen hours a day."

I thought the idea might not have occurred to him before this, but he grinned like a kid with a new bike. "Yeah," he said. "Yeah, it does, an' I love it."

He picked up his pike. "For now, I'm gonna run this across the lake to my mother. She thinks I've forgotten how to fish since I went to school."

"That'll change her mind for her," I said, and then, because his eyes showed he was hungry for more information, I told him what I was planning to do. It wasn't complex. I would drive up to North Bay and ask around, see what signs of the Freedom for Hire people I could come up with. Somebody would know something. Maybe a gas-station attendant, maybe the barman at one of the beverage rooms, maybe the manager of the local bush-plane service. I would follow up as far as I could.

He asked the obvious question. "How will you follow them, always supposing you can trace them?"

"I'm just going up to my house to throw the canoe on the car. Anyplace they're hiding I can reach with a canoe."

He didn't say anything more. He just stuck his hand out to me and we shook. "If anybody needs me, Marcel Dupuis at North Bay will know how to get hold of me," I said. Then I thought about Sam. "Listen. One other thing. I can't take Sam with me. I'm going to have to move quietly. One bark out of him and we're both gone. Will you take him for a couple days?"

"Yeah," he said, Indian again. I knelt and fussed over Sam, rubbing his big head so that he squirmed against my hand eagerly like a puppy. I would miss him where I was going. George watched without saying anything. He feels the same way about my dog. We both know how good he is in support.

At last I stood up, raised a finger to let Sam know that this was official, then went through the handing-over procedure. When I'd done it, George said "Come," and Sam went to his side. George nodded to him, then shook my hand and wished me luck and I was on my way, alone.

My house was still the way I'd left it. The soil is sandy and thin, and in August it's too hot for grass to grow, so you couldn't have guessed it was three weeks since I cut it last. I unlocked the house and dug out my backpack. I keep it ready to go, sleeping bag, fly dope, pot, plate, billy can, and a bare minimum of supplies. On impulse I threw in a couple of extra cans of meat and a bag of flour, which I slid into a plastic bag. Anything can happen in a canoe. Your gear had better be waterproof.

That was it. I paused for a moment in the kitchen, checking there was nothing else I needed, then took my combat jacket down from behind the door. It seemed silly now, in eighty-five-degree heat, but if I did head into the bush, the nights could get cooler fast. Besides, it was appropriate wear for the occasion.

FIVE

♦

I drove into North Bay around one-thirty, past the doughnut shops and motels that reach out down the highway
to greet you. It's not a pretty town, but it's prosperous,
as mid-north Ontario towns go. There's a military base
close by, and the town has a good sand beach on the
north shore of Lake Nipissing, which is the size of a
small sea. Now, in late August, the holidaymakers were
everywhere, happily storing up sunshine on their skins
to take back to the office and brag about.

I went directly to the police station and found Marcel
Dupuis at the counter, tying trout flies. When he heard
the door open, he scooped everything into the open desk
drawer in front of him and leaned against it, but I knew
about his hobby, so I just grinned.

He stood up and stuck out his hand. "Hi, Reid," he
said, speaking English now that we were face-to-face.

"Hi, Marcel. Looked like a Royal Coachman. You
have any luck with those Limey flies?"

He shrugged. "Me, I fish pickerel like a good Frenchman.
No, I 'ave a customer, 'e pay me twen'y bucks a dozen."

That took care of the formalities, and we switched to
the missing men. The detective had checked all the gas
stations and restaurants around the fringe of town, trying
to get a make on the car and its four people. Nothing. It

was nominally his day off, and he had gone home, so there was no chance to talk to him, but it wasn't necessary. If he said he had done it, it was done. The next move would have to be mine. I discussed it with Marcel.

"I figure they'll have a camp set up somewhere away from any road so nobody will hear them shooting."

Marcel brushed his big French mustache and thought about it. "That make sense," he said. "If they wan' it quiet like that, they can' be near a road." He sat down, took out his half-finished fly, and held the clamp between his knees as he tied on the hackle. I waited. He was like a lot of men, I guessed. His thought processes were clearer when his hands were busy.

At last he said, "It means they go somewhere by canoe, or they fly. An' I guess they save time, fly."

"That's my reading. Is there any other plane service started up, besides the one at Heron Landing?"

He looked up and frowned. "No. Jus' Pete Robinson at the Landing. Unless dey 'ave a frien' wid a plane."

I'd thought of that one. If they did have their own wings, I'd lost them for keeps. Any nonprofessional tight enough with Dunphy to fly his men into the bush wasn't about to tell me where they'd gone. "Any idea who else has a plane?"

He shrugged. "You know 'ow it is. There's planes in an' out d' lodges, Americans, guys from Toron'o. Could be one of dem."

"I guess I'll try Robinson first, then make a sweep of the lodges, ask around, see what I come up with."

He whipped the knot on his hackle and unclipped the finished fly from the clamp. It looked perfect, but he held it up critically, then snipped an invisible extra hair from the hackle and laid it aside. "I don't see no other way," he said at last.

"There's always the chance they've taken a room in a motel somewhere. Maybe right in town, waiting for their buddies before moving on, something like that?"

He tucked the fly into a wallet made of coarse sacking, hooking it into the fabric. There were others in there, all identical.

"I'll get on to that," he said. "Take a couple hours on the phone."

"Thanks, Marcel. I'll go talk to Pete Robinson. I'll call in for messages. If you do find them, maybe you could keep tabs on them until I get back."

"Sure," he said. He put his fly-tying tackle into the drawer and reached for the yellow pages.

I thanked him and left, driving away with all the windows down, trying to blast the heat out of the car.

Heron's Landing is a smaller version of Murphy's Harbour. The locals live by renting cottages to the summer tourists and going into the bush to cut pulpwood in winter. The biggest industry in town is Robinson's Air Service. They have two planes, equipped with floats in summer, skis in winter. Pete Robinson flies one; his wife flies the other. They do most of their own maintenance.

If people looked the part, the way they do in movies, Pete would be six feet two and lean, with his face crinkled up from staring into the sunshine all day. Instead, he's built like a fireplug, short and thick and strong and given to bursts of savage bad language. I don't think he means any of it; it's automatic, like prayer to a priest.

He was changing the engine oil on the Cessna when I arrived, swearing in a low hiss. He looked up and frowned at me, trying to remember who I was. When it came to him, he wiped his hands on a piece of pink rag and came over. "Hi, Chief Bennett, from Murphy's Harbour, right?"

"Right, Pete, how's business?"

We shook hands, and he shrugged. "I was doin' fine until they raised the goddamn premiums on insurance. Now I'm flying the first three months of the year just paying those bastards. Aside from that, we're makin' out." He stood watching the oil run out into the broad funnel of the wheeled container, then asked, "What brings you up here, anyways? No fish left down in Murphy's Harbour?"

"I'm supposed to be on vacation in Toronto, but my lady's out of town working, so I got out of the city fast as I could."

The oil trickled to a stop. I noticed that even at the end it wasn't black. It looked fresh enough to use again. He took care of his machines. It was why he'd survived forty years in the business without falling out of the sky. He reached out and screwed the sump plug back into place, then tightened it precisely with a wrench, tight and safe but not overstressed. Professional all the way. This wasn't a guy you could fool with devious questions. I had to rely on his honesty.

"Have you been out this morning, Pete?"

"Yeah. Took a party from Ohio into Gull Lake. Fat old guys. Had to make two trips, one for them, one for their supplies." He turned and grinned. "If they drink all the bourbon they've got along, they'll never catch a damn thing."

He waited for my polite chuckle, then said, "Not the guy you're looking for, right?"

"Right. The guy I'm looking for is a long, thin Georgia cracker name of Wallace. He may be in the company of two other men. One around nineteen, long hair, around five ten. The other is forty, fair hair cut short, mustache."

His face never changed. He didn't jump in too quickly or strike a pose while he pretended to remember. "No, nobody like that. What'd they do?"

"Wallace is wanted for assault with a deadly weapon. A knife."

Robinson lifted a liter of oil and stood with it in one hand, looking at me very straight. "And that's why you're chasing him to hell an' gone?"

I owed him a little more, and I paid. "Not exactly. But it's how I'll be able to keep him if I find him."

60

He opened the oil container and tipped it into the engine. I waited, and finally he spoke, softly. "Can you tell me the reason? Or is it a p'lice matter?"

He turned and looked at me while I tossed the coin in my hand. Telling him was a breach of security. If he was talkative, the story would be all over the region in a couple of days. But if I didn't trust him, I was at a dead end. The great Ontario middle north had swallowed up Wallace and Dunphy and Michaels the way a jukebox swallows quarters. No choice. "Pete, this is confidential. But I need your help."

He nodded slightly. "I'll try."

"These guys are dangerous. They're off somewhere in the bush training to be soldiers, with real guns. I've followed them this far, and they've vanished."

"You tellin' me they're terrorists?" He didn't chuckle or express surprise. He was a sensible guy wanting facts. It looked as if I'd made the right decision.

"Not in Canada. They're training as mercenaries; then they'll head out somewhere and hire out."

"Bastards," he said, and frowned. "I worked a lot of places before I saved enough to set up here. One o' them was the Congo when they had their troubles. They had mercenaries in there. Ex–French Foreign Legion guys mostly. They were worse than the rebels; shot and raped their way through the whole goddamn region. Animals."

It was like talking to the survivor of a bad firefight. I said nothing and waited until his old ghosts had settled down. At last he blinked and said, "I haven't seen anything like you're talking about. But I'll keep it quiet, ask around. I'd like to see the bastards outa business."

"Me, too. Appreciate anything you can do. I'm heading back to North Bay. I'll check in someplace and stay in touch with the police there."

He nodded, not speaking, then turned to his engine and poured in more oil. He looked grim. That made two of us.

I did what I could on the way back to town, stopping off at two lakeside lodges where I saw there were float-planes drawn up. Both of the pilots were there to tell me they never took passengers except family members. One of them was a stockbroker from Toronto; the other was younger, with violently ginger hair that I realized was dyed when he told me he was a guitar player in a rock group. He was harder to believe than the other guy, but I asked at the bar and found he had arrived the previous night and hadn't left the lodge since.

At four I was back in North Bay, checking into the Northern Lights Motel on the edge of town. It was small but had a phone in the room. I used it to call Fred's apartment first, talking into the phone for three seconds after the beep, then staying silent for two and talking again. It triggered the mechanism, and I was listening to Fred as she told me she missed me and wondered if I was back in Murphy's Harbour fishing. She left her phone number, and I wrote it down and tucked the paper into my shirt pocket.

Then there was a second message. This one was from Mrs. Michaels. "Hello, Mr. Bennett. You were right about Jason phoning. He called this morning at around nine. Said he was flying out to the training ground. He sounded, oh, you know, kind of down, flat, something. Said he was going to grow up. Not to worry about him, he was with professionals. They would make sure he was trained to a hair. That's exactly how he put it—to a hair. Said he wouldn't be calling for a few weeks but not to worry." Her voice faltered here; then she cleared her throat and said, "I'm afraid this isn't very helpful, but he wouldn't answer any questions. Just told me not to worry." Another pause. "You have my number if you want to reach me. I'll call again if I hear anything more."

That was the end of the tape, so I hung up and thought about my next move. And I also thought hard about my motivation. Why was I following this up? The smart thing to do would be to cut my losses and head back to Toronto. I'd traced the kid this far. Now he'd vanished. By the time he came back into town, maybe a month from now, he would be fitter and wiser. He would have a war to go to, maybe even a safe little war from which he would come home with all the anger burned out of his system. It might even improve him. Hell, it had improved me.

And then I remembered his mother's face. That was a pretty good motivation, all on its own. On top of which, this was a request from Simon Fulwell, a guy I liked and respected. And besides that, the biggest reason of all if I was honest, I had nothing else to do but go back to Toronto, which I didn't want to do, or go back to the Harbour and do some fishing. Neither idea appealed to me. No, I would stick around a little longer, see if I could come up with a lead, then maybe get the police to come with me and arrest the mercenaries for possession of illegal weapons. In the bust, I could cut young Michaels loose, by force, if necessary, and steer him toward a legitimate military career. It's not everybody's choice, but for kids like him, or the angry eighteen-year-old I'd been, it's a chance to get your head straight and develop some pride.

A young father walked by outside with his three-year-old skipping alongside and a bucket of fried chicken in his hands. It reminded me that I hadn't eaten since the corned-beef hash eight hours ago, so I dropped into the motel coffee shop. It was early for dinner, but I ordered fish and chips. I've found that two good meals a day is all I need. In town with Fred, who was a great cook, I'd got into the habit of eating to her timetable, three times a day. It was good to get back to my bachelor habits. The place was licensed, so I had myself a Labatt's Blue and thought some more about finding young Michaels.

In the end it came down to waiting. The trail had died. Short of rushing off madly in all directions, I had no choice but to wait for a while to see if he came back into town, where I could hope to catch him at the airport, or to learn where he was by asking a lot more questions. I decided to do it that way. It seemed a better way to pass the time than sitting in Toronto, wondering how serious Fred was about being a one-man woman. I guess I'm no more neurotic than the average man, but it seemed to me that actresses have a harder time staying monogamous than most women do. They spend their working lives projecting themselves as someone else, and if they're as attractive as Fred is, it's somebody sexy. I guess I've been a policeman too long to ever put my suspicious nature behind me. We had a good thing going but a lot of miles between us. And while I was crazy about Fred, I wasn't sure any woman could feel the same way about me.

After my dinner I walked downtown to the police station. A new man was on duty. I didn't know him, but he was expecting me. He was young and eager and bored with the quietness of a Sunday afternoon inside. He stood up when I came in and stuck out his hand. "You must be Reid Bennett. I'm Wally Kelso."

We shook hands and smiled, and he said, "Got a message for you from Robinson out at Heron's Landing. He said you'd be calling in for it."

"Great. Thanks. What did he say?"

Kelso shrugged awkwardly. "Well, he's kinda ornery, you know. He wouldn't tell me. Said to tell you to call. You wanna use the phone?"

"Please." I took it and rang Robinson. His wife answered, and there was a long, echoing wait while she went outside and shouted to him and he picked up the extension in his hangar.

"Yeah," he said. "That Reid Bennett?"

"In person."

"Yeah, well, I got a lead for you. I flew a prospector into the area of—well, that don't matter. He's lookin' for gold, and the less people know about it the better. But anyways, while we was on the way up there, he told me he saw something last month up around Berry Lake."

The hair on my neck started to tingle. I was on the trail again! "Over the Quebec border, isn't it? What'd he see?"

"Says there was a couple guys there in a camp. They were dressed in military gear, he said. You know the kinda caps the Americans wear? Soft but kinda tall, with a stiff front on them."

Fatigue caps. "Yes, I know what he means. What were they doing?"

"Well, he was on the other side of the lake, just coming in from the portage out of Laroche Lake. He was plannin' to cross and head on into Lac Glace. Anyways, he says they were running around there over the rocks; playing soldiers is what he said. An' then they started blasting away with automatic weapons."

"Bingo," I said, and he laughed.

" 'S what I thought. Gotta be your guys training."

"What did he do? Did he talk to them, what?"

Robinson grunted. "He don' do a lot of talking, this guy. Me an' him go back a long ways, so he opens up to me when we meet, but he says he pulled his canoe back out of the water and went around them, went back over the portage and skipped on to another lake to the west of them. Went on his way from there."

"Good, so they don't know he saw them."

"Doubt they do," Robinson said. "He's kinda cagey. His canoe is all painted brown so it won't show up. He doesn't want people seeing him, and mostly they don't."

"Sounds like my guys, okay. Thank you, Pete. That's what I've been waiting to hear."

"Figured as much. What're you gonna do now?"

"Head in there, quiet, like he did, see if I can get the kid out." The words came out without thought, but as I spoke, I knew it was what I'd planned all along. Action made more sense than sitting around brooding over Fred.

65

"How're you planning to get in?"

"I've got the canoe with me," I said. "How far is this lake?"

He laughed. "About two weeks if you're fit. About two hours if you've got a coupla hundred for my time."

"You're on. I'll head out there now."

"Nah, I've gotta party to pick up this evening; it'll make it too late. If you still wanna go in the morning, be here around seven."

"See you at seven. And thanks."

"You're welcome," he said formally, and hung up.

Kelso was watching me carefully as I put the phone down. "Good news?" he asked casually.

"Yeah. Thank you. It was. Looks like I know where I'm going to spend my vacation."

SIX

◆

I spent the rest of the afternoon preparing to head into the bush. Having my survival gear along was a start but if I was going to be two weeks' travel from help, I'd need more. To start with I needed precooked foods. I wouldn't be able to light fires to cook anything, a jungle-fighter like Wallace would sniff the smoke from a mile away. I would have to eat prepared rations.

C rations would have been perfect but the only outfitter in town who was open on Sunday didn't have anything like that. So I picked up half a dozen cans of beans and a bag of dog biscuits. They're as good as army hardtack.

When I'd packed I spent a little time thinking about young Michaels. He might react to the pressure of training in one of two ways. Maybe it would be too tough for him and he would be glad to see me. Or maybe, perversely, he would be loving it, anxious to stay on and prove himself to his new buddies. If that happened I wasn't sure what to do. The smart thing would be to try and find out from him when he was due back in North Bay and have his mother there to talk to him. Either that or I could truss him like a turkey and lug him out in my canoe. That had two strikes against it. First, it was illegal. Second, canoes are unstable craft and it would be impossible to move him faster than his buddies could come after me. I could end up dead in some nameless lake.

That thought made me slow down and reassess my reasons for going. It wasn't the money. That was just a bonus. I needed this score to prove to myself I could still do it. Getting past Wallace would help me feel useful if Fred decided to make me redundant.

Wallace and Dunphy were a challenge. Wallace particularly. He was the same age as I was and well trained. I guessed he had been in 'Nam at the same time as me. Going up against him was playing marines, only doing it on turf I knew better than he did. I was born here and my father had taken me camping and fishing from the time I was old enough to sit still in a canoe. To Wallace this was just the boonies. He, and Dunphy, could live here but without empathy. They would use the same gear they planned to use on their assignments. I expected they would have inflatable boats and outboard motors and firearms, but they wouldn't have thirty years of knowing the woods and lakes. I had the edge in experience. I hoped it would make up for their edge in numbers.

I was up at five-thirty, gave myself the last hot shower I would have until I got back out of the bush, then shaved and drove out to Heron's Landing.

Robinson was having breakfast and he poured me a coffee while his wife threw some extra bacon into the pan. She was a carbon copy of him, short and powerful and talkative. Her vocabulary wasn't as graphic but they were well matched. I'd have trusted her to fly me anyplace. They had a large-scale map of the area I was going into and I studied it as I ate. There are towns in the area, on the Ontario side of the border, Temagami, Temiskaming, New Liskeard, except around New Liskeard the terrain was all the same, bush, with very few roads or settlements, especially on the Quebec side. Two hun-

68

dred miles out there wasn't much on the map except natural features like lakes and hills. It would be rough going, all of it and I would be alone. I folded the map when I'd checked it and handed it back but Robinson shook his head. "Keep it. I've got another."

After breakfast we lashed my canoe against one of the pontoons of his floatplane and loaded my gear. He nodded when he saw the rifle. "Don't normally like to see guns outside hunting season," he said, "but you're up against a rough bunch here."

"Shouldn't be any trouble." I minimized, "I just want to see one of their men and talk to him, bring him out if he wants, otherwise leave him to it." I strapped myself in.

"All set?" Robinson asked and when I nodded he began his preflight checks.

We took off and headed north-northeast over the endless string of lakes and the bush that covers all of this part of Canada, from here to the tree line. We passed a couple of lodges within the first five minutes but soon left all roads behind and had the country to ourselves. Except for a few fishermen and maybe a prospector there was nobody below us now.

"How're you planning to get out?" he asked me. "You want picking up?"

"Might be smart. If I do bring the kid out they'll come after me. I'd like to get out faster than I can make it by canoe."

"That's what I thought." He turned and grinned at me.

I pulled the map out of my pocket and checked it. There was a round lake, two lakes south of the one he'd marked as the prospector's sighting. "How about here?"

"Yeah, Pool Lake. I can land there. When?"

I thought about that. I needed twenty-four hours to get from my drop-off point to somewhere close to the camp, maybe another twenty-four to contact the kid, that would take me to Wednesday morning. Then I had to get out, over two portages and into the third lake, possibly with military rifles trained on me. That meant traveling at night, and hoping they didn't have passive infrared equipment with them. Three days in all.

"Thursday morning, first light."

"Okay." He nodded, businesslike. "Same rates okay?"

"Sure." I checked the map. "I'll be on the east shore, close to this point at the north end. But don't land unless you see a fire on the other shore down at the water's edge on this point. Looks rocky, is it?"

"Yeah. This is a new lake, geologically speaking, bare rock on both sides, bush to the water's edge at the north end, where the overburden built up as the ice moved south."

"Okay. Then I'll build a fire on the west side and wait on the east, seven in the morning on Thursday."

"You got it," he said.

We flew on for another hour, then he pointed ahead. "There it is, Pool Lake. I'll make a circuit, keep your eyes open, see if there's any action, if you don't see anything I'll set down."

I nodded and started watching carefully. It was only a formality, I knew that. If men were down there practicing jungle warfare they would be invisible from the air. I would have been and I knew Dunphy would be. But I had to go in somewhere, so unless I could see boats drawn up on the shore or a fire I would go in.

Robinson made his circuit and turned to look at me. "Looks clear."

"Yeah. Put me down close to the north end, unless you know where there's a portage somewhere else."

"Not on this lake. But it's red pine bush, clear under the trees, mostly, you shouldn't have too much trouble."

"Okay then, north end, please."

He nodded and turned south again for his run in, setting us down gently with a noise like heavy fabric ripping under us as the pontoons broke the tiny waves. We slowed and rocked back on the pontoons and then he opened up again and taxied up to within a hundred feet of the shore before turning and cutting the motor back to a slow tick.

I stepped down, over the canoe and unlashed it from the pontoon, settling it on the water, then swung my pack out of the backseat, and my rifle, and stepped down onto the pontoon and dropped everything into the canoe. Then I shook hands with Robinson.

"I'll see you Thursday. An' take care, eh," he said.

I nodded and stepped into the bow of the canoe where my weight would be closest to the center to help keep it balanced. I had two paddles lashed inside and I freed one of them and shoved off from the pontoon. Robinson reached over and slammed the door and turned away, opening up and taking straight off south ignoring the faint wind from behind him.

I crouched as the slipstream hit me and stroked out to the shoreline. There was a tangle of brush at the closest point but a little farther on was a deadfall lying almost submerged. I pulled the canoe alongside and checked the tree to see if it would take my weight. It did and I stepped ashore dry-shod and pulled the canoe around to a bare spot and beached it. Then I slung my rifle, lashed the paddle back in place, picked up the canoe and set out over the spongy duff of fallen pine needles, canting the canoe as far back as I could swing it so I could see ahead of me, seeking the best route. I didn't bother with a compass bearing. The sun was bright and I kept it over my right shoulder as I headed due north. The canopy above me was too thick for much direct light to fall on the forest floor but from time to time I got a glimpse of the shadow of the canoe and I kept to the right of it, walking steadily with that needle showing me where northwest lay.

After twenty minutes I stopped for a breather. I had crested a slight rise and the trees were giving way to rock that was bare except for lichen and occasional blueberry bushes. I set the canoe down, carefully, so that it didn't clunk, and sat beside it, making my plan. I had to stay under cover. That meant staying off the next lake until nightfall. I checked the map again, measuring how far I had to travel. Another thirty minutes of portaging, I reckoned, would bring me to the water's edge. The lake, with no name marked on my map, was about a mile broad at the base and tapered to a point at the north end. That probably meant it would be swampy there so I would check before landing. If necessary I would backtrack a quarter mile, halfway to a point on the west side. The point itself would be a dumb place to go ashore. It looked as if it might be bare, the kind of spot my enemy would use as a landfall if he was exercising on this lake.

I checked myself when I thought "enemy." I was thinking like a marine again. Good. I'd need to be that sharp if I was going to survive a meeting with Dunphy and Wallace—out here where there were no witnesses.

I decided to travel up the center of the lake. It cut down the chance of detection from either shore. My canoe is fiberglass and I don't make a lot of noise when I paddle. Besides, until I got close to the north end I would be too far away from shore to make a good target, even for an experienced sniper. Unless, of course, they had laser sights. How well equipped would they be? Good question.

After my break I picked up the canoe again and set off north. It took half an hour before I caught a glimpse of water ahead. I lowered the canoe and slipped out of my packstraps. The whole load weighed about a hundred and forty pounds so I was glad of the break. I stood there, letting the sweat dry on my body in the gentle warmth. The day was bright but this far north it was cooler than I had grown accustomed to in Toronto and I was glad I'd brought my combat jacket. I would need it when dusk fell.

The ground between the pines was almost completely clear. There was nowhere to hide the canoe so I did the best I could. I dragged it back thirty yards farther and turned it upside down, smothering it with handfuls of duff that I picked up. There was a chance then that it could have been mistaken for a smooth rock sticking out of the forest floor. It wouldn't, not if Wallace had trained his people properly, but I had to hope that they wouldn't be doing business this far south. If their camp was still located at the north end of the lake they would be up there, slugging through the swamp. With Wallace in charge they would probably be living in it, learning how to survive discomfort and come out of it fighting fit and fighting mad.

When I'd covered the canoe I put my combat jacket on and went down to fill my water bottle at the lake and to drink my fill.

After that I moved back and sat with my back to a tree about a hundred yards from the canoe. If anyone found it they would generate all their excitement away from me, giving me a head start in my race back to my pickup point.

It was only about nine in the morning and the day stretched ahead of me, empty, if I stayed lucky. And I thought about the men I would be facing. I speak good French. If one of the recruits saw me I might be able to pass myself off as a prospector. If I was lucky he would let me go. But I would have to be very lucky and the guy would have to be very green. My best bet was to stay out of sight. Once Wallace and Dunphy had me I was in for real trouble. They might not kill me but the least they would do is work me over so I needed a hospital.

The best way to pass time is to put your watch in your pocket and keep your mind empty except for what is going on around you. What I did was watch the birds. An osprey was flying over the lake in lazy circles, riding an updraft that took him one wing flap per circuit to negotiate. Finally he closed his wings and fell on a fish, a bass by the look of it, that he levered away through the air to his lookout tree where he ate and waited, like me.

When the sun had passed behind me and was throwing shadows at ninety degrees from the angle I'd noticed when I sat down, I broke out the dog biscuits and crunched a few of them, washing them down with water from my canteen. I spun it out until dusk, then walked down close to the water.

I still couldn't see anything but now, at dusk, the wind freshened. I stood and listened to it, trying to shut out the hiss of pine needles clashing together, listening for man sounds. And suddenly I heard them.

They were faint, so faint that I realized they were traveling most of the length of the lake, which was funneled toward me by its shape. There were three of them, three times the r–ri–rip of a triple gun shot. It meant three things to me. First, I was in the right place. Those were battle sounds, not hunting shots. Second, Dunphy was teaching his men the British combat technique. Limeys don't hose anything down. They fire a couple of quick shots on every sighting, making their ammo count. And third, because the shots came in triplets it probably meant they were equipped with ultramodern automatic weapons, the H. & K. probably, set up to fire three shots on every trigger press. I was where I should be, and I was in danger. These guys had enough equipment to leave me dead.

I passed the last half hour of daylight by protecting my supplies. The ammunition I had with me: .38 for my pistol in the right pocket of my combat jacket with the gun on top of it; .308 for the rifle in the left. I also filled both breast pockets with dog biscuits. Then I took a line out of the pack and tossed it over a branch. That took time. Red pine doesn't have branches close to the ground, like a maple. The lowest was thirty some feet over my

74

head but after a dozen tries I managed it and then tied my pack on and hoisted it ten feet clear of the ground where no bear would be able to tear it up.

By now it was almost dark and I carried the canoe quietly down to the water's edge and waited. It was cool but I didn't wear the combat jacket. If the canoe tipped I would have to swim a half mile and you can't do that with pockets full of hardware. I tied it to the life jacket and put it into the stern of the canoe. Then, when darkness finally settled on the water, I pushed off softly onto the blackness of the water and headed north.

As I paddled I kept listening for more gunshots but there was no sound anywhere except for the lonely yodel of a loon and the soft swish of my paddle. I glanced from side to side as I paddled, making out the tree line on both shores, keeping them equal in size, trying to stay out in the center as far as possible.

After half an hour I could see the trees meeting ahead of me and I paddled slower, taking care not to clunk against the side of the canoe. I was wondering whether the trainees would be out on a night exercise. It seemed likely. The shots had come late in the day. That could mean they were playing at ambushes, one group stalking another in the darkness, a game they would have to play for real when they headed south on their assignment. I wondered too if they had heard the aircraft. The wind had been blowing from them to us and Robinson had kept low when he circled the lake but the roar of an aircraft engine carries a long way over water. Up here there were not many other sounds to drown it out.

When I judged I was three hundred yards from the north shore I turned in to the west, halfway to the point, taking the extra precaution now that I knew for sure there were men around. The darkness was almost total but my night vision is good and I was able to find my way to shore without running onto a rock or tangling myself in the deadfalls that reached out into the water.

When I reached shore I sat for a moment, listening to the silence. Nothing was moving and I pulled the canoe broadside to the water's edge and stepped out onto a spongy mass of roots. It sagged under my weight and my left foot went into the water but I was wearing running shoes, the best thing for canoeing, so the water didn't bother me. I got out and picked up the paddle and my rifle and then hoisted the canoe by one of the cross braces and dragged it silently over the duff until it was clear of the water and I could carry it into the trees where there was a tangle of low branches.

There was nowhere to hide the canoe so I lifted my jacket out, turned it over, and slipped the paddle underneath. I put my jacket on, grateful for the extra warmth now that I wasn't using any energy. The hard part was about to begin.

SEVEN

◆

Now that I was ashore, alone, close to the enemy, I felt a bit like the dog that caught the car. What now? Sure I was in position to get the job finished, but the danger almost outweighed the advantage. I still had to locate the mercenaries without being seen, then isolate young Michaels and try to talk sense to him. And I wasn't sure he'd listen. He might just whistle up his buddies instead for a pickup game of kick the messenger.

I stood and thought it all through, working out my plan. The first consideration was their perimeter defense system. If they were serious about teaching these guys how to fight, they would have set up trip wires and booby traps around their camp. Maybe they would even have explosives wired up, something to get their people used to the nerve-shattering noise that's a part of every contact with the enemy. It wasn't likely they'd be using claymore mines. They didn't want their recruits dead, just smarter. But even a nonlethal charge would be fatal to me if I set one off. They would be all over me like a cheap suit.

In the end I did the wise thing. I waited, hidden among the thickest part of the brush that I could worm my way into. First I went back to the water's edge and drank my fill. Then I snake-crawled under the brush and lay there waiting for daylight. Slowly I let myself relax, and finally, in spite of my intentions, I slipped off into sleep.

Reveille came a little before dawn. Not a bugle call but a sudden explosion of gunfire and shouts. I jolted awake and lay listening, checking the direction and distance. A quarter mile on, I judged, at the apex of the lake. I sat up, resting my back against a tree trunk, and listened to the male roaring. It sounded like Wallace cursing out some recruit.

"You're dead, asshole," he shouted. "If I was the enemy, you'd have holes through your head. Where's your weapon?" Familiar sounds to anybody who has ever been through military training. The recruit must have tried to answer, but he was shouted down, and then a chorus of voices rose in a chant that made my hair prickle. "Kill! Kill! Kill!" they shouted like good little robots, and then changed it to a formless roaring as they ran for thirty seconds, which ended when the lake exploded with activity as they hurled themselves into the water.

I edged out of my hidey-hole and went to the water's edge to look at them. Eighteen men in the water, two on the rock. They were too far away for me to make out faces, but one of the men on the rock had a swagger stick under his arm and colorless hair. The other one was bending from the waist, shouting and clapping his hands like a swimming coach, swearing at the swimmers. Wallace, I guessed, with Dunphy playing his role of colonel.

Wallace kept them in the water for ten minutes, letting them out and ordering them back in three times before he formed them into two ranks and doubled them away over the rocks and back to their camp.

It was my cue to move. I figured they would be eating breakfast, shaving and hitting the latrine for the next twenty minutes. After that it would be soldier games that could send them out into the bush. If I moved now, I could be close enough to check which way they went and even to see which was young Michaels's hooch. I took out a few biscuits for breakfast, then moved up the side of the lake, gnawing as I went.

The trees opened up as I approached the head of the lake. It was difficult to stay in complete cover, but I kept low and moved from tree to tree as carefully as ever I had done in 'Nam. In one way the terrain favored me. The duff was a thick brown carpet. If anybody had grubbed down through it to dig a foxhole in the sand underneath, they would have thrown up a gray pile that would have stood out like a flower bed in the middle of a living-room rug. Another factor in my favor was timing. The recruits would not be looking for outsiders. Even this early in their training they would know that the only person out to ambush them was Wallace. At this moment, breakfast time, they would be relaxed, thinking he was getting his chow. But I kept my eyes wide open for booby traps. I'd seen my share of them in 'Nam and avoided them all. I wasn't about to make any mistakes now.

At last I saw them, and I was impressed. About eighty yards ahead, on a slight rise among the trees, there was a cluster of hooches, one-man shelters made from military-style ponchos strung over poles, about eighteen inches high, each protected by a twelve-inch pile of loose rock stacked around it. Wallace hadn't made them dig fox-holes. It was impossible where they were sited because of the rock. Instead, they were camped high, but blending into the background. If I hadn't been searching carefully, I might have passed them by without seeing them.

I stopped to unroll the hood of my combat jacket and throw it up over my head, lacing it loosely at the throat. Then I went forward, keeping an even closer lookout for wires.

The first one was about ten yards on, strung a few inches above the ground. I stepped over it carefully, then pushed on, down on my belly now, my rifle in front of me, checking for the second defense line.

It was about fifty yards out from the camp, and I stayed on the outside of it. There was no need to get closer. It wasn't close enough to recognize faces, but if Michaels appeared, I would probably be able to pick him out. I had to hope that when they started their exercises they wouldn't move out in my direction. It was possible but unlikely. They probably had a pathway through their perimeter that they would open by day and close at night. This wasn't the spot. I squeezed lower to the ground and waited.

Somewhere close by, the other side of the ridge where the hooches lay, I could hear men's voices, the cheerful off-duty voices of soldiers at their breakfast. And then there was the smell of good coffee, so alien to the forest that I could pick it up over the hundred yards or so from the cook fire. It made my mouth water, and once I smelled it, I knew my wait would soon be over. They would drink it and start their day.

Within minutes they had finished and were straggling back to their camp, lollygagging as they took the only minutes of relaxation they would have all day. I watched them, counting. Sixteen came back, all dressed in combat gear, with the high-top hats that had alerted Robinson's friend to the fact that they were military. They all carried rifles, automatic weapons that I recognized as the new British bullpup assault rifles, possibly the most effective infantry weapon in the world. My .308 and my pistol wouldn't cut it against them at short range. They had enough firepower to shred me.

I swallowed quickly and strained to see their faces. All of them appeared young as far as I could tell from this distance. The oldest would have been around thirty. Then I recognized the youngest, Jason Michaels. At least he had the same general description his mother had given me, and I picked him out by his slouch. Two days' training hadn't made a soldier out of him, although he was carrying his weapon professionally. But he looked out of place. I guessed he was in deeper than he liked. Big, noisy men who couldn't be bullied with his money were making him work hard, and his body wasn't used to anything more strenuous than a session with a girl in some motel room. He went to his hooch and crawled into it. I swore under my breath as I watched. It lay close to the center of the cluster. It would be impossible to creep in and get him out at night without waking his companions.

The men stood or sat around and smoked, chatting to one another in low, growly voices. They weren't relaxed. They hadn't worked together long enough; they hadn't fought together. I was reminded of a ball club at training camp. They were all jostling for recognition, each man acting a little larger than life, hoping to be the one who pleases the manager better than the rest. It bothered me. Any one of them would hold me if he could, just for the pat on the head he might get from Dunphy.

I also kept checking for sentries. If this was for real, they would have left at least one man in their campsite while they went for breakfast. He would go down later. And there were two missing from my count at the lake. That might mean there were a couple of guys on KP, or it might mean they had scouts out. I hoped they weren't circulating in the woods. It occurred to me again that I would have been better off turning Mrs. Michaels down and sitting in Toronto drinking beer and missing Fred.

Then Dunphy and Wallace walked up onto the rock. Wallace bellowed an order, and they all stood at attention, first grinding out their smokes on the soles of their boots. Michaels was the last man to reach the group, and Wallace strode over to him and chewed him out in a low, sneering hiss. I watched the kid's back stiffen as he tried to stand up straight, tried to avert the evil eye.

Wallace roared at him. "What's the matter, rich kid? Didn't the butler wake you up in time? Gimme ten." And then young Michaels was on the ground doing push-ups. He did a quick ten and stopped. Wallace shouted again, and he did a further fifteen, growing slower and wearier with each one.

Then Wallace said something quiet that made everyone except Michaels laugh out loud. And finally they turned and doubled away over the rock and down the way Wallace and Dunphy had entered, chanting an exercise song as they ran. God. Boot camp one more time.

I lay and waited until their chanting had died away, then counted to a thousand, slowly, waiting to see if they had left a guard at the camp. If they had, he would move now, with the boss away, stretching himself and maybe grabbing a quick smoke before Wallace had time to come back and catch him at it. But no one moved, and so I slowly stood up, moved back, keeping as many tree trunks as possible between me and the campsite. I hopped over the trip wire on the perimeter and moved away to the west around the rock.

As I moved, I heard the sound of an aircraft, the same trapped bumblebee roar that Robinson's Cessna had made the day before, but far off and faint. I stopped for a minute, wondering if it was bringing in supplies or new recruits, but the sound faded in the distance. An overflight, I thought, somewhere to the west of me.

About a hundred yards past the rock I moved back to the east again, heading for the shore of the northern lake. The going was harder here; the trees were smaller and tighter together than I was used to in my own area, northern jack pine mostly. I found it hard to walk and ended up on hands and knees, keeping down under the worst of the branches. I wondered what the group's agenda was for the day. Would they be on an exercise, reds versus blues, one group stalking the other with blank ammunition? Or would they be getting weapons training? Whatever they did, I hoped it marched them away from their base. I had a little sabotage in mind, something that would save me a lot of trouble if I was seen.

About thirty yards north of the rock, in a clearing they had slashed from the trees, I found the messing area. They had built a fireplace of rock slabs, and beside it was a big supply tent and two smaller tents, two-man jobs. Wallace and Dunphy lived there, I guessed, with perhaps the two men I had missed on my recount. Perhaps those two were the group's cooks, inferior to the two principals but important enough to warrant separate accommodation. I waited for a couple of minutes within a hundred yards of the tents, but nobody stirred. They were all out together on the morning's work.

At six forty-five precisely, the shooting started. Rifle-range practice by the sound of it. In every case there was a shout of command and then a crash of rifle fire, always in the distinctive triple-burst patterns. It sounded as if the men were being trained two at a time, each man firing a full magazine in those efficient b-b-bub bursts, then waiting for a report from the range officer.

The sound was coming from two hundred yards north of me. At first I wasn't sure of the direction in which they were firing. It figured to be away from their camp, so I was safe from stray bullets, but it was reassuring after a minute or so to hear the whine of a ricochet off a rock to the east of me. They were firing across the lake at targets set up on the far shore.

Now I had to work, carrying out the only project that would buy me time and safety if they saw me and started pursuit. I edged on down toward the water, and there, about twenty yards from the lake, tied to stout trees, I found their boats. There were three of them, inflatable rubber dinghies, each with a twenty-horsepower Mercury outboard.

I worked quickly, opening the cap of each fuel tank

and tipping in a handful of sand, wiping the top of the tanks carefully so that there was no trace of the sand on the outside. It meant they would start and run for perhaps a minute before the fuel filters or even the carbureters choked up. With any luck they would be stranded out on the lake, paddling to beat hell while they swore and tried to clear the engine. It would give me a chance to get away in my canoe.

The shooting was still going on, but I didn't linger. Instead, I ducked back the way I had come, rounding their camp on the west side. Only this time I didn't pass it. I squirmed in close, checking again for guards, and when I didn't see anybody, I went into the center of it and flapped up the end of Jason Michaels's hooch. It had a pack inside it and his mess tin. I opened the lid of the tin and placed the photograph that his mother had given me inside it, face up. I wasn't sure how smart the kid was, but if he had any brains at all, he would know it meant his mother had sent somebody to look for him. It would alert him to be on the watch for me. It was a gamble, but it was one I had to take.

Then I was through for the morning. Now I had to wait for nightfall, keeping alert in case they started moving out around the camp on an attack-and-defense exercise. To be sure I wouldn't be spotted, I retreated all the way back to where I had spent the night and crawled under cover in my thicket. If they did play games, they wouldn't be looking for me. Their attention would be on the campsite.

The day dragged as I lay still, listening to every sound in the bush, expecting any moment for a man to come creeping through the trees and point his assault rifle at me. I've done it before, plenty of times, but always for real, armed and ready to kill if I was seen. This time was different. I was walking the very boundaries of the law, able to defend myself if I had to but not by killing. These men might be misguided losers, but they hadn't committed a capital offense, yet. I had the feeling they would if Dunphy caught me. I had humiliated him in Toronto, and with his record, I didn't think I would survive if I was captured.

As the hours slowly passed, I listened for activity of any kind. Around nine the shooting stopped, and the men doubled back into camp. I guessed they were stripping and cleaning their rifles, but I was too far away to see. Then, promptly at ten, they broke into another chant, which faded as they doubled away to the north. And then I heard the first sound that made me anxious. They ran down to the water, six at a time, carrying their rubber boats.

I listened as Wallace shouted instructions for them to splash out into the water and climb aboard. Then they started paddling. That was a relief. If they tried to use the motors, they would soon work out that they had visitors, and the rest of the day would be spent clearing the area. I would have to abandon my canoe and back off, going as far west as necessary to bypass the swamp I'd noticed on the map. Probably it wouldn't be possible and I would have to swim it—dangerous. But necessary. I'd be forced out and wouldn't have any other choice.

For hours they paddled up and down the lake. Every twenty minutes they would head for shore and make a mock attack, beaching their craft and crunching up through the bush. If they were practicing stealth, they were earning about three points out of ten. The noise they made would have alerted an enemy in seconds.

Through it all I could hear Wallace shouting, hectoring, keeping up the kind of DI pressure that makes recruits hate. He was good at his job, I had to say that much for him. Even his mother would have hated him.

By late afternoon they had improved enough that I could no longer hear any splashing as they paddled, and I was shocked to find them coming ashore just a hundred yards south of me, on the point I had noticed on my map.

The crashing came closer. I swallowed quickly and waited, huddled tighter to the earth than I would have been under incoming fire, waiting for the shout of recognition that would alert me to get up and run, not sure what good that would do me, anyway. Then I heard a man swear, the angry shout of someone at the end of his patience. And then another man laughed. They were thirty yards from me, and I raised my head and checked them. One was holding his face, swearing over and over in a weary monotone while the other one said, "Why don't you look where you're goin', faggot!"

"Goddamn trees," the first one said. He took his hands down from his face, and I could see blood on his cheek. "Why're we working out here, anyway? We'll be in the jungle or rice paddies or something."

Then the second one said, "If you can't take a joke, you shouldn't have joined." The standard soldier's response to trouble. And the youth in his voice made my neck tingle. It was young Michaels, weary but proud. It wasn't his face that had been gouged, and he was certain it was because he was the better man. And he was only twenty-five yards from me.

I watched him as he stood stretching his aching back. Then the other man turned away, and Michaels called out, "Wait up. I'm gonna take a leak."

The other man was angry, following the party line. "Can't you do that on your own? Need the goddamn butler to undo your zipper or what?" Then he moved back the way he had come.

I lay still, breathing very shallow. I'd lucked out. Twenty guys in camp. Two of them had come close to me, and one of them was Michaels. If I could count on this kind of luck, I could clean up at the tables in Las Vegas.

Michaels unzipped and relieved himself, and I took my chance. I slithered out of the bush, coming up ten yards behind him. He was fastening his pants when I hissed at him, very low. "Jason."

86

He lifted his head and glanced around, not seeing me. He wouldn't have lasted a day in 'Nam. I hissed again. "Over here. Keep quiet."

Now he saw me, and he raised his gun. I left my rifle on the ground and held one finger to my lips. He stared at me, but he didn't cover me with his rifle, and I moved closer.

"I'm here to see if you're okay."

"Who are you?" Not the response I'd been looking for. It sounded as if he had confidence in himself. That could be trouble.

"A friend of your family." I didn't narrow it down to his mother. That might have given him all the prompting he needed to raise his gun and hold me.

"How'd you get here?" His mother was right. He didn't take kindly to adult interference. Either that or he was bemused by his training. I began to wonder if I'd moved too soon.

"That's not important. I followed you to see if you're all right. If not, we can get out of here. I've got a plane coming for us."

He lowered his rifle all the way to the ground, resting the butt and holding the tip of the barrel at arm's length from him as if the whole thing were a burden.

"Who sent you? Who are you?"

This wasn't a time for explanations. I decided to lie. I could explain later when we were flying out together in the floatplane. "Wallace is out to get you killed," I told him. "He hates your guts because you're from a wealthy family. You've got to get away while you've got the chance."

His lip lifted in a sneer. "Who the hell are you?" he asked contemptuously. "You talk like my mother sent you to try and scare me into going home."

"Wallace is wanted for attempted murder." Just a small exaggeration. "And Dunphy is a psychopath. He did a year in military prison for assaulting one of his own men. I'm telling you, these are bad people."

87

"And now I'm one of them," he said, and raised his rifle.

He'd left it too late. He had to hoist it by the muzzle before he could aim it at me, and before he had it half-way up, I had my .38 out of my pocket and jammed into his face. "Move and you're gone," I said. "Now listen."

His eyes rolled helplessly, and he let the rifle drop. I nodded. "Good. I'm going to leave the gun on you to remind you what you've gotten yourself into as a mercenary. People will be trying to kill you. No flowers, no flags. Just a bullet in the head if you're lucky and tossed aside for the village pigs to disembowel."

He licked his lips. I could see that he was trembling. Good. With any luck my twenty-five grand was within reach. "This Freedom for Hire is a scam. Dunphy doesn't have an army. He's a clearinghouse for recruits. He gets the hiring pay. It's an embarrassment to him if anybody comes back to claim it. On top of which you're rich and he's not. I'm warning you, you're dead if you go with them."

He still said nothing, and I lowered the gun. "Now I can get you out of this. All you have to do is come back here tonight. Sneak out of camp and join me here. Clear your throat quietly and I'll hear you. I'll get you out, and if you still want to play soldier, you can join the regular army. Okay?"

He nodded so quickly that I knew it was the fear in him making the decision. So I added the clincher. "And don't think you can go back and get the rest of them on your side. If you say you saw a man in here and didn't stop him, they'll say you were too chicken to bring me in. And if I'm caught, I'll tell them about this meeting."

His lips were dry, but he nodded again and whispered, "Okay."

I handed him his rifle, and he backed away, watching me fearfully. I was the first real threat he had ever encountered.

EIGHT

I lay hidden, listening for the sounds of men coming back into the bush, wondering whether Michaels was more afraid of me than he was of Wallace. My meeting with him hadn't been as clean as I would have liked. I had expected anger. Well-adjusted young men don't skip out on their family to go and kill people. But I hadn't expected the hatred he showed for his mother. It was warped, and I didn't know which way he would bend under pressure, whether the new resentments he was building up against Wallace would be enough to make him duck out and come with me or whether he would see me as a hireling of his mother's and hang me out to dry. All I could do was to lie low and wait. It was tense.

The only sounds I could hear were encouraging—shots and whistle blasts from farther down the lake, as if the men were off practicing their attacks in other areas. But I knew Wallace was smart. Even if Michaels had told him about me, he might carry on, lulling me so I would be off guard if he sneaked back with the kid at night.

Eventually I relaxed enough to pull out some of my dog biscuits and gnaw on them. They were some nationally advertised brand that promised to keep your pet young forever. The makers had been generous with the beef flavor, and they went down not badly, although my dentist wouldn't have liked the strain they put on my teeth and they did make me thirsty.

Around dusk I heard the men returning to their camp. Fortunately, Wallace had kept them using the paddles, so they still didn't know they had problems with their outboard motors. That was my ace in the hole if things fell apart later.

I heard them splashing ashore on the rocks at the north end of the lake, and then there was a command, from Dunphy, judging by the crisp English intonation, and a chorus of shouts, and they all hurled themselves into the water. Good training. They had worked all day and were looking forward to a rest and some chow, but he had sent them swimming, in their clothes, I guessed, from the speed with which they hit the lake. Dunphy was a professional. He was teaching them about the real world of patrols and attacks and perpetual discomfort. I listened while they spent ten noisy minutes in the water before doubling back to their messing area, chanting all the way.

It was half an hour later that they returned to their hooches. I guess they'd been given permission to light a fire and dry their clothes, because I soon caught a smell of woodsmoke and was able to pick out a glow in the treetops around their campsite. There was some laughter and the occasional half shout of men at horseplay, but these died away within an hour, and then the glow vanished, and they settled down for the night.

I crept out from under the branches and eased back to the spot where I had met Michaels earlier. I wished Sam had been there with me to warn me when anyone came close, but I did the best I could, straining my ears for noises as I sat and nursed my rifle with my back to a tree.

The hours dragged by, filled with the slow, quiet sounds of the bush, the trailing of a porcupine and the scurry of smaller creatures and the low woofing of a horned owl.

Out on the lake the loons were calling. Their lonely yodeling is the eeriest sound in the north, and I felt my hair rise as I sat there, willing Michaels to arrive and my long wait to be over. I was too close to the camp, much too close for comfort.

I checked my watch at a little after three, deciding that if he had not shown by five I would use the last of the darkness to head south off this lake. I had tried, and if he didn't show, I had failed. Hanging around wouldn't help.

About an hour later I heard the sounds of a man in the bush, the low crackle of sticks underfoot, each crunch slow and separate as the walker eased forward, trying to be silent. I raised myself into a crouch, ready to dive away if somebody flashed a light on me. I had the safety off my rifle, ready to slam off a couple of quick shots if I had to, keeping their heads down while I ducked away into the wood. The sounds seemed to come from one man's progress, but I wasn't sure.

They grew closer, the crunch underfoot mingled with the swishing of branches as the jack pines tugged at clothing and sprang free. Then, finally, I heard a low, gentle humph, a man clearing his throat.

I warbled a tiny low-pitched whistle three times, then waited, and a man's voice said, "Over here." It was Michaels. I eased out through the tangle, making very little noise, enough to alert a trained man but not enough to make him fire. Then the voice came again. "Where are you? We haven't got all night." It was the right imperious tone to make me certain he was alone. He sounded scared. He wanted to get out.

I squirmed further, and when he spoke, I was almost under his elbow. He said, "I'm over here, let's go."

I lay silent for a half minute longer until I was sure there was nobody with him, then whispered, "Come this way," and wriggled past him toward the branches where I had hidden my canoe. He swore softly but dropped

91

to his hands and knees and followed, and within a minute we found the canoe. "To your right," I whispered, and took the front end, staying low, although the branches were less thick here and I could stand almost erect without getting snagged.

He hadn't done much canoing. That was obvious, even in the dark, from the way he handled his end, so when we got to the water, I held the stern on the shore and told him, "Get in the bow, grab a paddle, and sit still till I'm in."

He clumped in, almost falling, swearing as he rocked but doing it softly. He was acting scared, and that was good. It would make him easier to handle. Then I put my rifle aboard and stepped over the stern. One dig with the paddle and we were offshore. Michaels was a clumsy paddler, changing arms constantly, not trusting me to keep us on course. It would almost have been easier to tell him to ship his paddle and forget it, but I didn't want to argue. Voices carry like bell notes over the water.

We made it to the south end of the lake in the glimmer of the false dawn. I ran us ashore up onto the duff that stretched to the water's edge, and Michaels stepped out and towed me in, lifting the bow and running the canoe half its length out of the water. I picked up my rifle and came forward, stepping ashore at the water's edge. Michaels pulled the canoe farther on shore, then straightened up and laughed softly.

"Made it," he said, and stuck out his hand.

I took it but not enthusiastically. We still had a day and a night to stay out of sight. Then we had to hope his ex-buddies weren't looking for us on Lac Laroche when Robinson arrived. If they were, we'd have to let him go without us, and it would take two weeks to get out of the bush on our own, even without resistance from Wallace and Dunphy. We hadn't made it yet. Not in my terms.

"I just hope you're right," I said. And then I heard the sound that told me he wasn't, the ripping silk sound of an outboard motor starting up at the north end of the lake, close to the camp.

Michaels swore. "They've missed me," he said.

I glanced at him. His face was just becoming visible in the growing light. He looked the same as he had the day before, spoiled and rich and expressionless. He didn't have any fear showing, and I didn't think he was that courageous. It made me wonder.

"Why would they head down here right away?" I asked him. "Have you set them up?"

"Shit, you're paranoid," he said, and his tone was huffy, but there was no fear in it. And there should have been unless he had lied to me. I frowned and glanced around quickly. I didn't trust him, not now.

"Why are they heading down this way?" I asked again. And this time I raised the muzzle of my rifle and nudged him under the chin. "Have you set this up?"

"For God's sake! Why would I do that?" It was a liar's answer.

"For kicks," I guessed out loud. And then I heard the sound I'd been waiting for, the dying splutter of the outboard, followed by a man's voice cursing and then the faint put-put-putting of someone tugging at the motor, trying to start it.

Michaels had learned something from Wallace. He ducked sideways and batted the muzzle of the rifle away. But he hadn't learned enough. I let the muzzle swing away but followed through on it, completing the motion so that the butt came up and caught him under the rib cage, hard. Michaels fell backward, arms and legs convulsing as he struggled for air. I turned back to the shore, staring up the lake to where the rhythmic splash of paddles was drowning out the splutter of the motor not starting. I must have listened for almost a minute before Michaels got his breath back in a sudden howl of

93

inrushing air. I prodded him with my toe. "Stay put or you get seconds," I said, and he let himself go limp.

The movement of my head let me catch another sound off the water, the quiet splashing of another inflatable boat, much closer than the first one, only three hundred yards out, pulling toward me from the direction of a rocky point to the west side of the lake. I'd been set up. These men knew where I was, and they were coming to get me, making a military exercise of it, something they could crown with the pleasure of taking a real live prisoner and then interrogating him. I had to get away, fast.

I turned and stuck my rifle muzzle under Michaels's chin. "Are they all out there? Or are some of them in the bush?"

He had trouble speaking, and the first words he managed were "Don't shoot. Please. I had no choice. They'd have torn me apart."

"Who's out there? How many boatloads?"

"On this lake, two," he said. "The other boatload went down the west lake."

"Stay where you are or I'll knock your head off."

I turned and knelt down on the pine needles, bringing my rifle up to the aiming position. I was torn. I couldn't shoot the men. This wasn't war, even though I would become an instant casualty when they found me. I had to slow them down and escape. That was all I could do.

The foremost boat was coming at me fast, as the men in it strained at their paddles. It was only about two hundred and fifty yards from shore. But it was bow on, and that gave me my break. I lined up carefully and shot out the float on the starboard side. The boat spilled sideways as my heavy round tore through all the flotation chambers. Men tumbled into the water, yelling with alarm, and then, as the reaction came and the drag of the down side pulled the boat sideways, I put a second round through the other side, collapsing all but the bow and stern compartments.

The water was filled with struggling men, but I was

safe. They would hang on to the remaining chambers, and soon the other rubber boat would pick them up. They would be wet but safe, and I could escape while they made their way to shore. I stood up, proud of my shooting, and turned back to Michaels when Wallace's voice said, "Nice shootin', asshole. Now what?"

I spun to face him, but he was too clever to be visible. "Drop the rifle," he said, and I did it, knowing he could kill me in a second, long before I could place him and snap off a shot. I had no choice. This was a time for waiting, not fighting.

"Good," he said when I had let the rifle fall. His voice was almost playful, making the word sound as if it had about eight ohs in it. "Now take two steps forward an' put your hands up on your head."

I did that, too, and then he stepped out from behind the thickest tree around, an old white pine that would have soaked up all the force of my .308 even if I'd fired at him. He was wearing camouflage fatigues and a cap and carrying one of the assault rifles I'd seen among his men. He kept it on me while he jerked his head at Michaels. "On your feet, kid."

Michaels struggled to his feet, moving painfully. Wallace laughed. "That was dumb, what you did. You gotta expect a man to use the butt."

Michaels said nothing. He bent to pick up my .308. Wallace ignored him, turning back to me. He was smiling, but it was a mask, the face of a Klansman giving the order to lynch someone. "You must think you're pretty good, boy." I kept silent, and he moved closer. It was my best chance—let him talk himself off guard and grab his rifle. "Yeah, you figure you can walk in an' talk one o' my guys into desertion. Is that what they taught you in the marines?"

Suddenly he fired off a three-round burst into the ground at my feet. He missed by inches and laughed when I started.

"Next time the feet," he said. "Then you can lie there an' worry while the guys come ashore. Seems to me they could be pissed at you, boy, getting 'em all wet. Might wanna dry their boots."

I said nothing, watching the tilt on the muzzle of his rifle, waiting to jump if he aimed at my legs. He was out of my reach, and all I could do was try to evade his shots. It was undignified, but I believed him. He would blow my feet off next shot unless I dodged. Saving my feet took priority over saving my face.

He fired again, but I was out of the way, and he laughed again. "Hell, boy, you quite a dancer."

I had moved far enough that I could see Michaels. I had hoped he might cool Wallace down, that his city sensibilities weren't ready to see me mutilated for Wallace's amusement. But he was standing with my rifle under his arm with a grin on his face, glad to be revenged for the thump in the gut I'd given him. I'd have to look somewhere else for help.

Out on the lake there was a lot of shouting going on. I guessed the inflated dinghy had reached the one I'd blasted. They would pick up the survivors and head for shore. I was certain they would all want to warm up by putting their boots to me.

I tried my last hope. "You don't think I'm doing this out of love for the little bastard, do you?" I asked. "His mother's paying me ten grand for getting him out. If you let me take him, it's yours."

Wallace laughed and fired another burst, but wild, not even trying to scare me, "She is like hell, boy," he said. "She's offerin' twenny-five grand. Can't you get nothin' straight?"

I didn't say anything, but I was wondering where he had got his figures from. Did Michaels know what the price for his return would be? And if so, how? And why had he told Wallace? Was he going to buy his way out of his situation after the gang of them had dealt with me?

96

"If you say so," I said. Not contradicting him but not agreeing. "All you have to do is let him out. I'll take him back, you collect the money, I'll give you all of it."

"Hell, boy, don't worry your head 'bout that," he said. "I'll get the money. Me an' young Jason, we unnerstan' one another."

I waited to see if he was going to come closer, but he didn't. He was being too careful, even stepping back a pace as he raised the barrel of his gun to cover me at knee level. "B'lieve I'll aim a little higher. How's the knee sound?"

I did all I could. I shouted, "Get him," and dived aside, but he only laughed and stood his ground, swinging his aim to cover me. Then there was the crash of a shot, and I drew myself up automatically on the ground, making myself small waiting for Wallace's second shot. Only he wasn't in charge anymore. His rifle went flying out of his grasp as he yowled in pain and rolled on the ground, clutching his right hand. I dived for the rifle and held it on Michaels, who was standing staring at Wallace with his mouth open.

"Drop it," I shouted.

He dropped the gun, and I waved the muzzle of the bullpup at him until he had edged back to where I could pick up my own rifle. I needed it. I was bluffing with the bullpup. I hadn't checked it but guessed it had blown up, maybe from an overcharged round, and that the action was useless, it had shattered, injuring Wallace. But now, with my own rifle in one hand, I glanced at the assault rifle and saw it was like new except for a smear of blood on the stock. Then I heard the most welcome sound of the morning. George Horn's slow Indian voice saying, "I gotta find myself a good lawyer."

He was back in the trees, about thirty yards off, carrying his family's hunting rifle, a worn old weapon so beat up that the barrel shone like stainless steel. Sam was standing at his heel.

I laughed, a quick gulp of release from the tension of

the last minutes. "I'll get you the best that money can buy." I had a load of questions to ask him, but they could wait. Right now we had to get ahead of the boatloads of mercenaries. They would be ashore in a couple of minutes, and we couldn't beat them all.

Wallace was standing, nursing his bloody right hand, moving it slowly up and down, cradled in his left in that prayerful way you do when there's nothing else to ease the pain.

I told him, "Sit down, Wallace," and he swore but sat, and I whistled at Sam, but he ignored me until George gave him his release message. Then he bounded over, wagging his tail. I patted him and pointed at Wallace. "Keep."

He crouched in front of the injured man, snarling, and Wallace craned back away from the menace. Behind me on the water the shouts were getting louder. I turned and saw that the second rubber boat had almost reached the one I'd sunk. Men were waving and shouting, but they were only two hundred yards away. Time was running out. George was standing on the trail. "We gotta go, Reid."

"Right." I swung my rifle to cover Michaels. It wasn't really necessary. He was shaking. This wasn't the kind of game he had trained for. He didn't know that friends got hurt when the bullets start flying. The sight of Wallace with a couple of fingers missing from his right hand was more than he'd bargained for. "Okay, Jason. We're heading out. You run ahead of me, keep up with my partner. Don't try to duck aside or I'll shoot you in the arm. That way you'll keep running, but you'll never disobey me again. You got that."

"Okay. Okay, for Christ's sake." He was shaken enough to enunciate every syllable. "If we've got to go, let's go."

He turned and headed toward George. I paused, looking at Wallace. He would be a handicap. He was injured and angry and would be hard to keep moving, but on the other hand, he was a hostage, and if we could get him out of the bush, I could arrest him and prevent his doing anything to George Horn, legally or otherwise. "On your feet," I said.

He looked up at me, and his eyes were filled with hate. "Fuck you," he said. "I ain't goin'."

"In that case I'll have my dog tear your face off." It isn't a trick Sam's trained for. His attack work is all counterattack. I knew he would hold Wallace forever if I gave the command, but he wouldn't grip anything except arms or legs. I knew that, but Sam's appearance doesn't give the fact away. He looks rugged with his torn ear, a battle scar from a previous firefight. Right now he looked ready to eat Wallace where he sat.

Wallace said, "I'll get you, Bennett. I'll shoot your dog and cut your goddamn heart out."

"Later. On your feet," I told him, and touched Sam on the head. "Easy, boy." He fell back a pace and relaxed as Wallace stood up, still holding his right hand, with blood dripping out between the fingers of his left.

I turned and called to George. "Have you got a canoe at the other side?"

"Yeah." He didn't say anything more, just hooked his arm ahead silently. Indian again.

I turned one last time and fired my last two rifle shots high over the heads of the oncoming boatload of men. They swore and shouted, and someone in the stern stood up and returned fire, wildly, hosing down the waterline, hoping for a spinner that would put one of us down. Dunphy trained his men well. Fortunately the shots hit the rocks and jumped over our head, buzzing away like a swarm of killer bees.

George led the way, with Michaels behind him, moving at a jog trot between the well-spaced pines. Wallace stumbled behind them, a pace or two in front of me. He started to slow down, and I hissed at Sam, who barked angrily, and Wallace picked up the pace again.

George Horn's long, loping pace never faltered, so I swallowed hard and kept up. We had twelve men behind us, wet, humiliated, scared, and ready to kill without any more provocation. We had to be gone before they could cross the portage.

The thought reminded me that there was another boatload out somewhere to the west of us. It was unlikely that they would be in the bush this far south, but I didn't want to chance it. I panted, "Seek," to Sam, and he took off away from us in a big looping curve that carried him fifty yards ahead. It meant he would be the first casualty if the mercenaries were ahead of us, but as much as the thought worried me, I had to use him. I didn't want George Horn harmed, and as point man, he was the most vulnerable. I just hoped that we were alone.

We ran until we reached the rock where I had rested two days before. George stood and waited for us to catch up. Wallace and Michaels both sank to their knees and sucked in air. I stood, while George listened silently. My own blood was pumping too loudly for my hearing to be acute, but I trusted George's fitness. After a minute he said, "Can't hear them. They may not know which way we've gone."

"Hope you're right," I said. I was looking at him as he stood, every muscle taut in concentration, and then I saw his nose twitch.

"Smell something?"

"Yeah," he said, and I turned my head to look back the way we had come. Far off over the trees I saw the sign he had picked up first.

"Smoke," I said.

He nodded again. "Yeah. I'd say they've set fire to the bush. Now we really have to run."

NINE

♦

I didn't argue. The bush was bone-dry, and the wind was out of the north. It wasn't strong, but the fire would strengthen it, whipping the flames ahead faster than we could run. We had to hope we had enough of a start to reach the canoe before the flames overtook us.

"Let's go," I told the prisoners. "You run or you roast."

They didn't waste energy arguing. They heaved in one more long breath, then got up and ran behind George, who had picked up the pace even more. We had half a mile to go and nowhere to hide. Sam was still running ahead, but he stopped and cocked his head back the way we'd come, his nose twitching. Then he whined once in his throat and looked to me for directions. "Good boy. Seek," I reminded him, and he cantered on again, ignoring the threat from behind us.

A quarter mile farther on, the smoke reached us, dry and sweet, almost pleasant in its first faintness, carrying memories of campfires and outings in the canoe with my father. George paused a second and waved us on, then ran even faster. We were almost sprinting now, running like quarter-milers at a track meet. I found myself dragging behind under the weight in my pockets and my rifle, but I hung in. I would probably need everything I had before we were free.

About two hundred yards farther the fire itself started crowning through the tops of the trees over our heads, setting the trees off like tinder, roaring like a hungry animal. The smoke grew thicker, choking us, cutting down our ability to run. The heat seared our faces, making us all lower our heads as we ran. Wallace fell. He lay motionless until I reached him and kicked him in the rear end, not hard. He needed prompting, not hurting. "You wanna be left here, looking like Charlie after a napalm strike?" I shouted.

He groaned and took one more long breath before struggling to his feet, his face dripping with sweat, flecked with ash that was falling on us like black snow, starting fires of its own in the duff under our feet. I glanced around. The fire surrounded us now, burning lower on the trunks of the trees. The few dead pines still standing were burning like torches. The heat was unbearable, and I took a moment to flip up the hood of my combat jacket, cutting down the pain on my neck and cheeks. We had only minutes left to reach water. Otherwise, the men behind us would find our bodies next day, black and tortured, arms and legs drawn up like a fighter's in the agony of dying from superheated fumes in our lungs while our bodies cooked in their own fat.

George and Michaels hadn't paused, and I had to blink hard through the smoke to see them running on a hundred yards ahead. I dug deep into what was left of my strength, thanking heaven that I'd kept myself in shape. All those lonely hours of running paid off now as I called on the most my body could give me.

A tree suddenly crashed across our path, flashing the duff into a carpet of flame, but we couldn't stop. First Wallace, then I, jumped it and kept running, through waist-high fire, choking and stumbling, trying to breathe without inhaling, keeping the heat and smoke out of our lungs. Wallace fell again but rolled and ran on, the back of his combat jacket scorched, his hair whitened with ash as it singed at the tips. I plunged after him. And then the sheen of water broke through the trees ahead.

It gave us the strength we needed to complete the run full tilt into the water. George and Michaels had already launched the canoe and were standing offshore about ten feet. Wallace and I both paused to duck under the surface to douse our scorched clothing. The air close to the surface was almost clear of smoke, and I crouched neck-deep when I came up, filling my aching lungs with cool air.

I looked around for Sam. He was up to his knees in the water, whining gently. He had outrun the fire and patrolled the water's edge, combining duty with survival. Now he waited for his next command. I called him to me, and he swam out while George brought the canoe broadside to us. I hoisted Sam in, and he curled down in the middle, still keening low in his throat, worried by the fire, wondering if I'd got the message yet.

"Pull back to paddle depth," I shouted, and George dug into the water, bringing the canoe in to where the water was three feet deep, where he and Michaels could reach bottom and balance the craft while Wallace and I got in. I held it for Wallace, who still couldn't use his right hand, then said, "Hold on tight, George. I'm coming in." He and Michaels strained down on their paddles, and I leaped high in the water and sprawled as far across the canoe as I could, trying to keep my weight central. It rocked and shipped water, but I curled myself in without sinking us.

"Pull," George said, and he and Michaels dug into the water and dragged us away from the shore, slowly, with the canoe down to its gunwales in the water, overloaded to its absolute limit.

There was no chance to pick up speed. We inched out, the veins standing out on Michaels's neck, his paddle blade almost bending as if the water itself were as thick as mud. I didn't move. We were out of immediate dan-

103

ger now. We could choke in the smoke that lay like cream across the surface of the water, but we would not burn. My trying to paddle with my hands would only tip the canoe, so, instead, I eased my handkerchief out of my pocket and soaked it in the water in the bottom of the canoe, pressing it over my mouth and nose. Sam was panting, his mouth open, tongue lolling. There was no way to make him a smoke mask, so I reached my free hand out and patted him gently, telling him, "Easy," over and over to soothe him.

After a minute or so the water began to get choppy as the wind, sucked up and reinforced by the fire, swirled at the surface of the lake. "Hold it here," George shouted, and Michaels stopped paddling. He and the others took off their caps and soaked them, covering their mouths and noses as I had done. I noticed that Wallace's right hand was still dripping blood, and then, as he moved his left hand to resoak his hat, I saw that he was missing the last two fingers on his right. George's bullet had hit his hand where it curled around the trigger guard. In a weird way I was glad that Wallace had not lost his trigger finger. I didn't like the man, and he would have killed me, but the only trade he had was fighting. A worse injury to his hand would have been as bad to him as a wheelchair would be to me. I felt sorry for him, but glad he could still work, just as long as he practiced his craft somewhere else, far away.

We sat there isolated in our slopping canoe, scooping handfuls of water to our mouths as the hot, dry smoke coiled past us, thicker and thicker, searing our throats, making our eyes burn and run with tears. We were distressed, but we were safe from the fire and from Dunphy's men. They would have to wait until the bush cooled before they could carry their inflatable boat over the portage and search for us on the lake. When that happened, we would be in deep trouble. All our natural cover would be gone. George and I on our own could have escaped, rolling in the ashes until we were camouflaged so well the men would have had to step on us before they saw us. But with Wallace and Michaels we were vulnerable, and I wasn't counting on any mercy if Dunphy caught me.

I wanted to question George. I wanted to know how he had found me. How did he happen to be in the right place at the right time to save me? How did he plan to get us out? I needed answers before the fire burned past us and we had to hide from Dunphy's men. But as the smoke swirled about us, I needed oxygen more, so I concentrated on breathing through my handkerchief and soothing Sam, who was sneezing and panting in the smoke. Wallace had a field dressing in his pocket, and after a while he pulled it out and tried to wrap his injured hand, working clumsily with his left. I tapped him on the shoulder, and he turned and swore at me but gave up and let me wrap the wound, tugging the dressing as tight as it would go.

The sky darkened over us as the fire spread down both shores of the lake we were on. And the wind picked up, growing stronger as the fire spread. I glanced at George, and he nodded, understanding without words. Yes, we were catching the wind. Yes, we were floating toward the south shore of the lake. More water splashed into the canoe. I didn't panic. It had flotation chambers in bow and stern. Even if it sank it would support us all in the water. I sat and worked at bailing, splashing as much water as I could back out of the hull and downwind.

At some point I checked my watch. It was seven-thirty. In Toronto people would be kissing one another good-bye and leaving for the office. Disc jockeys would be reporting on traffic tie-ups and making jokes. And here enough lumber to build a small town was turning to ash while every creature in the bush burrowed down or ran through the treetops to avoid the killing flames as we sat in our swamped canoe and waited for a chance to go ashore and survive.

To pass the time, I took out the dog biscuits I had packed into my breast pockets. They were damp and softened from the ducking I'd taken, but I handed them around, and we gnawed between gasps of air. Sam got his share, gratefully. Wallace took his with a sneer. A soldier's life, dog food and pain, but he was old soldier enough to eat while he had the chance.

It must have been nine o'clock when the smoke started to thin. It was as if someone had unfastened the flap of a tent. The gray light that had hurt us for so long, filling our eyes with tears, began to brighten. One by one we took the wet cloths down from our faces and breathed the cleaner air.

"It's passed us," George said.

"Okay. Do you have a rendezvous with the aircraft, what?"

"Yes. Tomorrow morning on this lake. The time you set up."

"That's going to be too late," I whispered. "The rest of these guys will be down here by this afternoon. We have to get away."

His face was streaked with ash and soot like a child's attempt to draw war paint. He ignored it, speaking hoarsely. "There's nowhere to go, Reid. We can't hide on this lake."

As he spoke, a gust of wind scooped a hole in the last of the smoke, revealing the shoreline to our west. He was right. A few trunks were standing, smoldering, trailing smoke downwind, but all of the ground cover was burned away. We would stand out like targets if we went ashore. And we still had twenty-four hours to put in before we could escape.

"The only thing to do is head down the lake and go south. Let's do it."

George nodded and called out. "Get paddling."

Michaels glanced around, rocking the canoe. "We won't make it across the lake. This thing will sink."

"It won't sink. It'll fill up is all," Wallace drawled. "Do's you're told, boy."

His authority was still there. Michaels dug his paddle into the water, and we inched southward over the choppy water. Wallace and I did our best to bail out the water that splashed in. We managed to keep the canoe half-empty, but we were submerged to our thighs. My legs began to stiffen with exhaustion and cold, and Sam had to sit upright to keep his head clear of the water, but we were safe, while the fire roared down both sides of us, consuming the forest faster than we could paddle.

We landed at last at the south end, beaching the canoe on the shore and stepping out carelessly into the water. "Pull it out and empty it," George commanded, and Michaels heaved the bow up onto the scorched ground, and all four of us tilted it so that the water ran out enough that we could lift and tip it completely.

I looked around. The fire had passed only minutes ago, it seemed. The ground was still smoking, and the trees were standing as black pillars, the last of the embers glowing as the wind raced by them to fan the flames that were half a mile to our south by now.

Wallace looked around him. "Jesus. Look at that."

"Nice guy, your boss." I said. "He'd've cooked you just to get me."

Wallace swore. "He figured I'd split with you," he said. "I owe the son'bitch." He turned to George and said, "I owe you as well, Tonto. You can't live long enough to get away with this." He held up his bandaged hand.

George ignored him. "Which way?" he asked me.

I waved my rifle at Wallace. "You and the kid sit down on that rock. Don't try to take off or the dog will run you down. Okay?"

He turned away without speaking and sat down on the rock. Michaels joined him, and they sat there staring at me angrily while I walked off a few paces with George and took out my map. "There's another party out on the lake to the west of here," I said. "I guess the fire beat them off, but we can't go that way. That leaves us heading east, or south behind the fire. I believe that south's better. When Robinson comes back, he'll see the fire, and he'll be watching for us on the water. If we go east, he may not swing by that way. He'll figure we've burned."

George grinned. "He was damn near right, Reid."

I reached out and bumped him on the shoulder. "Listen, thanks for being here. I was gone if you hadn't shown up, and they wouldn't have needed to burn the place."

"I figured you'd need me. I talked about it to the band chief. He said I oughta follow you. Bring Sam so he could track you down. So I did. Then, when we got to your packsack, I figured I'd wait till you got back. Then, early on, that guy there came ashore in a little boat. So I sat back and waited."

"I owe you," I said. "I've got twenty-five grand coming for delivering the kid back to his mommie. You're in for half of it."

He grinned again. "Yeah? Hey, anytime. That's better than legal fees."

"But more hazardous to your health," I said. "Look, we'll move on now, behind the fire to the next lake. Go ashore somewhere and wait for morning. If Robinson comes back on time, we'll wave him down."

"What if this guy's buddies come lookin' for us?"

"They'll be looking for bodies. I figure they'll move slowly, maybe not get to the southern lake till tomorrow midday sometime. They don't know where we are, and this is a big area."

"Right." He nodded and stuck his rifle under his arm. "Hey, we can let them carry the canoe."

"Of course. What are prisoners for?" We both smiled,

covering up the problems of the next twenty-four hours, and I went back to Michaels and Wallace. Wallace had a tobacco tin on his knees and was trying to roll a cigarette with his left hand and the unbandaged index finger of his right. "Smoke if you want," I told him. "It's too late to worry about fire now."

He looked up at me through narrowed eyes but said nothing. He was tough and proud of it. I knew firsthand the pain he was going through, but he was not going to let it show.

"Okay, Jason. You're on canoe detail," I said. "Pick it up and let's go."

Michaels stood up. He was scared and showed it. "Go where? What for?"

"We're heading out," I said briefly.

"Why don't we wait here? They won't find us."

"They will," I told him.

"You don't know that?" His old rich-kid arrogance was starting to show through. "They'll probably think we're dead. We nearly were."

"They'll mount a search-and-destroy mission," I said. "Pick up the canoe, we're moving out."

Wallace leaned sideways and spat like a ballplayer. "Now you better start workin' me over, tough guy, because I sure as shit ain't going nowhere with you."

I looked at him, seeing that desperate southern pride in his face. Guys like him have won more Congressional Medals of Honor than any other Americans. When you see "Death Before Dishonor" tattooed on their arms, you know they mean it. And he knew I was a copper, that I wouldn't use any more force on him than I had to. He'd beaten me unless I could bring him along. And if I didn't, he would tell his buddies which way we had gone.

"You'd rather stay here and lose your whole arm to gangrene, would you?" I asked pleasantly.

His face tightened, but he sneered again. "You a doctor's well's a cop? Y'ever seen gangrene in 'Nam?"

109

I was thinking as I spoke, trying to make him think this was planned but improvising the answer. "George, you and the kid head south. I'll catch up with you when I'm through here," I said.

George looked at me in surprise, but I didn't give him any signal, and his own intelligence steered him right. "Don't shoot him," he said, and Michaels gasped. "Use your knife, we don't want his buddies hearing us."

I nodded, and George turned to Michaels. "Grab the canoe, let's go."

Michaels was trembling. "You mean you're going to let this man kill him?"

"Pick up the canoe," George said.

I waited until the kid had the canoe on his back, blind to what I was doing. Then I spoke softly to Wallace. "On your face, tough guy."

"Or what?" he drawled, and I rapped him on his good arm with the barrel of my rifle.

"Or I hit your right hand next time. Okay?"

He swore, but he lay back and rolled over, keeping his hands extended in front of him. "Hands down your back."

He did it, and I told Sam, "Keep," and he craned forward, snarling. Wallace swore, but he lay still. I took the lace out of one of his boots and tied his thumbs together with it. It probably came under the heading of cruel and unusual punishment, the shape his right hand was in, but it was only a shade of the punishment he would have given me if George hadn't stopped him.

I don't like inflicting pain, so I didn't truss him any further, or even gag him. I just slashed the laces on his other boot, then heaved his boots off and threw them away. When his buddies came to search for us, they would find him, but he would be slowed down in following them. The ground was going to be too hot for bare feet, and it would take half an hour at least to find his boots. It would splinter him away from the others, about the best advantage I could hope for.

Then I told Sam, "Keep," and jogged away after George Horn and Michaels, following the clear trail they had left through the solid carpet of ash that covered the ground. The wind was still strong, and already it was picking up the ash in a cloud, resettling it. With luck our trail would be invisible by the time the mercenaries paddled down the lake behind us. I hoped so. We had to be out onto the lake before they caught up. Once that happened, we were safer. They would take hours searching for us. With even more luck we could be a couple of lakes south by then.

When I was a couple of hundred yards into the ruined forest, I whistled for Sam and went on jogging. He caught up to me within another fifty paces, and soon I found George and Michaels humping solidly over the smoldering ground.

Michaels was flagging, so I called a halt, and he lowered the canoe. "No need to sweat it," I said. "Nobody's going to find us now."

"What did you do to him?" he asked in a frightened voice.

"I tied him. They'll find him and come after us. But he can't do anything on his own."

"I don't want them mad at me," he said, and tried to grin. "They got pretty rough last night. When Wallace found your pack, they came asking questions. They're bad people." I wanted to hear more about it, but for now that was enough.

"Relax, we're on our way out of here. Grab the bow. I'll take the stern." Then I said to Sam, "Seek."

Sam ran on ahead, moving warily over the smoldering ground. He stopped and whimpered once as he tried to run over a rock and found it hot, but mostly he avoided the bad spots.

George kept up the pace, and we marched quickly down toward the lower lake. The fire had died down around us, but in front it was a wall of flame, holding us back, too close to Dunphy's men for safety. The back of the fire was traveling slower than the front. There it was crowning through the treetops, but here it was lingering, consuming everything burnable. We had to wait for the path to be safe enough and cool enough to follow.

It worried me. The mercenaries would be on the lake behind us before we could get out on to the next one. I took out the map Robinson had given me and checked it. The news wasn't good. We had two miles of land to cross before we got to the lake. It was a safer spot. There were islands on it that wouldn't be caught in the flames. We could hide on one of them. If the men came after us, they would have to search every one of them. That would take all day unless we were unlucky and they hit on our island first. But still we had a mile to go, a flaming mile that would take four or five hours to burn down. That would give them plenty of time to catch up to us, and if they did, George and I were as good as dead.

"Lemme see the map," George said. I handed it to him, indicating our only hope with one finger. "Looks as if this portion might be swampy. If we can reach that, we can take to the water."

He looked at it, narrowing his eyes. "Leads right into the next lake," he said. "But this's been a dry summer, Reid. Might not be's wet as we need."

We looked up, locking eyes thoughtfully as we considered our next step. And then, faint in the distance, Wallace's voice was shouting, "Down here. Down here."

George grunted. "Sounds like we've got company. They'll be on us like a duck on a June bug. And there's no place to hide."

TEN

♦

I turned to check behind us. I still couldn't see the mercenaries, but already a burble of shouts had sprung up. I figured they were coming ashore close to Wallace. He would point them after us. It was certain he had looked up when Sam left him and saw which way he ran. His buddies would start by doubling after us, faster than we'd been able to move.

"Okay, Jason. Pick up the bow and move."

"Into that?" He pointed at the wall of fire. "You're crazy."

He was shaking with fear, and I couldn't blame him. "Better run into it than have them throw us into it dead," I said. "That way we've got a chance."

"They won't kill me," he tried in a whisper. "I'm with them."

"These guys are killers. They'll kill us two for sport and kill you to shut you up."

I bent and picked up the stern of the canoe. "Right, grab the bow."

He was slow getting to his feet, but he must have been thinking as he did it. I was right, and he knew it. He'd probably already heard some soldier stories from the men behind us. They'd bragged of the villages they'd burned, the people they'd interrogated, the methods they'd used. He knew where he stood. I just had to make sure he stayed more scared of them than he was of the flames.

When he had picked up the bow, he stood looking at me nervously. I took a moment to explain what would happen. "Two hundred yards into that fire there's a swamp. It's a wide area, and we can get out into the middle of it, safe from the fire and safe from your ex-buddies."

"Two hundred yards? Through that?" The fear bubbled out again.

"Thirty seconds at most. Then into the water. Then into the canoe and downstream."

George was ignoring us, looking back the way we had come. He was just as scared but wasn't going to show it. "Someone's moving. I can see them back maybe six hundred yards," he said softly.

I set down the canoe and told them both, "The only protection we can have is to wet our faces and hands. Then breathe shallow and bust a gut running."

"How'm I gonna wet my hands?" Michaels was almost crying.

"The way you're almost wetting your pants," George said.

Michaels gasped. "You mean piss on my hands?"

George propped his rifle at his side and did it. So did I. Then, reluctantly, Michaels did the same thing. Then George opened his jacket and tore a strip out of his shirt and drew it over his head just like an old Russian woman's babushka. "Pull the hood out of your combat jacket and tie it as small in front as it'll go," I told Michaels, and he did it while I did the same.

"What about Sam?" George asked quickly. "He'll burn for sure?"

"When we hit the fire, he goes in the canoe," I said, and bent to pat him. "Heel, boy."

Sam heeled, and I picked up the stern of the canoe, then realized what had to happen. "Swing behind me, Jason. I'll break the trail."

He gulped and made the turn, bringing the canoe stern on to our direction. "Okay, let's move." I set out at a jog over the smoldering ground. Sam followed, whining low in his throat, baffled by my actions. Around us trees were still burning like Roman candles, showering us with sparks as we moved downwind of them over the blackened duff. Every step we took turned over fresh fuel, and the flames picked up behind us. Michaels was whimpering to himself as he ran, a litany of fear. "Oh, God. Oh, Jesus. Oh, God."

We gained on the fire, entering a zone where the branches close to us were in full flame, reaching down almost to our heads. I checked the run and turned back. "Sam. In," I said, and patted the canoe. He jumped in, sitting up anxiously. "Good boy. Down." I gestured with one finger, and he settled flat into the bottom of the canoe. He was heavy, close to a hundred pounds, and Michaels swore. "Fuck the dog. Shoot him."

"I'd shoot you first," I shouted, and as if on cue, we heard the angry *zizz* of bullets over our heads, followed by the clatter of gunfire as the sound of the rifles trailed behind the bullets.

George snapped off three quick shots, standing up, ignoring the flames, working the bolt calmly as if this were a moose hunt. Then he said, "There's eight more of them. Let's go."

We turned and ran on, right into the flames. If Jason was whimpering. I couldn't hear him. The roar of the fire was like endless surf on a beach. But the heat was even more vivid. It dried my mouth at once, then my lungs, so that each breath was pain, each step a separate struggle. The fire was licking at us, the flames of the burning branches flicking out at us, casually eating up any hair that showed on our arms or in front of our hoods, filling us with animal panic.

I tried to ignore it, tried to keep my mind clear, functioning high and cool as if I were up somewhere looking down on the three runners, pushing them on with my willpower, thrusting them toward the center of the hell we were in. My jacket started to burn, and my hands, with the urine boiled off them, hurt as if I'd stuck them into a stove. I raised one of them over my face and kept on, pace after pace, until the end of the canoe dropped behind me. Michaels had let go.

I turned to shout, but George had beaten me to it. He was standing over Michaels, his denim jacket smoking. He kicked Michaels once, then grabbed the end of the canoe and waved me on, but I paused another moment, and Michaels got up and stumbled after us as I pushed on, wondering why I was slower, not realizing that I was stumbling because of the softness of the ground under my feet, and then, without thought, I burst through a stand of blazing cattails into knee-deep water.

I flung my end of the canoe ahead and plunged under the surface, then came up and lifted Sam out of the canoe and dunked him under. He came up, kicking and whining, as Michaels and George Horn found the water and dived in. We bobbed there for another minute while the trees above us blazed; then I waved and staggered on, leaving Sam swimming until the water was mercifully up to my chest. Then I lifted Sam into the canoe and stood holding it as George slid himself aboard, pulling himself smoothly over the stern. Then Michaels climbed in, over the side, rocking the canoe almost upside down, filling it with water. When he was in, I went to the bow and pulled it under me, heaving up, over the prow and full-length on top of the canoe, then swinging my body under my arms and in, still facing the wrong way but out of the water. "Hold it still," I shouted, and Michaels and George froze as I turned around.

"Okay, keep in the deep part." I shouted it back through the smoke that covered us all, almost masking the others from me. I grabbed the paddle and eased forward, feeling for the bottom and glancing up to see if any trees loomed up ahead. None did. We were in the middle of the little creek, safe from the flames. If the creek ran all the way to the next lake, we were safe. For the moment I didn't question that. My map might have shown me, but long-range planning was out of the question. We had to stay out of the fire itself. Even if the creek left us stranded, we were clear of the flames and hidden from the mercenaries. We had won, for now.

Michaels was using his fatigue cap to bail, slopping water out of the canoe but stopping every second or third stroke to splash some of it on his own face. I didn't bother. We had burns. They would be painful but would get no worse as long as we stayed out of the fire. If we could use the time to get away to the next lake, we'd have beaten off the worst of our problems. The men behind us would not find the creek before the fire had burned out. We had half an hour to escape, and I dug into the water, not pausing to wipe my streaming eyes.

We were lucky. Within minutes we had reached an area where the creek widened into an expanse of water-lily pads with a few reeds almost out of sight on the fringes. The fire still roared, but it was a hundred yards away on either side. The smoke continued to swirl over us, weighing us down but with no heat in it to compare with what we had left behind. We were free.

Michaels was sobbing to himself, not in pain but in panic, nursing his hurts, fearing for the future. I glanced back at him and saw George, his brown face burned red, skin peeling from blisters on his cheekbones, but he grinned at me and stopped paddling long enough to give me a thumbs up. I winked, realizing that my eyelashes had gone, and turned back to my paddling, keeping us moving downstream toward the safety of the lake ahead.

We came upon it gradually. The lily pads on either side spread apart behind us, and the water roughened. I stopped for a second and waved my paddle in the air, and behind me I heard George laugh. Then I dug firmly into the water and moved ahead into the safety of the open lake.

The smoke still clung about us, hanging low over the water, turning and coiling like some creature in a science-fiction movie. It was gray and thick and choked us, but it meant nothing. We would not burn.

I turned back to look at George, then pointed on ahead, the way we were facing. He nodded and dug in with his paddle while I unflapped my pocket and took out the map. It showed nine islands, two of them lying close to the north shore, where they might be in danger from flaming fragments carried on the wind. Of the others, two looked as if they were little more than rocks. That left us five to choose from if we stayed on this lake. From the look of the map we didn't have a lot of choice. The portage to the south of us was close to three miles long, and there would be no trail. We would have to slash our way through unless the forest favored us with red pine with clear space under the trees. We wouldn't cross it before the fire caught us.

To the west we had only half a mile to travel, but the contour lines showed that the going was steep and we would be racing the fire. It wasn't a gamble I wanted to take. To the east there was no chance. The closest lake was four miles away, and it was long and narrow, a gouge left by the glaciers of the last ice age, lying north-south and ending three miles north of the next lake. From the air it might look like part of a chain, but with a fire and a gang of killers against us, it was no escape route.

I looked up, trying to make out the position of the sun through the smoke. There was no chance. The air was equally gray everywhere, so I looked back at George and drew my finger across my throat. He shipped his paddle and bent to splash water on his face, then to pat Sam's head.

Michaels looked first at George, then at me, then swore. "You're lost, aren't you? Lost. We've gotta wait here until the fire's gone and then run like goddamn rabbits again, haven't we?"

"You wanted combat. This is it," I said.

"This is bullshit," he said savagely. "I shouldn't have taken any notice of you. I should have stayed where I was."

"If you had, you'd have been doing this for real at the end of your training. Only the guys hunting you down would be better at their jobs than your buddies are." Talking was difficult in the smoke, but I wanted him cooled out by the time we got him home, certain that he had done the right thing in running away. If he was, I'd be free to take the money and go home with no arguments from his family.

He coughed in the smoke, then burst out, "Who in hell asked you to come after me, anyway? I was doing fine until you turned up."

"So was I. Sitting in Toronto doing nothing. Then your mother came and asked me to get you out, and I've had one hell of a vacation ever since."

He narrowed his eyes and looked at me, tears from the smoke running down his face, but angry. "My mother asked you to do this?"

"Right. She'd already hired a detective, but when he couldn't find you, she dug up my name and came after me.'"

He began to smile, slowly and painfully. With his teary face and the pain showing in his eyes, he looked like a game loser making the best of a bad thing. "My mother. Sharp dresser, around forty-five, dark hair, big wedding ring with diamonds?"

"That's the one," I said.

"You dumb bastard." He laughed bitterly. "That's not my mother. That's my father's girlfriend."

Explaining only makes you look foolish, so I saved face. "You thought it was a good idea when I came after you."

"Like hell. I wouldn't have come at all, only Dunphy questioned me after Wallace found your pack. Then they got rough, and I said I would come and lead you back to it so Wallace could catch you."

"You realize that you're expendable now that you've done that." I was keeping the pressure on, knowing he had broken already but was afraid of the fire, and of his buddies, wondering whether they would take him back now he had run away. "How did you get up here?"

"Flew, of course. The colonel had a floatplane, big thing, it was down at the town dock in North Bay. We went aboard and came up here."

"How often does that happen? That people fly in?"

He shrugged. "I'm not sure, but we had fresh meat in camp, so I guess they come in pretty often."

George caught my eye. That gave us a new problem. If Dunphy had an airplane at his disposal, he could hunt us down faster than we could run, even if we could get off this lake and head south.

"Do they have a radio at the camp?"

Michaels shrugged. "I don't know. I never saw one. I was too busy training, anyway."

"Okay, how come Wallace was on his own, waiting for me where we came ashore?"

"He found your pack in the trees when we were on our exercise. Dunphy wanted to bobby-trap it with a grenade, but Wallace said no, he would wait."

"Why on his own? If he'd had a couple of men with him, we'd have been caught for sure."

Michaels sniffed, embarrassed. "That's what Dunphy said, but Wallace told him he wanted to do it on his own, have some fun."

I knew his idea of fun. "And Dunphy thought that some of you tenderhearted recruits might have gotten upset?"

Michaels couldn't meet my eyes. He glanced down at his blistered hands. "I didn't give the orders. I just jumped when they told me."

"And asked how high on the way up. There's hope for you yet, Jason. You could come out of this with a set of balls." I wanted him humiliated. His sense of worth would rebuild quickly enough once we got back to the city and he could flash around in his sports car. Right now he needed to be humble, so I didn't spare him. I snorted and turned back around, blinking my eyes against the endless smoke.

We sat there for an eternity. I didn't bother checking my watch. We were safe until the smoke cleared; then we would have to find an island and hope we could hide out, moving south when it got dark. If George had some rations in his pack, we could manage for a few days or live on fish until we hit a highway a hundred miles south. It would show Michaels what he was letting himself in for as a soldier.

George heard the sound first. He said, "Listen," and I cocked my head, trying to shut out the roar of the flames and the crash of falling trees that had settled into the background of our lives, like the noise of a car motor when you're driving.

"Plane," he said at last. "Hear it?"

Within a few seconds more I did. "Yeah, sounds heavy, not Robinson's Cessna."

"Right. Maybe we oughta find an island and get under cover, Reid. Sounds like a Beaver."

"That's it," Michaels said. "That's the plane I was telling you about, the one we flew up in."

ELEVEN

◆

A pocket compass is no use while you're moving. You have to sight on a landmark and make for it, but there was nothing visible through the smoke, so I trusted to luck, matching my paddle stroke with George's so that the canoe didn't swing in a circle. It seemed from the map that the islands lay almost completely down the lake, one behind the other; if we missed one, we would hit another. Right now it didn't matter which as long as we could get off the water before the smoke cleared.

The sound of the plane died away as it headed north, over the fire and on to the safety of the upper lake. I strained my ears but couldn't hear the change of note that would have meant it was landing.

That much was a relief. Unless it was Dunphy's plane, it wouldn't land. It would circle and check for life. Dunphy's people would probably stay out of sight. They didn't want strangers butting into their private war.

George saw the island first. He called to me. "Off to the right, Reid, stop paddling."

I shipped my paddle, and he swung the canoe to the right and forced us forward until I could make out the loom of the trees against the smoke, green trees, safety. Then I dug back into the water, and we raced to land, coming up to a shelving rock that let us beach and step out, careless of the ankle-deep water. Sam sprang out on command and lapped at the water, wagging his tail. He could sense the safety even better than we could, and it put an end to his fears. I stooped to bump him on the back and tell him he was a good dog, then told him, "Seek." He set off to check the island for us while we drew the canoe out of the water and bent under a tangle of branches that forced us almost to our knees. That was a bonus. If the whole island was the same way, it would make it harder for Dunphy's men to search. We might just manage to hide out, even if they came ashore and looked for us. With luck they would already be tired from searching other islands. They would want to believe we were gone and wouldn't struggle through any more brush than they had to.

George had a pack in the canoe, and when we had made our way inland for about fifty yards, he pulled it out and said, "Let's try to cover the canoe, branches, duff, anything."

We scrabbled the ground for debris and built the best hide we could. It wasn't perfect, but it broke the lines of the canoe, and if they searched in poor light, they would miss us. Then he waved us on again, and we moved ahead until we came to a bare rock where we could stand upright. "This'll do," I said, and we all collapsed and sat with our backs to the rock, choking in the smoke, trying to catch our breath.

George did the practical thing. He opened his pack and took out a can of bully beef, opened it, and cut it into four equal portions. He handed two of them to me. "Sam gets his. He's earned it," he said. Then he gave one to Michaels, and I fed Sam and sat and nibbled my own ration, thankful to be out of combat for a little while at least.

Michaels was young enough that he wolfed his meat down and sat looking enviously as I made a meal out of my bit, doing the best I could to let it fill me up. When

I'd finished, he swallowed hungrily and asked, "Is that all we've got with us?"

"For today," George said. "I wasn't counting on feeding a crowd."

Michaels swore but did it under his breath, a sulky sound that made it seem to be our fault he was hungry. A rich kid's trick. I ignored it. "Why would your father's girlfriend want you brought back?" I asked, more to take his mind off his hunger than to know the answer. I hadn't examined the check very closely but figured it wouldn't bounce whatever happened.

"I turn twenty-one the day after tomorrow," he said.

"And they want you home for milk and cookies, what?"

"They want me home to sign the papers that make the old man my heir if I get blown away."

George frowned, his legal training showing through the burned face and the bushwise confidence. "Sounds like an unusual setup, him inheriting from you."

Michaels laughed shortly, then caught a mouthful of smoke and coughed, spoiling the impression. "Not really. But I wouldn't expect you to understand."

"Listen, kid," I told him. "George saved your ass this morning and just fed you. On top of which he's got a better education than you have, so watch your mouth and answer the question."

Michaels looked at me quickly, surprised, then away. "Sorry," he mumbled. "It's kind of complicated, that's all."

"Make it simple for us," I suggested.

"Yeah, well, my grandfather, that's mom's dad, he didn't like my father, so in his will he left money to me when I'm twenty-one. The old man's got business problems, and he wants my money as collateral for some deal he's cooking. He's been squeezing me ever since I turned twenty. Finally I'd had enough of it, and I figured I'd scare him, so I heard about the colonel, and I thought I'd go along with him for a while, just to make the old man sweat."

124

"And your mother?" It sounded as if he was short on affection of any kind, but you expect a boy of twenty to respect at least one member of his family. That's the way it happens in working families, anyway. Maybe the rules don't apply to the rich. Most rules don't.

"She's a wimp. He's been screwing that bitch for years, and she just does nothing."

"But you phoned this girlfriend before you flew out. Why?"

"I didn't. I phoned my mother," he said and clamped his mouth shut.

"Yeah. You've thrown a scare into all of them," I said. "They didn't think you had the guts to do what you did. You've shown them."

"Yeah." He was bitter. "That's fine, only now they're going to say that I didn't have the guts to stay there."

"Those guys would have killed you," George said softly. Like most Indians, he didn't waste words, but he could see where they were needed.

Michaels spluttered with anger. "That's your fault," he said. "I saw you shooting at them. I saw them fall. You killed a couple of them."

"Winged 'em," George said carefully. "Just winged a couple. One in the leg, another one in the arm."

"That's illegal." Michaels was shouting now, and I looked at him, and he dropped his voice. "You can't go around shooting people."

"That's what you signed up to do for a living," I reminded him. "Or don't foreigners count?"

George laughed. He knew what he'd done, and as a law student it frightened him, but this wasn't the place to show fear. "Cowboys 'n' Indians, right?"

"How hard did you hit those guys?" I asked.

"One in the hip. One in the upper arm. They're down."

"Which means they would need a couple of the others to go back to base with them. Good. That leaves them with no boat to spare."

125

George shook his head. "What I've seen, they won't use the boat; they'll walk 'em back to the shore and keep 'em there. It might give us an extra hour, but that's all."

"We've already had that. As soon as the fire burns down, they'll be onto this lake and looking for us. We're going to have to move at night, head south all the way down to a highway. I didn't see anything within a hundred miles when I flew in, did you?"

"There's nothing," he said. "I figure we'll take four nights at least, longer if we hit any long portages. Check the map?"

I pulled it out and looked. We were almost at the south end of it already. It stopped at the north end of the lake below us. Before I could show it to George, Michaels interrupted. "You mean we've gotta go four days and nights with nothing to eat?"

"See any pizza parlors around?" George grinned.

Michaels swore. "I'm not going." Hunger was stiffening his backbone. "I'll take my chances with the guys. I was getting on fine with most of them."

"Forget it, Jason," I said. "You've deserted in the field. The penalty is death, and that's the business Dunphy's in."

He stood up and threw up his arms angrily. Sam raised his head and looked at him. I reached out and stroked Sam, feeling the crispness of the burned ends of his hair. "We can do this either of two ways," I said easily. "You come with us of your own free will, or you come with us tied up in the canoe. Either way I can't leave you here to be shot."

He sat down again, his arms folded tightly as if he were in an invisible straitjacket. Maybe he was. I ignored him and spoke to George. "What do you think the fire'll do? Burn right down to the highway?"

He shrugged. "The bush is dry enough, but if the wind changes and it burns back on itself, it'll go out; might take a couple days."

126

"If it does, we can move by day as well as night, make it that much sooner."

He shrugged. "Robinson's coming back tomorrow. He'll report the fire, and they'll send guys in to fight it. We could join up with them if we're lucky."

"Let's hope they do. Otherwise, Robinson'll never get to us. He's going to think we're dead." I let the thought lie there, and we all sat silently until George cocked his head.

"Plane," he said. "Sounds lower this time."

We all sat and listened carefully, and suddenly the note changed as the pilot cut back on the power. "He's landing," Michaels said quickly. "They've spotted us."

"He's not on this lake," George said. "He's a mile or more off." And then, inexplicably, the power picked up again with a roar, and George laughed out loud. "Hey, you know what that is, don't you?"

I nodded. I knew, but Michaels shook his head. "What, what?" He squawked it in his spoiled-boy voice.

"That's one o' those converted Cansos, flying boats turned into water bombers. They're adapted so they can scoop water from a lake and drop it on a fire," George said. "That means we've got a chance. If he's in the district, we might get his attention."

"How?" Michaels was sneering to cover his anxiety. "What're we gonna do? Light a fire?"

I ignored him. "Let's get back to the water."

George ducked away under the branches, but Michaels hung back. "What if the guys are out there?"

"We'll shoot 'em," George said. I've known him long enough to know he was kidding, but Michaels didn't. He started swearing to himself prayerfully as if George and I didn't exist.

We wrestled the canoe back out to the water's edge. From there, with a clear vista ahead of us, we could see that the smoke was clearing. Visibility was still limited, but I could make out the shape of the next island in the chain, a hundred yards from us.

"Be a while before he can see us," George said. "I figure we should get out in the lake and I'll spread out my sleeping bag."

"What if they come after us before we're seen?" Michaels worried.

"They'll be in that rubber boat. We can sink it," George said. "You worry too much."

Worrying is uncool, so Michaels shut up, concentrating on putting the canoe in the water. I checked the wind and then the map. The wind was northeasterly, and the map showed that the land to the northeast was a narrow band of bush between us and the lake we had left behind. That meant the smoke would clear earliest in that direction. The sun was starting to show, and from the time, I judged it was southeast.

"We head around the island and out about a hundred yards is our best bet," I said.

"Right." George was grinning, his blistered face happy now that there was something definite to do. "Let's hope he overflies this lake."

"Got to," I said. "He's likely trying to douse the fire southwest of us, choke it off between the two lakes. He'll pass over us either coming or going."

George grinned again. "You got it, Pontiac. Let's hope he has."

I put Sam in the canoe; then Michaels sat in the center, and I took the stern. George sat in the bow, facing me, holding his sleeping bag, which was bright orange on one side, green waterproof on the other. "When he flies over, grab the end and spread it," he told Michaels.

Michaels was sulky. "He won't see this."

"Stands out like dog's balls," George said cheerfully. "Jus' do it."

"It won't help. They'll just think we're waving, being friendly."

"Not here they won't," I said. "This isn't Toronto.

People help one another. If we can get his attention, he'll land. He'll figure we've got problems."

"And we've got problems to burn," George said. He was opening up, the way he usually did with me, kidding, glad of the chance to exercise his city manners, to show that he had leaped the first hurdle to making it away from his home.

He stopped and listened, cocking his head up and back. "Sounds like he's coming back. Yeah!" He pointed up into the smoke. "There. Wave!" He and Michaels opened the sleeping bag; then George closed his end, and Michaels caught on, and they opened and closed it rhythmically, making a splash of orange through the pall of smoke. The plane passed us, a big old white flying boat looking as huge as a flying house. I waved my paddle at it, and George and Michaels tipped their signal toward it, trying to expose the most possible surface to it.

Michaels shouted, "Hey, down here," and George shook his head.

"The only people can hear you are your buddies," he said. "Keep it quiet."

The plane sailed past, about three hundred feet up. Michaels swore. "They haven't seen us."

"Could've," George said. "They've got a ton of lake water on board; they can't stop yet. Maybe they'll come back."

Michaels sat, slumped, his arms between his knees, defeated. "No, they won't," he said. "They've missed us."

George laughed. He was just as tense as Michaels, but he said, "You must've been an inspiration to your guys, Jason. Always smilin'."

Michaels swore, but he straightened up, looking around to see if the aircraft was still in sight. It wasn't, but as we waited, the engine note faded, then grew again as it turned back. I held my breath until the white shape loomed through the smoke a hundred yards away, lower now, down to fifty feet over the water and only a few yards to the south of us. The big bomb-bay water doors were hanging open under the hull, but as we watched, they retracted.

George stood up and waved his groundsheet, snatching it out of Michaels's hands. I sat tight, hands on the thwarts, doing my best to damp down the sway George was putting on the canoe, so intent on keeping us afloat that I couldn't even watch the plane. George hooted, "Hey, they've seen us."

"Motion them to land," I said. "And sit down before we're all swimming."

He sat, and as the plane roared past us, waggling its wings, we all three made the instinctive motion of flattening our hands and lowering them toward the water.

The aircraft passed out of our sight into the smoke, flying straight and true. "He's checking his landing run," I said. "He's coming down for us."

"I sure's hell hope so," Michaels said. "I don't need any more of this."

George grinned at me, but we said nothing. We waited, and after a minute the aircraft came back again, lower still but farther to the west. The pilot was waving to us now, pointing back behind him, closer to the north shore. I waved with my paddle and dug in hard, jolting us ahead into the teeth of his slipstream that made the smoke curl around us in a long spiral.

Michaels was laughing now, an excited hee-hee-hee sound, like a teenager responding to his first dirty joke. I had a guy like him in my platoon once. He never stopped giggling until he tripped a booby trap.

About a hundred yards farther the smoke started to thin. And then the visibility cleared right up so we could see the north shore, a rocky section, the narrow area I had noted on the map.

"We're too close to land," Michaels said shakily. "They could see us."

"We won't be here long." George had laid down the sleeping bag and picked up his rifle. He eased the bolt back a quarter inch and checked the chamber, then recocked and pushed the safety on. I did the same with mine. Michaels looked at us both and licked his lips.

I heard the plane reach the end of its southward leg and turn back toward us, the note beginning to rise in pitch as it approached. And then the motors slowed, and the big gull-shaped boat bounced down over the chop on the lake off to the west of us about thirty yards. It slowed at once and bobbed to a stop about fifty yards past us.

"The other side," George shouted. "The door's there."

I laid my rifle across my knees and struck out for the rear of the boat, bringing us around the end of the hull, close enough that George had to reach up and push the bow away from it.

There's a big blister on the side, but it was closed, and George reached out his rifle and caught us against the float. "They've gotta cut the motor."

He was right. The port motor stopped, flicking over slower and slower, the tips of the prop blades passing within a foot of the door that clicked open at the bow. George pushed off strongly from the float and grabbed at the opening. Then he ducked out of sight into the hull. Next Michaels pulled us farther ahead and climbed out, shoving off so hard from the canoe that I had to stroke back with the paddle to reach the hull. I got closer to the door and called, "George, get Sam in first."

George's head stuck out of the doorway, and he reached down for Sam's chest as I hissed and Sam straightened and poised to jump in. Sam gave a little kick and disappeared inside, into George's arms. Then I pulled ahead again and held the doorway, walking the canoe backward under me until I could reach George's pack and shove it through the door. I stuck my rifle ahead of me and climbed aboard, pushing the canoe behind us along the hull and clear of the propeller.

The interior was tight. Cansos were designed in the thirties, when engineers relied on angle iron to hold things together, and there was barely room to squeeze in behind the pilot. He was craning around to me. "What's happening? We figured you had an emergency." He was lean and old enough to have flown his aircraft on anti-submarine patrols in the Second World War. He seemed irritated that we didn't have any walking wounded.

"Police," I said. "There's a gang of guys with guns after us. Thanks for picking us up. Can you get off as quickly as possible."

"Guns?" He looked across at the copilot, a guy my age. "Guns? We don't want any part of this."

"I'm sorry. This is a real emergency. Please get us airborne and I'll explain."

I was digging in my back pocket for my billfold, and I flipped out my Murphy's Harbour ID. "I'm Reid Bennett; the young guy who got in first is my deputy, George Horn."

The pilot still didn't move. "That's fine an' dandy, but I'm not here to get shot at."

"Let's do it, Jack." The copilot was grinning. He wanted a real war story of his own. "If they're for real, let's swing around and take off downwind."

"It's not procedure," the pilot said. And then George shouted to me from the rear compartment, where he was looking out of the starboard blister.

"Boat coming. Six guys, all armed."

"Shut the hatch," the pilot said, and he poured power onto the starboard engine and we swung back downwind. I fastened the door clamps and leaned over him, peering out of his window. A rubber boat filled with mercenaries was about a hundred yards off, just coming into view through the smoke, and as I watched, one of them stopped paddling and pointed at our canoe. Then five of them turned as if on command and aimed their rifles at us.

The bullets sprayed through the fuselage behind the wing, and as the aircraft swung around, they started striking the stern, flicking and tumbling through the fuselage. "Get flat," I roared, and George and Michaels hit the deck.

The pilot was swearing, but he was still cool, struggling to start the port motor. It coughed and caught, but before he could kick the power on, we had swung right around and were heading toward the rubber dinghy, with the bullets coming right through the windshield, punching starred holes in the ancient Perspex.

I crouched and unclipped the side door, sticking my left hand out a few inches into the slipstream and loosing off three shots from my Colt. I heard the copilot give a whoop of delight, and then the port motor picked up power, and we swung south, bringing the rubber boat into my view. It was the far side of the blur of the propeller blade, so I held my fire until we were passing them at thirty yards range. The tangle of support wires on the float was in my sight line, but I chanced it, snapping off two more shots, aiming behind them to allow for our speed. I missed, but close enough that the shooters ducked and their aim was off. One of them was down already. I'd been luckier with my wild shots. None of them was paddling, and that was saving us. The recoil of the rifles was jinking their boat, throwing their aim off by the inches that stopped them from hitting me or the pilot, but most of the shots were plunking into the fuselage and wings.

"Shut the door," the pilot shouted. "I gotta get us up."

I swung it to and clamped it as the noise of the motors picked up, and we bounded forward, skipping over the waves like a pebble on a pond. I stretched as tall as I could in the confined space and saw we were heading back into thick smoke and then through it, a hundred and fifty yards on, I saw the bulk of an island with trees rising sixty feet high.

"Through the gate," the pilot shouted, and the copilot flipped open a flap in front of the throttles. The pilot shoved the throttles all the way forward, pressing them grimly as if he could force us off the water physically. And still we bounced, and the trees got taller and taller ahead of us. And then seconds before we reached the trees, the bounces stopped. We climbed agonizingly slowly, still staring up at the treetops, and the pilot dipped one wing to raise the other, matching the rise of the trees that straggled back from the shoreline up the rocks. The propeller chopped through the tops, sending a shower of greenery back over the starboard float.

The copilot let out a yelp, but the pilot said nothing, bringing the wing down again and climbing for thirty seconds before he eased the throttles back. Then he looked around at me. "I'm taking you right down to North Bay, and I'll have the police waiting," he said grimly.

"Good." I bumped him lightly on the shoulder. "And thanks for a nice piece of flying."

"Yeah," he said, but I could see his satisfaction. "Now what the hell's happening?"

I told him, keeping it as brief as I could, "I'd like to alert the Quebec police right away, make sure they get up here and pull these guys in. They'll need military reinforcements. These guys are professionals."

"Okay. I'll get you patched in," he said. "If we act right away, we've got them bottled up."

I blew out a long sigh of relief. My job was done. Jason was on board, and Freedom for Hire was on the endangered species list. Great. Then the copilot interrupted. "Trouble," he said. "The oil pressure on the port engine's dropped right off the clock."

TWELVE

◆

"Feather it," the pilot said crisply. The copilot did something, and the port engine slowed and stopped, the propeller blades revolving forward, edges into the wind. The pilot increased the power on the starboard engine and changed the trim on the controls, acting automatically, completely calm. "How's the other motor? Any sign of damage?" he asked.

The copilot opened his side window and stared out for an age, then slapped the window shut and turned back. "Looks fine," he said. "But we could have a gas leak. They hit us a lot of times."

The pilot cocked his head back toward me. "This means no North Bay. We'd make it okay, but it would take us the biggest part of four hours. I'm heading for Arrow Lake. We've got an emergency depot there with spares."

I nodded, and he spoke to the copilot. "Call base."

The copilot worked the radio and then nodded to the pilot, who took over. "Yeah, Madelaine. George Foster on Able. Two miles south of that fire at Laroche. We've got an engine problem. I'm making for Arrow Lake with the port motor dead. Alert the guys and patch me through to the OPP, can you? Over."

He sat silently for about thirty seconds, then spoke

again. "Yeah, Corporal. This here is George Foster of Flameout. I'm just south of Lac Laroche. There's a big fire there, about a thousand hectares, an' more important, there's a buncha guys with automatic rifles. They fired on my aircraft, knocked out one motor and other damage." He paused, then said, "I have a policeman on board, name of Bennett. Talk to him."

He gestured to the copilot, who pulled off his headset and handed it to me. I put it on, and he indicated the microphone switch. I nodded and spoke. "Reid Bennett, police chief from Murphy's Harbour. Who is this? Over."

"Corporal Hicks, Kincardine detachment. Over."

I asked him to get his tape recorder going and then gave him a quick summary of what had happened, including the fact that we had brought Jason Michaels out. I also advised him to bring in military reinforcements wearing the heaviest protection they had. Flak jackets would be no use if the Freedom for Hire people were using the new armor-piercing rounds designed for their bullpup rifles.

It took about ten minutes, and by the time I'd finished, they had a superintendent patched in, and I had to run through some of it again at his speed. He told me there would be an investigating team at Arrow Lake when we arrived. I would be debriefed by experts. I was glad George Horn was with me. As a law student, he would know how to handle the trickier questions, like why we had returned fire. Unless we were careful, the press would try to turn this into a gang fight. The best thing to do would be to make mileage out of the fact that the Freedom outfit were mercenaries. Even to the liberal press that's a dirtier word than police.

When I was through talking, I went back and checked on the others. Jason was sitting with his back to a bulkhead, in shock. George was calm. He was lifting out a bilge plate, checking for holes below the waterline. He looked up when I moved in behind him. "We took about

136

fifteen hits, couple down where they'll be trouble," he said.

"I'll tell the pilot. You two okay?"

He grinned. "Apart from I've never been shot at except by some fool I was guiding on a moose hunt, yeah. The kid's shook up, though."

"I'll smooth him down. We want him on our side. The OPP is going to have a couple of detectives waiting when we land. We have to get our stories straight."

"D'we lose an engine?" He jerked his head toward the port side.

"Yeah, lost oil pressure. Bullet through the line, I guess. We were lucky. They were out to get us."

"Nice guys." He laughed and this time it was a touch shaky. I bumped him on the shoulder.

"Thanks for everything, George. I'd have been in a lot of trouble by now if you hadn't shown."

"You would have been dead," he said. "That guy Wallace is meaner'n a snake. Glad I was there."

We shook hands, and I turned to Michaels, patting him on the shoulder and crouching to his eye level. "Nice going," I said. "You stayed cool under fire. Not many guys do."

He raised his head and looked at me. For a long moment he said nothing; then he grinned weakly. "Yeah, I did, didn't I."

"You did fine. But it's a bad business you were in. The detectives are going to be waiting for us when we land. They'll want to know all about what happened. Just tell it like it was."

He frowned. "It was like I said. Wallace found your pack and waited. I wasn't really part of it at all. Oh, he leaned on me, but he would've been waiting for you, anyway."

"Mention the fact that he leaned on you. This man is bad news, and we want him locked up. He's done enough that he's going inside for a couple of years. He deserves it."

"All right," he said uncertainly. "He's gonna be mad."

"By the time he gets out, you'll be off in Europe or somewhere. It's me he's going to threaten. It happens all the time. Comes with the uniform." That was true. If all the people who have threatened me over the years ever keep their word, they'll have to form a line.

I reported back to the pilot about the bullet holes in the hull, and he nodded. "There's a slipway at Arrow Lake. I'll land and taxi right out. This thing's got wheels as well, you know."

He didn't want to talk, and I took the hint and went back to join the others. I sat and patted Sam for a while, rubbing his coat until all the singed hair had broken away. His fur had saved him. His nose was dry, and he was panting heavily, but apart from losing a quarter inch of hair all over his coat, he was unharmed. Then I flopped out on the deck, remembering other flights in and out of combat zones in 'Nam, and soon I was asleep.

The change in engine note woke me with a start, and I looked up to see George staring out of the starboard blister. "Must be Arrow Lake," he said. "There's a big wide slipway down there."

I stood up and joined him, stretching the stiffness out of my joints. There were a dozen or so cars clustered around the hut at the top of the slip. "Looks like word's got out," I said. "We'll have reporters to contend with."

"Say nothing," George told me. I turned and looked at him. He was just a kid, the age of the guys in my platoon eighteen years earlier. His eyebrows were singed off, and his face and lips were blistered, and all his brand-new legal wisdom was in his eyes. "We could be in a mess of trouble. Guys like those can afford the best defense lawyers in the business."

"I'll have a word with Jason," I said, and turned away. Michaels was still sitting against his bulkhead, looking as if he hadn't moved in two hours. I crouched next to him and repeated George's warning, and he nodded. It

138

should have been reassuring, but it wasn't. He was weak and spoiled, and his grandfather's money was going to protect him.

We landed smoothly; then Foster lowered the wheels and taxied right up the slipway, skewing his angle of approach sharply to compensate for the missing power on the port side. He and the copilot got out first. Then George, carrying his pack and rifle, then Michaels, then me, with my Remington, then Sam. I'd been right. There were four newspaper people there, snapping photographs of us, and a man with a TV camera. There was also a uniformed OPP man and a couple of guys who looked like cops. They nodded at me, and I steered the others toward them, ignoring the press people.

The OPP man took over, quietly discouraging the reporters. He couldn't keep them away. They thrive on drama, and we all three had cameras jammed into our faces, but we followed the detectives into the hut at the top of the slipway, and then the uniformed man shut the door from outside, raising a hubbub from the press.

"You're Bennett?" one of the detectives asked me. He was a big man, soft-spoken, dressed in a suit that looked as if it had cost him ninety-nine dollars with two pairs of pants. I nodded, and he stuck out his hand. "Sergeant Tracy. Forget the gags, I've heard 'em."

"Hi. Reid Bennett. This is George Horn, and this is Jason Michaels."

He nodded at both of them but concentrated on me. His partner stood there, chewing gum quietly, watching me.

"What the hell's goin' on?" he asked.

I told him, making it like an official report, explaining who the mercenaries were, how I'd come to follow them up, what had happened at the lake, what weapons they were using, and the degree of discipline I'd observed among them. Then I took out my map and pinpointed the location of their camp.

"At the moment there must be twelve of them still fit and in action," I said. "George here put a couple of them down with arm and leg wounds. I lucked out with my revolver. There were sixteen, that's four out, counting Jason. And don't forget they've got those new Enfield assault rifles, and they're hard-noses."

"We've got a combat group from Petawawa Armed Forces base and a chopper full of Sûreté Québec tactical guys heading up there," he said. He turned to the other man. "Get in touch, tell them what Mr. Bennett had to say."

The other one nodded without speaking and went out, through the clamor of the reporters at the door. They all craned up, flashing quick shots inside the building.

The detectives waved to a bench that was most of the furniture in the hut. The rest was a work area filled with tools and drums of oil. "Take a load off," he said.

We sat gratefully, and he asked each of the others to go over their own stories. He asked a few questions, solid questions, breaking out extra details they had overlooked, then turned back to me. "This is a hell of a case," he said. "I'll call the Crown in North Bay to prepare charges. I've never handled anything like this before."

"It's a war," I said. "I can understand them shooting at me, but blazing away at an aircraft is nuts."

"Yeah." He nodded me away from the others, and I walked with him to one side where we could speak quietly without being overheard. He stood there a moment, staring at me sightlessly while he got his thoughts in line. "Seems to me there's two things to do. First is get them bottled up. Second is to negotiate. No way I want any guys in there trying to fight it out with them. What do you think?"

"The best move would be to capture their camp. You can starve them out. They only have one working boat; it would take weeks for them to get out in that, and

140

they don't have any rations with them. If you can head off their air support as well, you've got them."

He nodded. "Okay. I'm gonna need formal statements from all of you, including the charges you want laid. But like I said, that should be done after conferring with the Crown."

"Right, no sweat. Only my reason for tangling with them was to bring out Jason Michaels. I want to pass him back to his family and collect my pay. Until then, please don't separate us out. I don't want him running out on me."

"He likely to do that?"

I shrugged. "He was flaky enough to join that crowd; he could be flaky enough to run. And he comes into a mess of money in a couple of weeks' time, so he could keep on running."

"Crazy prick." The detective shook his head. "Why would a rich kid do anything's dumb as joining a cocka-mamy outfit like that?"

"For kicks, I guess. Anyway, please, don't split us up."

"You got it." He reached out and rapped me on the arm with his fingertips. "Meantime, I figure you should all get a doctor to look at those burns. You're kind of marked up."

"Thanks, and if you need anything from me, count on it."

He walked back to the others and said, "You guys need looking at. I'll have an officer drive you to the clinic, get something on those burns. Meantime, I'd appreciate it if you don't say anything to the press. Last thing we need is a bunch of TV cameras up there while we're trying to subdue these guys."

George nodded. Michaels said nothing, but he stood up obediently. For the first time I checked his outfit. Up until that moment he had been only a thing to be moved. Now I saw him as the TV audience would that evening, young, singed, dressed in combat gear like everyone wore in Vietnam. In the eyes of Joe Citizen he was a soldier. I had to disguise him for his own good. "Listen, Jason," I told him. "There's a boiler suit behind the door; slip it on."

"Why?" He was truculent now. Dunphy and Wallace were miles away, his money was back within reach, and he didn't have to take advice from anybody. I started to wonder if I'd done anybody any favors by getting him out.

"Because your ex-buddies are going to be the bad guys in tonight's news, and the fewer people know you were involved, the better off you'll be."

He sneered, his peeling face drawn up tight. "What the hell would you know about it?"

"I've already been where you're headed," I said. "And it took most of the last seventeen years to live it down."

The detective spoke. "It's good advice, kid."

Jason whirled to look at him. "Who're you calling kid?"

The detective laughed. "I got daughters bigger than you."

George grinned, and Jason bristled, but he slipped the coveralls over his uniform, and we all went out, Sam at our heels. The reporters clustered around, shooting more pictures, shouting questions. A cluster of them had formed around the two fliers, who were giving them a blow-by-blow of their war story, but that didn't stop the reporters from diving for us as soon as we came out. There seemed to be more of them than there had been, but maybe I was being more observant now that the action was over. We got into an OPP car, George in front, Jason and I in the back, with Sam between us. Then the constable gunned the motor away while another uniformed officer struggled to stop the press from following.

He didn't succeed, but we reached the clinic in Fayette and left the driver of the car at the door to keep the press out while a doctor checked us over. He gave us salve for our burns, tutting over us like an anxious mother. None of us had anything to say except me. I asked him what to do for Sam, and he smeared a little of the salve on Sam's nose and told me to put oil with his food for the next few weeks. That would bring his coat back to life.

It was half an hour later that we got back to the car. In the meantime, the townspeople had turned out to see what was going on. Maybe they saw the reporters and figured Tom Selleck was in town. In any case, they were disappointed when three scorched-looking guys got back into the scout car, along with Sam, and the OPP man drove us away, back to rejoin the detectives.

Jason was annoyed. "Look, I don't need this," he said angrily. Take me to the nearest hire-car place and I'll go home."

"Can't do that," the constable said easily. "Sergeant Tracy said I was to take you to the office. He wants statements."

Jason swore and settled back in his seat, arms folded across his chest. I ignored him and asked the constable, "What's been happening while we were inside?"

"The sergeant'll say." The OPP man didn't even lift his eyes to check me in the mirror. He just drove carefully, ignoring me. Jason blustered at him, but I didn't bother. He was smart enough to do his job as requested, and dumb enough to enjoy it.

We were all famished. I wanted to stop at a greasy spoon to get some burgers—half a dozen for Sam—but it wasn't possible with the reporters along.

We got to the nearest OPP post, a one-story wooden shack on the highway, trailing our kite tail of reporters. The constable spun us to a stop next to the door, and we went inside.

Tracy and his partner were in the front office, talking to the duty corporal. They looked up when we got in, and Tracy said, "All fixed up? Good."

"Listen, I'm a citizen," Michaels said, and Tracy waved him down.

"There's a lot of that going around, son. I need some more information from you guys."

"What's been happening?" I asked him.

"Good news, bad news, I guess," Tracy said. "The good news is that most of the guys surrendered with no trouble. The bad news is that their leaders, Wallace and Dunphy, have disappeared."

THIRTEEN

◆

Jason was the only one to react. He gasped. Dunphy and Wallace scared him. He wanted them in jail while he got his inheritance and jetted off to Fiji or somewhere.

"When were they last seen?"

"Just after Dunphy set the fire." The other detective spoke now. He was younger than Tracy and tense. His delivery was staccato, and he jerked his finger in his collar when he spoke, lifting his chin as if it gave him more authority.

"They all claimed that Dunphy did that, of course," I said.

"Waddya expect?" Tracy said. "They're in enough Dutch without an extra attempted murder charge. They say that the supply plane arrived and Dunphy waited there. Told them to go after you; four of them were to bring Wallace back if they found him. The others were to stop you three, any way they could."

"They sure tried," George said.

The young detective looked at him condescendingly. What did an Indian know about anything? He ignored him and spoke to me. "Four of them took Wallace back. The plane was waiting. Wallace told them to follow you; he was going to hospital. Dunphy must've been on board. Anyways, the guys didn't argue; they went back,

145

and when they didn't have a boat to use, they went all around the lake. The whole bunch of them was together close to the place where they fired on the plane."

"Like sheep," Tracy said. "The chopper has a PA system, and as soon as they heard the order to lay down their guns, they did it."

"Well, that's good. But how about the other two? Does anybody know where their supply plane is based?"

"From what I hear, they don't know anything." Tracy gave a quick chomp on his chewing gum. "Buncha dummies."

"I guess you've already alerted hospitals about Wallace's wound."

"Of course." The younger detective almost sneered. "An' we also evacuated the casualties. One hit in the thigh, one in the top of the arm. The other one got a bullet through the chest. Y'ask me, it's you guys we should be investigating. None of you's got a scratch."

Tracy made peace. "Okay, so skip it, Lloyd. These guys were defending themselves, that's all." He sighed and turned to me. "I'll have to ask you all for formal statements, please. Plus you'll have to appear when they come to trial, but you can go for now."

"Right. Jason, you go first." I nodded to the young detective, and he led Jason off to a side office.

Tracy said, "Okay, Reid, isn't it? I'll take your statement; then you can stay with the kid until we're through with Mr. Horn."

George grinned and sat on the bench, patting Sam's head. I winked at him and went and told my tale for the record.

When I got back out, Jason was waiting, with George. The young detective took George away, and Jason turned to me. "We can go now, right, they're through with us here?"

"We'll all go together. Maybe the officers will take us back to North Bay. My car's there, and we can drive home."

He shook his head. "No, that'll take hours. I'll call my father. He'll send the company jet."

I looked at him, weighing up whether he could run out on me. He met my eyes boldly. Maybe he would run, maybe not. But he had taken his fill of orders. He was back in his own world now, a world most of us never know, where company jets are laid on at the snap of a finger. He didn't need me anymore.

"Who'll come up to meet you?" I asked.

"Meet me? What is this? You think I'm a lost kid. You have to turn me over to my mommie?"

"The contract I took was to get you home. If you decide to zip down to New Orleans for some crawfish, then disappear again, I haven't completed my deal."

He thrust out his arms angrily. "What am I? A package? You don't have to deliver me anyplace. I'm my own man."

"Okay. Just have your daddy's private pilot bring a receipt for one Jason Michaels, alive and well. After that you can fly down to Rio."

He tried to outstare me but broke off eye contact and turned away. "Don't you trust me?" he asked over his shoulder.

"After this morning? Would you?"

He turned back with an attempt at a laugh, and I knew he was planning to vanish. "You can talk to my father. I don't deal in pieces of paper." He turned away, to the counter, and asked the constable behind it if he could use the phone. The officer handed it to him, and he called a Toronto number, collect.

When it rang, he didn't wait for the operator to inquire about the charges. "It's Jason, Margaret. Put my father on."

There was a twenty-second pause, and he spoke. "Don't worry. I'm fine. We got away, no trouble." His father must have heard the news, but Jason overrode him. "No trouble. I told you. I'm up in the sticks north of North

Bay. Can you send the plane there for me? Yeah, North Bay." No please, I noticed. As rich as he was, he didn't have to ask for favors; he just ordered. I wondered again why he had joined up with Freedom for Hire. Dunphy must be a hell of a salesman.

He listened a moment longer, then said, "Good. And there's someone here wants to speak to you." He turned and beckoned me with one finger. I picked up the phone.

"My name is Reid Bennett. Is this Mr. Michaels Senior?"

"Yes. What's up, Bennett?"

"I was approached by a woman who said she was your wife. She gave me a check for services rendered in finding and bringing out your son. Jason tells me I could have been mistaken about her identity. I just wanted to know whether my agreement with her is complete upon delivering your son to North Bay."

"I heard about that," he said. "Yes, that will be enough. Put Jason back on." Bad manners apparently ran in the family.

I handed the phone back to Jason, who listened for a few moments, then said, "Good. And have him bring some clothes for me, would you?" He nodded into the phone and said, "Good," and finally, "Thanks," and hung up.

When the detective was finished with George, Tracy got the same uniformed man to drive us to North Bay. None of us talked, and after a while I dozed, stiff and itchy in my dried-out clothes. George nudged me when we reached the airport. It's a tiny place, and as we drove up, I could see a Lear jet with some kind of company logotype on it waiting on the tarmac. I glanced around behind our car. Two others were trailing us, and I leaned over and told the OPP man, "Can you stop at the front and try to keep those reporters back for a minute?"

"It's a free country," he said. "I don't want no hassles with the press." He sounded jocular, the cutup of the lunchroom, I figured, having a much more exciting day than usual, when he would be out on the highway flagging down speeders.

"Try, please, this case is complicated."

"Do my best." It wasn't a promise, just noise.

He wheeled in, and we ducked out of the car and inside, twenty yards ahead of the reporters. The small concourse was empty except for a fit-looking young guy in a flight suit with the same crest on it that I'd seen on the jet. He took a couple of quick steps toward us and stuck out his hand. "Hey, Jay. Good to see you. Got some threads on board for you."

"Thanks, Brian, let's go." Jason shook his hand briefly and went with him, not looking back until he reached the outer door. Then he checked himself and turned to lift a hand to George and me. "See ya," he said, and was gone.

The reporters were crowding into the building, and they ran to follow Jason, but an elderly *Corps de Commissionaires* man with Second World War medal ribbons stopped them at the door. Some of them argued, but the others turned back and followed us. "Sir, excuse me, who was that?" one of them asked, and then they were all clamoring questions at us. There wasn't going to be any peace, so I bought them off with a quick piece of fiction. "Didn't get his name. My buddy and I were up in the area where the fire started, and we met him. Then the water bomber took us out. I guess he's some kind of wheel. That's all I know."

They wanted our names, but George fielded that one. "Lookit, we've been off work two days with this fire. We gotta get home while we still got jobs."

After that we were free to ignore their questions as we retrieved our rifles and George's pack from the trunk of the OPP car. "Were you hunting?" one of them shouted. "It's not hunting season."

"We're Indians," George said.

149

They dropped away then, running to the side of the airfield fence to take long shots of the company jet that was taxiing downwind to the end of the runway.

"Alone at last," I said, and George laughed.

"I don't need publicity," he said. "Wouldn't sit too good with my professors. They figure students should be seen but not heard."

"Okay, let's get home." I whistled Sam into the car and we drove back down Highway 11 toward the Harbour.

As we drove, I asked, "What will the rental place charge you for the lost canoe? Any idea?" George shrugged.

"Whatever the traffic'll bear, I guess. Maybe you can call them from the Harbour, tell them to claim it on insurance and I'll pay whatever's necessary."

"Fine. Shouldn't be much, and I'll split the blood money with you, twenty-five grand between us."

"Big bucks, but we earned it." George grinned. "Now I know what it's like to be in a war."

"Not like television. You can't switch off and go to bed," I said. "Anyway, first thing I'll do at the Harbour is cash the check this woman gave me in advance, then clean up the guns, then sack out."

"God, you palefaces sure love your sleep," George said. "You sacked out in the airplane, then in the car.

"So what're you gonna do after that? You've still got three weeks before you have to make your mind up about coming back full-time." George's conversation pleased me. Normally he was like most Indians, not talking much about anything. Now we were chatting like any couple of guys in a bar. And another thing, he wasn't reliving the escape, polishing up the story, making the most of his exploits the way most guys his age would have done. I was proud to know him.

"Well, Fred's off on the prairies playing schoolmarm in some movie, so I figure I'll come back up here and fish. If the weather gets a little cooler, the pickerel will start running below the dam. Could stick a few of them in the freezer."

He nodded. "Yeah. My uncle tells me he's gotta new black-and-yellow jig, works like a charm. I'll get him to make you up a couple."

"Great." I grinned and drove in silence until we came to a highway diner. "Hungry?" I asked.

"Thought you'd never ask."

We went in and had a couple of burgers each, and I brought out some beef patties for Sam. Then we drove the rest of the way to the Harbour, and I dropped George at his mother's neat little house on the reserve and went into town, to the bank.

We're a very small community, and our bank is a converted frame house on Main Street, opposite the Lakeside Tavern and the Marina. I parked and went in and presented the check. Millie van Kirk, the teller, made a little moue of surprise at the amount. "Won the sweep, Chief?"

I knew from previous investigations that she liked to gossip, but I had to tell her something. Policemen who come into big windfalls are always suspect. "Payment for services rendered," I said cheerfully. "I found somebody's missing kid."

"Good," she said, beaming. She loved happy endings. "I'll have to clear it before I can credit it to your account. Tomorrow be okay?"

"Fine, take your time," I said, and went back to the car and home. My house seemed extra quiet now that it had known Fred's laughter, and my voice seemed loud when I called Sam in and settled him in the kitchen. Then I had myself a good long shower and cracked a beer while I got the gun-cleaning kit out and worked on the rifle, then my .38. It was mindless, cheerful work, and I was whistling to myself when the phone rang.

It was Millie. She sounded apologetic. "I'm sorry to trouble you at home, Chief," she said.

"That's okay, Millie. What's on your mind?"

"Well, it's your check." She hesitated and then blurted it all out. "Looks like whoever wrote it has stopped payment."

"Oh." I felt my anger starting to boil, but it wasn't Millie's fault, so I kept it in. "Thanks for the phone call, Millie. I might have started using it to pay bills with."

"Sorry, Chief. I've got it here for you if you'd like to pick it up."

"Thank you. And if you could find out when the stop-payment order went through, I'd appreciate it. Like the time as well as the date."

"No problem," she said cheerfully. Sure she was cheerful. She had two pieces of gossip now for the price of one. First the big check, then the turndown. What would the rumor mill make of that one? I wondered.

The more I thought about it, the madder I got. A deal's a deal. I don't make many of them, not about money, anyway, but when I do, I keep my end of it, and I expect the other party to keep his. Maybe if you're rich enough, the rules don't apply. Or maybe there had been some kind of screwup and a fresh check and an apology were on their way to me right now. Maybe.

It was already five o'clock. I'd missed the Michaels empire for this working day. Maybe I should wait until the morning and present myself at his office. I dismissed that one. They would kick me out without a kind word. No, the best idea was to go and call on him. Which left only one question. Where did he live?

I solved that one before going any further. I called Irv Goldman in Toronto. He's a former partner of mine, a detective in 52 Division, which is in the heart of the city, down where the slums give way to pink-painted renovations. Part of his beat is the financial district. He would know where to find Michaels.

He had come on duty at three and was in the office tidying up the paperwork on some stockbroker with sticky fingers. He stopped his running to answer me. "Michaels? It was his kid involved with those mercenaries, right? Saw it on the update when I started."

"Right. That's my connection with him. I got the kid out, with some help from George Horn from the Harbour."

We chewed that one over until he had enough news to take home to Dianne at the end of his shift. Then he got back to the problem at hand. "Yeah, while we were chatting here, I had my partner check out Michaels's home address for you. Rosedale, as you'd expect. Got a pencil?"

I wrote down the address and thanked him. "I'm going to play this one by ear. He owes me the money, and George and I got shot at earning it, so I want it. But I won't do anything physical."

"Please don't." Irv laughed. "You've used up all the goodwill there is in town, stirring up those mercenaries. I was listening to the superintendent when the news came in. He called you a goddamn cowboy. Said it was a good job you'd left the department when you did."

"He's right there, anyway," I said. "Thanks for the information, Irv. Say hi to Dianne for me."

"Yeah. Same to Fred. When's she getting back, anyway?"

I told him, and he groaned. "Take plenny o' cold showers," he advised, and hung up.

The doctor at Fayette had given us each a tube of salve, and I put a little on my burns, then dressed in a better pair of slacks, city clothes, pulled a light jacket out of the closet, and set out for Toronto with Sam in the rear seat.

Now that I had no timetable, I kept my speed down to the limit, checking the changes in the city as I eased into it through its thickening waistline. It seems there are apartments out for thirty miles these days, big filing cabinets for all the human material that keeps the money pumping out of the stone-and-glass towers downtown. At seven in the evening the roads were still filled with homebound cars, most of them with a tired yuppy and a briefcase full of problems to be checked out after supper and the mandatory half hour's quality time with the kids.

It made me think. No matter what kind of decision I came to about my job at the Harbour, there was no way I could ever be an executive. Being tied to a desk eight or ten hours a day would be worse than a prison sentence. I guess my options are narrower than some people's.

The Michaels house was in Rosedale, the old-money section of Toronto. Most of the old houses have been split up into the kind of apartment it takes two solid incomes to afford. More reason for sweating in an office, if that was your idea of a great life.

Sam lifted his head when I got out of the car. I wound the window down and told him, "Keep." It wasn't likely that any of the neighbors would try to rip anything off, but old habits die hard, and Sam was the only antitheft insurance I needed.

A housemaid answered the door, and I asked to speak to Mr. Michaels. I guess he didn't get many guys with burned faces knocking on his door, so she asked snootily who she might say was calling.

"Colonel Dunphy," I said on a hunch, and she left me standing in the hall while she tritch-tratched over a parquet floor the length of a tennis court to a front room. I heard her murmuring, and then a woman's voice answered, and the maid came back.

"Come in, please," she said. I'd have bet most of the male guests were called Sir in that house, but what the hell. I followed her and came into a big room lined with books. A woman in her late forties was sitting on a spindly-legged couch that had been bought for its looks, not its comfort. She had a silver coffeepot and one cup in front of her. She gave the maid an automatic smile and asked her to bring another cup. Then she waved me to a seat across from her. "Sit down, please. My husband is out, but perhaps I can help."

I sat and waited. If she was going to lead the conversation, I could learn something. She sat and looked at me and said nothing until the maid came back with another cup and saucer. She took it and asked, "Coffee?"

"Please." I got up and accepted the cup, then sat again.

"I assume you've come about Jason," she said.

"Yes. I was hoping to see your husband about a financial arrangement we had made."

"And what kind of arrangement was that, Mr. Dunphy?" Her voice was under tight control, and I could tell she had rehearsed this scene a number of times, and I wondered why. She had obviously never met Dunphy. She didn't like him, or she would have addressed me by his rank. What was going on. I decided it was time to change her line of thought.

"To begin with, Mrs. Michaels, I'm not Dunphy. I used the name because I thought your husband would see me if I did and would refuse to if I used my own name."

She cocked her head to one side quickly; it was almost coquettish, and I realized that she was still a very attractive woman and that staying that way took up most of her energy.

"Why would you assume that?"

"Because your husband has just reneged on a deal I made with his representative. I was to receive a sum of money for getting your son back from the outfit he had joined. I did that, at considerable risk and discomfort. Now I find he's stopped payment on the check I was given. I'm here to ask why and to get my money."

155

"What did this representative look like?" Her voice was icy. She knew what was going on, but she was getting some kind of masochistic kick out of having me draw pictures for her. Complex lives these rich people live.

"Is that relevant, Mrs. Michaels? I spoke to your husband this morning when I'd brought Jason out as far as a police station close to North Bay. He assured me then that our contract stood. Now I find the check has bounced, and I wonder what's going on."

"Was it a woman?" she persisted.

"Yes. And even if it makes you angry, I should tell you that she represented herself to be Jason's mother."

She put her coffee cup down and clenched her fists in her lap. "Of all the unmitigated gall," she hissed.

"Look, I'm sorry. In fact, I'm sorry I ever got involved in this whole episode. I could have put in the last couple of days far more enjoyably at the dentist. I got the boy away, under fire. I delivered him to North Bay, where your company jet was waiting, and then found I've been stiffed for my pay. I'm angry."

She cocked her head again, defiantly this time. "Welcome to the club," she said. "There is a great deal of anger under this roof."

"When do you expect your husband home?" The hell with her problems. She could sit here in splendor being mad. I needed the money to get George through his next year of law school and to give me a start on whatever new career I chose.

She countered with another question. The obvious one. "If your name isn't Dunphy, what is it, please?"

"Reid Bennett. I'm the police chief of a small town in Muskoka, currently on vacation."

"Thank you, Mr. Bennett. And how much money are you owed?"

She had stood up and gone over to a writing table. Good. She was about to write the check, and I was going to smile and leave. I thought.

"Twenty-five thousand dollars. I have the returned check here if you would like to see it."

She whirled around. "Twenty-five thousand dollars? You expect me to write a check of that magnitude? On your say-so?"

"I expect somebody to write it. My deal was to save your son from almost certain death in this cockamamy mercenary outfit. In doing so, I've been shot at and had people trying to burn me alive. I don't think there's a regular pay scale for that kind of task, but I wouldn't have attempted it for any less."

She had frozen, so I stood up. "Obviously this is something I have to take up with your husband, Mrs. Michaels. If you could tell me when you expect your husband, I'll go."

Now she went back to her couch and sat down again, glancing up and waving at me vaguely. "Sit down, please. It isn't that simple. I'm sorry."

When in Rome. I sat and waited for her to speak. She fiddled with her coffee cup, adjusting it into the very center of the tray, then looked up at me. "I'm sure you find all this very unusual," she said.

"'Unique, in my experience. I'd like to know what's going on. Like why are you mad at Dunphy? You've obviously never met him."

"You're very perceptive," she said, her voice just this side of sarcastic. Then she realized what she was doing and shook her head."I'm sorry, that came out bitchy. No, I wanted to meet Dunphy because of the hold he had over Jason."

I cocked my head as she had done. "What kind of hold? Last I saw of Dunphy he was trying to kill all of us, including Jason."

"He gave Jason a sense of pride that was lacking." She got up again and brought a cigarette box from a table against the window, opening it and flapping it at me. I shook my head, and she took a cigarette and lit up.

"Jason is arrogant, I grant you. But he has no sense of self."

"You mean you encouraged him to join a mercenary group so he could find himself? Something like that?"

"My husband did. In fact, he paid Mr. Dunphy a big bonus to take Jason."

I frowned. Who was it said the rich are different from the rest of us. "But didn't he know the boy would be in danger? What kind of a father would do that?"

She sucked on her cigarette with a greedy gasp. "I suppose I should explain," she said. "My husband is not Jason's father."

FOURTEEN

♦

I held up one hand to head her off. "Look, Mrs. Michaels. I don't need to know any of this. I'm sorry your life has been so complicated. As soon as I've been paid for services rendered, I'll leave."

"I wish I could do that," she said. She looked around. There was an onyx ashtray on the table by the window, but instead of getting up for it, she butted her cigarette in the saucer of her demitasse and looked up at me with a half smile on her face. "You put it very well. Payment for services rendered. That would suit me perfectly."

I stood up. "I'm a cop, not a marriage counselor, Mrs. Michaels. If you'll just tell me how I can contact your husband, I'll take it up with him."

"You can wait for him here," she said, and her sexuality made the hair tingle on the back of my neck. I don't have to brush women off as commonly as some men do, so I've never developed the skill. She didn't care, anyway; she had decided to play games with me.

"I've imposed enough on your time," I said, but she wasn't buying.

"Don't mention it. My husband won't be very long. Perhaps you'd care for a drink while you wait." She turned away to one of the lower bookshelves and moved a book, and the shelf swung open on a big array of

159

bottles. "What will it be? Vodka, scotch. No, let me guess." She turned to look at me, her left index finger on her lower lip. "I'll bet you're a vanishing breed. I'll bet you drink rye."

"I didn't come here to socialize. This is business, and I'd like to keep it that way."

She lost patience. "Don't be such a goddamn tightass. Have a drink with me." She took out a bottle of Canadian Club and sloshed a couple of tumblers half full. "Come on."

She was going to be mad no matter what I did. Better she should be mad and sober, but if I didn't make some concession, she would tell me nothing. "If you need company, I'll trade you," I said roughly. "You give me directions for getting to your husband, and I'll drink your rye."

She looked at me with her eyes wide with surprise. "Deal," she said hoarsely, and handed me the drink.

I didn't take it. "First, where can I meet your husband?"

"He's at the Yorkton Yacht Club. He may sleep aboard his boat, or he may be on the last ferry. I never know."

"Thanks." I took the glass from her and looked at it. She'd poured about six ounces. "Trying to get me hammered?"

"You look like a growing boy," she said happily, and I knew she was an alcoholic. She would have euphemisms for everything. Drinks this size would be "family size" or "executive specials." You never got a second drink; it would always be "the other half." Boy! This was a weird family. She raised her own glass, which was just as full, and took a quick gulp. Then she set it down on the coffee table and reached for another cigarette.

"I don't drink often," she said, "but when I do, it brings out all my vices."

For the moment she was happy, the bubble-thin happiness of the drunk with just enough booze on hand to keep the rats at bay. Soon she would get either maudlin

160

or murderous. I planned to be gone by then, but in the meantime I dug for information.

"Jason told me that he's about to come into money. Would this account for your husband's trying to get him out of circulation for a while?"

She lit her cigarette and held it in the corner of her mouth as she cocked her head back and blew smoke. She looked like a hardworking hooker when the fleet's in. "Inquisitive son of a bitch, aren't you?" she said in what she probably thought was a roguish voice.

"If it's going to help me get paid, I'd like to know."

"You'll get paid," she said, and laughed.

"I mean for services already rendered." I grinned to show her I wasn't mad.

She nipped at her drink again, grimacing slightly. Another sign that she was an alcoholic. I've never met a really dedicated drinker who likes the taste of the stuff. Moderate drinkers quit when it stops tasting good. Alcoholics punish themselves with every mouthful. "Let me tell you a story," she said, and then laughed and added, "A bedtime story."

"Go ahead." I wasn't going to flirt with her.

"Once upon a time there was a young debutante." She looked at me to make sure I wasn't laughing. "Really. We used to do that kind of thing in this town, once. Anyway, she fell for her tennis coach, and the next thing you knew, she couldn't button her school blazer. So her father, a tough bastard—you remind me of him in some ways—he did the proper thing."

"Which was?" I could see it coming, but as long as she was talking, I might learn something, and she wouldn't be rushing to pour more drinks.

"He bought her a husband." She laughed. "Really. The best that money could buy. Charming, intelligent, ambitious. And they got married, and people sent them toasters and place settings from the bridal list she opened at Birks, and six months later the baby was born."

"Sounds like a lot of people's stories." I wanted her mad enough to brag about her problems. That way I'd get through the crust and into the truth, the facts that would make sense of what was going on.

"You mean, and they all lived miserably ever after?" She laughed a little raggedly. "Yeah. Well, they did. At least the debutante did. The husband got to be really good at handling her father's money, built up an empire and took a mistress. The baby grew up pampered by the mother, hated by the nominal father."

"This still doesn't explain why the father would want him killed." I pretended to sip my drink. Two ounces was all I planned to drink. The rest could go to irrigate the dieffenbachia that stood in a corner.

"It does when you get all the facts." She was being very lucid all of a sudden. I guessed she was one of those people who need a drink to get them thinking straight. If she stuck to one a day, she'd be a genius.

"And what are the facts, Mrs. Michaels?"

She went coy on me. "Unless you're a lawyer or a whole lot squarer than you look, why don't you call me Norma?" she suggested, and I worked out that she must be in her fifties. The most recent star with the same name was Norma Shearer, last seen riding into the sunset in the middle thirties.

"Okay, Norma. What are the facts? This is one hell of an interesting story."

"I'm glad you appreciate that," she said. "The facts are that my late father could see how the company he had built was passing out of his control. He'd retired, and my husband had moved in on his territory, expanding and making money but stepping on Daddy's pride." I listened and nodded, knowing now how rich she was. Only the very rich around here refer to their old man as Daddy.

She was continuing, more theatrically now, as the rye took a tighter hold on her. "So Daddy changed his will.

162

He locked a chunk of the company off into a trust for Jason when he turned twenty-one."

"And Jason hasn't made a will?" Not many guys of twenty do. They all figure they're going to live forever.

"Exactly. And with the stranglehold that son of a bitch has on everything, he'll break the trust and keep the whole thing."

She was growing more tense, as if she were up on a high board over a swimming pool, wanting to climb down but ashamed to give in. Very good, Bennett. If the rich need analysis, they can pay some shrink. All you need is your money, remember?

"The only thing that doesn't make sense is why this woman would come to me pretending to be Jason's mother and ask me to get him back."

She drained her drink and reached for the rye bottle. "Beats the hell out of me," she said. "Why don't you go ask her? She lives at Prince Arthur Place. Her name is Alison Beatty."

The idea made sense. I would probably find Michaels Senior there with his shoes off and a drink in his hand. But this woman didn't need reminding of that. I shook my head. "No, all this is irrelevant to me. I got Jason out as I contracted. Now I just want to get paid what I was promised and I'll go." I stood up. "Thank you for your rye and your time."

She froze with the uncapped bottle in her hand and gave a little cry of distress. "You're not going? You haven't even finished your drink."

"I've had my quota. Thank you." I put the glass down, and she picked it up, setting down the bottle and holding my glass in both hands like a magician on stage. She smiled craftily and raised my glass to her mouth and licked her lips slowly, a move that reminded me of photos in girlie magazines I'd seen as a kid. Then she drained the glass. It's a pity burlesque is dead. She could have made a fortune.

I turned away and walked out. I heard her screech something, and then glass shivered against the wall behind me. It took all my self-control not to sprint over the parquet to the door.

I got back into my car and fussed Sam for a few moments. He sat up and pressed his big head back against the pressure of my hand. The contact cheered me. Women like Norma Michaels leave me with a hole in my gut. Loneliness isn't something she could dispel by dragging the iceman into bed. She should know by now that her condition was contagious. Misery loves company, but misery also makes misery. There once was a time when I might have taken my chances on that, but I had Fred in my life now. I didn't need any more ships that pass in the night.

I pulled away from the curb and headed out of Rosedale back into the real world where family problems aren't complicated by the weight of ten zillion dollars on top of everything else. The only productive thing I could do was to go call on Michaels Senior's girlfriend. If she lived in Prince Arthur Place, it might be hard to get in. It seemed to me that it was one of the newer condominiums that have risen from the ashes of unprofitable apartment blocks in Toronto. Thirty some floors of half-million-dollar pigeonholes with squash courts and saunas and beauty parlors in the basement and upkeep costs higher than most of us could afford to pay in simple rent.

I prepared my camouflage carefully. There was a Chinese grocery store open on Yonge Street, and I picked up a couple of bunches of freesias for a few dollars and had the clerk double wrap them for extra bulk. The package looked like the kind of bundle stars expect from their agents on first nights. Then I drove north to Prince Arthur Place.

It turned out to be two buildings artfully placed back-to-back as if to fight off the rest of the city. As I'd expected, they had a security man at the gate of the

164

parking lot, but I was lucky. He was a twenty-five-year-old gum chewer with a radio tuned to some rock station. He came out of his little house and said, "Yes, sir?"

"Hi. Like your music. I'm from out of town. What station is that?"

"CKNY," he said, warming up to me.

"What's the frequency? All I can find is guys yakkin'."

He told me, and I thanked him with a wave of one finger. But he wasn't bought off entirely. "Who're you here to see?"

I did a conspiratorial chuckle. "Anybody you'd care to recommend? Like the gal I'm here to see is kind of senior."

He laughed with me. "Most of 'em are, here. What's this one's name?"

"Ali. Ali Beatty. Asked me to come up next time I was in town, and here I am."

The security man was impressed. "Asked you up? Hey, I wouldn't have thought that. She's kind of snooty."

"Yeah, before she lets her hair down." I grinned again like a salesman. "Listen, she said not to let the guys in the office know, so I'm gonna tell them I'm delivering flowers." I held up the bunch. "Which is true, only she gets to ask me in for coffee."

He nodded thoughtfully. "Yeah, good idea. Old George inside, he's kinda nosy. Yeah, I'll tell him the delivery man's on his way."

"Good thinking." I flipped out a five-dollar bill, and he looked at it in surprise.

"For me?" I guess he didn't get much in the way of tips. George did all the Christmas collecting.

"Yeah," I said. "I'm feeling lucky." He snuffled a quick laugh and waved me through. I saw him lift the phone in his shack.

George was waiting at the door. "I'll take those," he said.

I shook my head. " 'Preciate the offer, but the boss said to take 'em on up."

He tutted. "And who would he be, this boss?"

I raised an eyebrow and stared him down. He was small and British, ex-service by the look of him, used to being ordered around. "Miz Beatty'll tell you if she wants you to know."

"All right," he said. "But she's not going to be pleased. She already has a couple of visitors up there."

"I'll be discreet," I promised, and handed him a five. He took it after looking at it as if he'd been expecting a twenty. Then I asked him, "What visitors are these? The boss said she'd be on her own. Got her sisters over, has she?"

"Two gentlemen, sir." My fin had bought me some respect, anyway.

"Two?" All my suspicions jumped out of hiding. "One English, officer type?"

"That's right, sir. The other an American gentleman."

"With his right hand bandaged?"

"Yes. Do you know them?"

"We've met. Which apartment is she in?"

He told me, and I held up one finger for a moment. "Excuse me," I said, and went to the door again and whistled short and sharp. Sam came through the window of the car and was at my side in seconds. "Good boy, heel," I told him, and I went in, past George, who tried to tell me Sam couldn't come in. I knew it would cause trouble, but I had enough, anyway, right now. "Those men are wanted by the police. Dial 911 and tell the police that Dunphy and Wallace are with Ms. Beatty. Dunphy and Wallace. Got that?"

"What's going on?" he blustered, but I stabbed him in the chest with one finger.

"Do it, George, or your ass is grass. That woman is in danger."

I only made it to sergeant in the marines, but apparently George had never risen that high. He turned to the phone, and I sprinted for the elevator. There was a broom standing beside it, and I dropped my flowers and grabbed it. Not much, but I might have to take on both men, and a bayonet thrust with a broomstick can be lethal if you know what you're doing. And I do.

The elevator was quick and silent. It ran me to the eighteenth floor in one take, and I came out carefully, looking both ways. She was in 1814, George had said. That was to my left. I ran down the hall on tiptoe and listened at the door. It was silent inside. Damn, I should have asked George how long ago the men had come calling. If they were after revenge, five minutes was all it would have taken, less if they hadn't done any more than kill her.

Finally I tapped on the door and waited. Nobody answered, and I tapped again and called, "Alison, it's me," in a voice as close to that of Michaels as I could manage. "I've forgotten my key," I said.

There was no answer, and I tried the door. It swung open. I hissed at Sam and told him, "Come," and went inside, checking around me very carefully. There was nobody there, but as I stood, I could hear water splashing and a tap running. I told Sam, "Seek," and he jumped ahead of me and sprang through the apartment. I waited, and he ran into all the open rooms and then stopped, out of my sight, barking.

Holding the broom like a rifle, I followed the sound and found him at the bathroom door. It was shut but not locked. I opened it and let him in, and he barked again, but it was his working bark, not an attack sound, so I followed him in and saw the bathtub running over. There was a woman lying in it, covered by a foot of water.

I reached in and grabbed her by the hair, pulling her up and out, limp as a load of blubber. I rolled her on her face first and pumped hard on her back, and she gouted out a great spout of water. Then I flipped her onto her back and listened for signs of life. There weren't any, but I set to with CPR. The water had been running cold. If she had developed hypothermia, there might be a chance to get her going again.

It still hadn't worked ten minutes later when the police arrived. Sam's barking alerted me, and I told him, "Easy," then called, "In the bathroom," and kept on pumping her chest.

They were both young guys, one black, one white. The black one said, "What's happening here?"

"Found her in the tub," I said, then bent to breathe into her lungs again. I did it and went back to pressing her chest rhythmically, and said, "Reid Bennett, police chief, Murphy's Harbour. My ID's in my left rear pocket. Can you get a cardiac unit up here?"

One of them turned to use the phone, but I shouted, "No, I think this was an assault. Don't touch anything. Go down and phone or call from your car."

The white guy left on the run, and the other one knelt opposite me across her body and gave the formal signal. "I know CPR."

"Good. Take over, please." I leaned back, and he went to work, smoothly and professionally.

I talked to him as he worked. "She's involved in a family that sent me after those mercenaries. Nod if you've heard of Dunphy and Wallace."

He nodded as he pumped her chest. "They were here. George on the door downstairs told me. I came up, and she was in the tub. All I've touched is her and the front doorknob."

"Good," he grunted, and bent to blow into her lungs. When he had straightened up and listened to her mouth, he flashed a glance at me. "Looks like we're too late. How long you been at it?"

"Maybe ten minutes. I got the guy on the door to call when I came up."

He nodded. "Don't try to leave, please. I'll have to get the detectives in soon's help arrives."

"Understood. I'll take over again when you need a rest."

He nodded and went on working while I knelt on the wet floor, watching for signs of life.

Nothing had happened when the paramedics arrived, but they took over from us, and I stood up and uncrinked my back. The black copper did the same thing, and I reached out and shook his hand. "Nice try, anyway. What's your name?"

"Harry Good. I hoped we could bring her around. I saved a kid last summer up at the conservation area in Pickering."

"We tried," I said. There were towels on the rack, but we were too long on the job to use them. Both of us wiped our wet hands on our pants, and I said, "Let's go out in the hall till the brains get here."

"Okay." He turned to the other copper. "Did you call the detectives while you were down there, Jeff?"

The other guy nodded. "They're on their way." He was a year or two older than the first one, sandy haired, with a mustache that looked as if it had come with the uniform. "You say you're a police chief, sir?" He managed to make the "sir" sound menacing.

"Right." I unflipped my billfold and showed him my ID. "I'm the guy who was involved in the scuffle with the mercenary guys up north. Two of them were seen here just before I got here. It'd be a good idea to grab George downstairs and find out how long ago that was. Also to get their descriptions on the air ASAP."

He wondered how to make me look small but couldn't think of anything better than "Of course. You stay here with Harry. The detectives will want to talk to you."

"Right." I turned to Good. "Shall we stand in the hall, Harry?"

"Be best," Good said.

We went outside with Sam while the other man took the elevator down. Good looked at me and allowed himself a faint smile. "Don't mind Jeff. He kinda takes the job seriously."

"The best way," I minimized. "Only it tends to take the fun out of life."

He laughed and brought out chewing gum. Juicy Fruit. "I'm trying to give up smoking. Wanna stick?"

"Thanks. My mouth tastes of dead woman and lipstick."

"Yeah," he said thoughtfully. "Come to think of it, when did you see a woman take a tub in full makeup?"

I thought about that. "I'm not sure. Any girls I know take showers, but it seems to me that they cream all of that gunk off first. No, I figure someone put her in there."

"Figures," he said, and stooped to pat Sam, who ignored him. "You really trained him," he said approvingly.

"He's all the backup I've got in my little place," I said, and he nodded, and we stood chewing gum and waiting until the detectives arrived. In an ordinary apartment block the neighbors might have opened their doors. Apparently people with enough bread for a bunk at Prince Arthur Place lose their curiosity. Nobody came out, and after another five minutes the elevator opened, and two detectives came in.

I was delighted to see them. One was a stranger, but the other was Elmer Svensen. He's my sister's boyfriend and a good buddy of mine. He'd bailed me out one time when a Chinese woman I was close to was about to cancel my check.

"Reid," he said. "Hey, kid, what's happening?"

"Elmer. Good to see you." We shook hands, and he introduced me to his partner.

"Reid Bennett. He's gonna be my brother-in-law come December. Reid, this is Joe Irwin."

"Hi, Joe. This is Harry Good. We've just been trying to get some life going into a woman who lives here,

170

Alison Beatty. She was lying in the bottom of her tub, which is still running over, by the way. We didn't touch anything except the woman."

"Any response?" Irwin asked. He nodded at Good curtly. Detectives don't mingle much with the troops. I guessed he was new to plainclothes and proud of it.

"None. This could be a homicide."

"Homicide?" Elmer frowned at me. "Makes you think that?"

"Dunphy and Wallace, the two guys in charge of the mercenary outfit I was tangling with up north, they called on her just before I got here today," I said. Down the hall a door had finally opened, and a middle-aged man stuck his head out and looked at us. "Maybe we should duck inside and talk," I said, and Elmer nodded.

"Harry, could you stand outside and keep the lions at bay? Joe, maybe you'll go down to the front office and call homicide. We don't know if this woman's gonna make it, but we've got enough work without taking on an extra case if we can avoid it. Then talk to that citizen down the hall, see if he noticed anything strange."

Both men nodded, and Irwin moved away to the man at the open door. The man asked, "What are you men doing here? And why is there a dog in the building?" Then Elmer and I went inside with Sam, and I shoved the door almost closed with one foot.

Both of us stuck our hands in our pockets, the automatic safety precaution at a crime scene. It stops you from touching anything. Then he said, "What the hell was happening up north? When Louise heard on the radio, she just about went out of her tree. You should've called her."

"Sorry about that, Elmer. I figured now she had your shoulder to cry on she wouldn't worry anymore."

"You kidding?" He grinned. "Anyways, tell me, how's this broad connected with the guys up north? She one of their girlfriends? What?"

"It's kind of complicated. And the first twist is that they have two other possible targets in town. It'd be smart to have someone at their door for a day or two."

He took his hands out of his pockets and found his notebook. "Who are they?"

"Michaels, not sure of his first name. He's the stepfather of the boy I brought back, plus the wife, the mother. They live up in Rosedale." I gave him the address, and he wrote it down. "Also the boy, Jason Michaels. They're teed off about him. He ducked out on them, and besides, it looks to me as if the stepfather had set the kid up to be wiped."

Elmer looked up in horror. "His own goddamn kid?" His reaction pleased me. Louise has a couple of kids, and it looked like Elmer counted himself their father. Good. They all deserved it. I was about to make the comment when the door opened and two more detectives came in. Elmer said, "Hi, George. This may be a homicide."

The other guy grunted. "It already is," he said. "She was DOA at St. Mikes."

FIFTEEN

◆

The homicide men were pros. It took them only a couple of minutes to get my story into a straight line that made sense to them. Then one of them went to phone for the investigation team to photograph and fingerprint the place. After that they went over everything again, getting all the details. Filling them in on Wallace and Dunphy took a couple of hours, and by that time the apartment had become the usual crime-scene zoo. But Sam and I were free to go.

I had considered dropping in on my sister, but it was after ten, and I was still tired from the exertions of the past couple of days, so instead I went back to Fred's place.

The light was flashing on the answering machine, and I played it back and was treated to Fred's voice. "Hello, machine. Good to talk to you again. Please tell Reid Bennett that his other half wishes he was here." Then there was a pause, and she added, "And tell him I love him and he can reach me at this number."

I scribbled down the number and then listened to the other calls. There were three more of them, all from her, spaced about twelve hours apart. The message was about the same on each, and I rewound the tape and called Saskatchewan. They're two hours behind Toronto out there, and I figured she might be out to dinner, but I was lucky. She picked it up on the second ring.

"Hi, it's your wandering boy, missing you like hell."

"Reid!" God it was good to hear her voice. "I was starting to worry about you. I called you at home, no answer. I just got off the phone from the police office at the Harbour. Somebody called Fred Horn said that you and his son had been up north."

"We went on a little assignment. If I get paid, I'll be earning as much as you this week. But how are you?"

"Aside from wishing you were along, fine and dandy. The director is fantastic. He's been changing the script as we go, fattening my part. This film could be big for me, Reid."

I swallowed my jealousy of some guy who could make her feel this good. "That's tremendous news. I don't know why you didn't get the lead in the first place."

"It's not sitting well with Ms. Famous Face." She laughed. "That's the only fly in the ointment. She's getting more and more difficult. The tension on the set is starting to build. But so far we're on schedule, and the weather's holding."

"I hate to think how long you're going to be there." Talking to her was difficult. I've never been comfortable telling a phone receiver how much I loved anyone.

"Not a moment longer than it takes. I'd rather be right there with you this minute than accepting an Oscar. I'm missing you, Reid. In fact, if this is what it takes, being an actress, I'm thinking of activating plan two."

"Flattering but no go, kid. I don't want you pining around unfulfilled."

She laughed. "Not much chance of that with you right there," she said. "But tell me about this assignment. What was it?"

I filled her in, leaving out most of the gory bits. I wasn't out to worry her. That's a coward's trick. There was still enough to tell that she said, "Listen, Reid. That's enough of that kind of work. Knock it off. You hear me?"

"Loud and clear." I laughed to show I knew she was kidding but made my decision right then. "In fact, tell you what. I'm going to sort out my payment tomorrow. Then I'll put in a day with Louise and her kids, playing big brother. After that I'll come out for the weekend with you. Will that be okay?"

"Would you?" I've heard her do a thousand different voices as we kidded around or as she read parts for rehearsals, but this one was the real essential Freda, warm and womanly. I gripped the phone tighter.

"Count on having me there on Saturday. I'll stick around until you get back into the thick of things, than vanish. I don't want to clutter you up. You're working."

"Worrying about my beauty sleep?" She laughed again. "Forget it. A good infusion of hormones does more for a girl's skin than any amount of sleep and cold cream. I'll be counting the hours."

"I'll call tomorrow night, around this time."

"I'll call you if you're a minute late," she said, then added, "This is for real, Reid. Don't let me down."

"You're stuck with me."

"Stuck on you, too," she said. "Good night, lover."

"Good night, lover. Until tomorrow," I said, and hung up the phone.

Sam was sitting beside the couch looking at me, and I reached out and patted his head. "How are you at second fiddle, Sam?" I asked, and he blinked at me.

Talking to Fred had made me restless, so I poured myself a solid Black Velvet and sat with it, watching the late news. My adventures were covered in a lot of detail. My name was mentioned as the guy who recently sorted out a gang of bikers in Murphy's Harbour, and the news people had done their homework and found out a lot of my history, starting with the fact that I'd been in the

175

U.S. Marines in 'Nam and going on with the story of the bikers I tangled with in Toronto before I quit here. They'd even dug out a photo of me from my Metro police days.

I groaned when I saw it all. The Canadian media is still bleeding over 'Nam. The Americans have made their peace, but our people haven't. Anyone who fought there gets painted with a broad black brush. It had been that piece of news that had made life impossible for me to stay with the Metro police a couple of years earlier. And now it was all coming out again. I'm proud that I'd gone and glad. 'Nam had turned me from being an angry kid into being a much quieter and saner man. But as I watched, I wondered whether Dunphy and Wallace were looking at the same pictures, making their plans to get even with me.

Probably not, I decided as I switched off the set. Most likely they were sneaking out of the country right now, back into the anonymity of some big American city. Extradition laws are so complex that they would be safe in the States even if the police tracked them down. I hoped that was what was happening but wondered why they had taken a side trip to kill Alison Beatty. What had she done aside from sending me after them? That might have been enough to earn her a beating from them if they'd ever met her again somewhere. But to go out of their way to expose themselves by killing her, that didn't make sense.

The weather had turned blustery, so I didn't sleep on the balcony. I crashed into Fred's bed and slept solidly. I was up at six-thirty and ran, with Sam alongside me, for a brisk half hour, then fed us both and got ready to tackle Michaels.

I figured the detectives would have located him no matter where he spent the night. He would know I was in town and would be perhaps a little fragile from all the publicity. There was a good chance that his relationship

176

with Alison Beatty would come out during the investigation. Reporters love that kind of story, lust in the boardroom. He might be a little gun-shy. Well, that made it tougher, but I was prepared to face him down, anyway. I owed George, who wouldn't collect unless I got my pay. A guy from his background needed all the support he could get for law school.

The early radio news didn't give much detail on the killing. An unnamed woman had been found drowned in an unnamed condominium. Homicide detectives were investigating. The usual minimal stuff. There was more in the *Toronto Sun*, a breezy tabloid that didn't mince words like the older dailies, but even it didn't add anything to what I knew firsthand.

The day was cool, one of those late-August mornings when you know the leaves won't be hanging on the trees for a lot longer and you start digging deeper into the closet for something warm to wear. I had dragged out a pair of cord pants and a good tweed jacket, but I was still out of place among the suits on Bay Street, the financial center where Michaels Senior did business. I left Sam in the car and went up to the forty-second floor.

As soon as I walked in, I realized that the news of Alison Beatty's death had just broken. Two women were leaning over the receptionist's desk making "Isn't it terrible?" faces. They finally gave up, and the receptionist fitted on a brave smile and asked if she could help.

"I have an appointment with Mr. Michaels," I lied cheerfully.

"Yes, sir, who may I say is here?"

"Reid Bennett. And please tell his secretary I have some important news for him." I smiled back at her and waited while she called and was told that Michaels had never heard of me.

She lowered the phone and said, "Mr. Michaels's secretary says you're not on his appointment list for this morning, Mr. Bennett."

"This is impromptu. He contacted me last night after the news you were discussing earlier. I said I would report to him at nine."

She mouthed a perfect O and raised the phone. "This is personal; Mr. Bennett has news for Mr. Michaels."

That worked. A middle-aged, capable-looking woman came out through the double doors for me and led me to a corner of the floor, the southeast corner. We went in through her office, and when she tapped on the inner sanctum, the curt voice I'd heard on the phone up north said, "Come in."

The woman opened the door and said, "Mr. Bennett, Mr. Michaels," and went out quickly.

He was sitting on the window ledge looking out over a view that took in all Toronto's waterfront and a panorama of the islands. He didn't stand up but turned around and looked at me, his eyes angry. "You've got news?"

"Not about your loss. I'm sorry."

"You presumptuous bastard," he said, but he still didn't stand up, so I knew he wasn't going to throw me out. Not yet. I studied him and waited. He was wearing a gray three-piece suit. Fifty, I thought, tall but running to fat. He looked as if he might just be giving up tennis for golf. After about thirty seconds he turned back to the window. "So what's the news."

"Well, it comes in two parts. One part affects me. The other part affects you."

That got his attention. He turned and stood. He was about six two, an inch more than me, and he used his height to bully. "What could you possibly know that affects me?"

"We'll get to that. First, let me get my own news into the open." I pulled the stopped check out of my pocket and held it out between both hands. "This was supposed to reimburse me for getting your son out of the hands of the Freedom for Hire organization. When I presented it, I found payment had been stopped. I want my money."

He didn't like that, and he moved to press a button on his phone, but I caught his hand. "You're stuck with this meeting until I get satisfaction. Why not sit down and think about that?"

He was stronger than he looked, but I had him. He wasn't going to lose face by tussling, so he sat, and I reached over and pulled the phone out of his reach.

"You come to me this morning of all days to ask for money?" He hated me with eyes that were almost colorless. He looked like an aging SS man in a late movie.

"I didn't choose the time. I'm sorry for your loss, but I almost lost my own life yesterday getting your son to safety. I was promised payment, and it was canceled. I came to find out why and, when I have my money, to give you some other information."

The pressure was good for him. He was becoming an executive again, not a grieving lover. "If you want another check, I'll give you one," he said contemptuously. "Or would you feel safer with cash?"

"Cash would be ideal," I said easily. "Can you arrange that?"

"I can arrange just about anything I want," he said angrily. "If you want cash, that's what you get."

"Good," I said, and waited.

He sat for about thirty seconds, staring at me. Then he stood up abruptly and came out from behind his desk and took down a picture from the wall. There was a safe behind it. He fiddled with it and took out a box, which he set on the arm of the couch under the picture and opened. I waited where I was, and he put the box back in the safe and whirled the wheel on the front. Then he turned and shoved a handful of bills at me. They were Canadian thousands and I counted them, twenty-five. Mission accomplished.

He spoke as I was counting. "I keep cash on hand for emergencies. This suits you, does it?"

"Fine, thank you." I shoved the bills into my left-hand pants pocket. They made a nice comforting bulge. "Do you want a receipt?"

He looked contemptuous again. "Of course I do. I have to account for money the same as anybody else." He opened his desk and took out a sheet of paper. It was blank, no letterhead. "Got a pen?"

I had a ballpoint in my pocket, and he dictated and I wrote. "Received from Alison Beatty, twenty-five thousand dollars for services rendered." Then I signed it.

"I want her name clear," he said. "So you better put the date of your meeting with her. What was that, Friday last? Forget the stopped check. That was an oversight."

I shrugged and wrote down the date of our meeting. If he wanted to protect his girlfriend's name, that was up to him. I had my cash.

"Fine with me. Thank you for being so understanding. Now for the second part of the bargain. I have to tell you that Dunphy and Wallace, the heads of the Freedom for Hire outfit, were seen at Ms. Beatty's apartment yesterday."

"The police told me that when they gave me the news of her death," he said. He folded the piece of paper neatly in three so it would have fit into an envelope and looked up with a calm expression on his face as if paying the money he owed me had laid to rest the ghost of his dead lover. "Is that your big news for me?"

"That's half of it. The other half is that they're obviously out for revenge over something. I think you should hire yourself a bodyguard for a while or get police protection. And it would be a good idea for your wife and son as well."

"I'm not going to cower in a corner because two men are suspected of killing my assistant." He tucked my receipt into his inside jacket pocket and stood up. "I should thank you for your good work in getting my son out unharmed, Mr. Bennett. But quite frankly, if I never see you again, it will make me very happy."

180

"I couldn't have put it better myself. Thank you for honoring Ms. Beatty's check. Good day."

I nodded to him and turned away. He said nothing, and I left the office, nodding politely to the woman outside. She was shuffling through the desk, trying to sort out the mess that Alison Beatty's death had created for her. She nodded back abstractedly, and I left. Somehow I couldn't get rid of my surprise that Michaels had paid up so readily. Was he in shock over his girlfriend's death? I'd expected fireworks, and he'd rolled over.

I guess I should have opened an account in Toronto and deposited the money, but instead I decided to drive up to my place. It would fill the time until my sister Louise was home from work and I could give George his money in big bills. His half would be more than his family made in an average year, and I guessed he would spread some of it around them, keeping only what he needed for his year at the university. In some ways he was still all Indian. They share everything.

The highway was almost empty now, in the middle of a week when summer was virtually over, and I didn't have to drive fast to get home in a little over two hours. I stopped at the station and found George inside, studying one of his textbooks. He grinned and snapped it shut. "I was thinking about you as I read up on banking law," he said. "How'd it go down there?"

"Good, financially. I got paid okay. But bad for the woman who retained me. Dunphy and Wallace came calling yesterday and drowned her in her bathtub. I found the body."

George whistled and stood up. "Why'd they do that? I would have thought they'd head south and keep on running till they got to Nicaragua or wherever the hell they work."

"Yeah, me, too. But they were seen at her apartment, calling on her, about a half hour before I got there. They could still be around. They might even come here looking for you."

He grinned and reached down under his desk, coming up with the station shotgun. "The thought had crossed my mind as well."

"Good thinking. I don't like the way these guys work. You've seen them."

"I'd be happier if they were in the pen," he said. That was a big confession from an Indian. He was as close to being afraid as he liked to admit.

"They will be. Every copper in the province is looking for them now."

"I'll bear that in mind," he said.

I winked at him. "So, now for the good news."

I pulled out the wad of bills, and he laughed. "Well, hot damn. Money. So that's what a thousand-dollar bill looks like."

"Twenty-five times over. Would you like yours now, or should I put it in the bank for you?"

He looked me in the eye. "Listen, Reid, this is heavy bread. I can't take half of it off you."

"If you hadn't come in after me, I'd be dead now and this money would still be in Michaels's safe. No arguments. Right?"

He shook his head doubtfully. "That's more money than we'd make in two years trapping."

"If you're going to be a lawyer, you're going to have to get used to earning big bucks. Better start practicing."

He stuck out his hand, and we shook. "Thanks, Reid. I was glad to help, anyway."

"For services rendered. Thank you for having the balls to come in after me."

So that was done. I went across and had Millie credit both our accounts with twelve and a half grand. It was the most money I'd had in the bank since I split the sale price of our house with my ex-wife. Millie chattered, delighted to be playing with big bills, and then I left and drove home. I was on top of the world when I got there, but I let Sam out of the car for a quick check around before I got out. And that brought my mood to earth. He checked around the door closely. Someone had been calling.

My hair tingled, and I called him back into the car and went down to the station to pick up George and my gun. He brought the shotgun with him, and we went up to the door as if we were on patrol. I unlocked it and shoved Sam inside. He ran through the house, barking everywhere, but I didn't realize why until he came back to me, letting me know the place was empty. Then we went in and checked it ourselves. It was still neat and clean, but the back door had been forced. Somebody had broken in.

"That was done since this time yesterday," George said. "Dad checked the house on his rounds, checked all the vacant places."

"The house hasn't been turned over," I said. "Maybe it was kids looking for booze." I opened the door of the fridge, which was largely empty except for half a dozen cans of Labatt's Blue. They were still all there. Next I checked the cupboard over the sink where I keep my liquor, one full, one started bottle of Black Velvet, plus some Montego rum I'd bought for Fred. All of them were there.

"Doesn't look as if they've taken anything." I checked the door for damage. "Looks amateur. The scar where they jimmied it is rounded, as if they'd used the spiked end of a tire iron."

"Sounds like kids," George said. "But they'd've ripped off the booze for sure. You don't think it was those bikers, do you?"

I shook my head. "They'd have trashed the place like they did the Corbett place that time. No, these guys must have been looking for something."

"Better check and file a report," George said. "Did you have anything valuable?"

"Naah, I don't have anything worth ripping off. Books, a few clothes, not even a good television set." I thought about it. "Listen, don't bother putting the break-in on the record. It's just going to sit there as an unsolved crime and there doesn't seem to be any harm done."

"You're the boss." He stooped and patted Sam. "So what's on now? You going fishing?"

"No, I just came up to get rid of the cash, kill time until my sister gets off work. I'm staying with her overnight, then heading out to join Fred for the weekend. I can afford it now."

"Hell, you could afford Hawaii." George laughed. "When you coming back?"

"Next week, early. I'll pick up Sam from my sister's place and head back out. Think we can go fishing?"

He grinned. "I'm sure of it."

He turned down my offer of a beer and left. I opened a Blue and wandered through the house opening drawers and cupboards, checking my belongings. I'd told George the truth; I don't have a lot to attract thieves. An old stereo with a few records, mostly country, one suit, a few pairs of pants and another jacket, my winter gear, a cheap camera, books. I could carry away anything important under one arm.

One of the last places I looked was the bureau in the bedroom. Fred had left a couple of things on top of it, suntan lotion and a pair of big costume-jewelry earrings, and I grinned when I saw them. Then I opened the top drawer. It holds socks and underwear, and underneath it in a tin box I keep souvenirs, some photographs and a locket of my mother's and my father's and my own medals and discharge papers. I could tell at a glance that the tin had been searched, and I stopped at once and went down to the kitchen for a pair of rubber gloves Fred had bought when she decided to clean my stove. They were stiff from the gunk in the stove, but they would prevent my smudging any new prints on the tin.

Wearing the gloves, I went through the contents of the tin. The locket was still there. It was gold and the only item a normal thief would have taken. The other items were all intact except for one thing. My marine dog tags.

I stood and thought about that for a minute, wondering why anybody would bother stealing five cents' worth of metal. Then I set the tin on the bureau and called George.

He answered at once, on a tinny-sounding phone. I guessed he was out back of the station again, fishing for pike. "Yeah, George, Reid here. Whoever it was has taken my service dog tags."

I could hear his puzzlement as he said, "Why in hell would they want them?"

"Beats me. But they didn't touch anything else. I've got the container here, it's metal, should hold prints pretty good. You want to print it for me?"

"Hey. Sherlock Holmes all the way." His laugh echoed on the line. "You want to bring it in?"

"Yeah, I'm just heading back to Toronto, so you can play detective while I'm gone."

"Good. I'd better come ashore and talk business. See you."

He hung up, and I picked up the box and the contents and put them into a plastic bag. Then I fastened the back door by driving a four-inch nail through it into the jamb and set off for the station, en route to Toronto.

SIXTEEN

◆

George already had the dusting equipment out, and we worked over the box together. He got a good set of latents off it, two sets, in fact, one of which we soon discovered was my own. The other looked as if it'd been made by an index finger and thumb. From the way the box had been sitting in the drawer, I decided they were probably made by somebody's left hand. George gave them to me to deliver to Toronto, and I took them with me when I shipped out.

It was two by the time I left, and I beat the rush hour into town and dropped the fingerprints off with Irv Goldman in 52 Division detective office. That's not normal channels. I should have taken them to forensics and then waited the usual three days. Instead, Irv promised to follow through and have them processed as if they were part of an investigation of his. Time saved, although there were still no guarantees they would be useful to us. Only a few people ever get fingerprinted. Convicted criminals, policemen, and a few security-company people. That excludes about 95 percent of the population, most of whom would scream like stuck pigs if you asked them for a sample to compare with your evidence.

I left Irv's office and drove up to my sister's house.

She wasn't home yet, but her kids are typical Toronto latchkey brats, and they were in the kitchen making peanut-butter sandwiches.

They dropped their makin's and hugged me to pieces when I arrived, complete with the candy bars I had picked up on the way. I kind of enjoy being an uncle and do my best to spoil the pair of them. Young Jack is ten, and he wanted to know whether Fred was going to join us.

"No, she's acting in a movie. She's out in Saskatchewan for a few weeks. I'm going out to see her on the weekend. I thought I'd come and see you all before I went, maybe ask you to take care of Sam for me while I'm gone. Could you do that?"

"Could we?" Little Lou is eight, with her mother's blue eyes, and her black hair in two tight plaits. She looks like the kind of little girl you used to see in cartoons twenty years ago. I hope that if Fred and I go into the baby business our youngsters will look like her.

"Sure. You just tell him, 'Heel,' and you can walk anywhere. He'll follow you; you won't need to say another word. He's like a shadow."

"Oh, Sam," she said, and sank down to kiss his head. He let it happen, blinking to show his embarrassment.

Louise bustled in at five-thirty. I gave her a quick brotherly peck of greeting, and she squeezed my arm. I guess we're closer than a lot of siblings. I paid for her education out of my Marine Corps earnings after our parents died, and she's always been grateful. I'm proud of her now. She's creative director at an advertising agency, and she looks great. She has our father's blue Limey eyes and our French Canadian mother's jet-black hair.

"Hi, stranger. Good to see you," she said. "You here to stay?"

"Better than that. I'm here to cook supper, as long as we barbecue."

"Sounds ideal to me," she said. "I'll fix a salad, you get the coals going."

Jack helped me, and I sent him back into the kitchen for a juice can with both ends cut out. I set it over the flames, and we had the coals going in a matter of ten minutes. That impressed him. "Elmer takes a lot longer," he said. "I'll have to tell him about using a chimney."

"Yes, makes the coals draw better. Now, why don't you ask your mom for the burgers and we'll get to work?"

He ran indoors for the meat, and I stood there nursing a beer and waiting for him to come back. When he wasn't with me within a few minutes, I ambled in after him to see if he'd been sidetracked by the TV. He hadn't. Elmer Svensen was standing in the kitchen with his partner. Louise was with them, looking shaken.

"Hi, what's up?" I asked, and Elmer looked at me and shook his head.

"Got a minute, Reid?"

"All the time you want, Elmer. What's on your mind?"

"Bad news," he said. He turned to Louise first. "This is messy, Lou. Could you take the kids outside, please?"

"Sure, if you think it's necessary." She took them by the hand and led them into the garden. When they'd gone. Elmer turned back to me.

"Norma Michaels has been found strangled."

"Strangled? That's the second homicide in that group in two days. First Michaels's girlfriend, now his wife. It's got to be tied in with this Freedom for Hire thing."

Elmer nodded, but he didn't comment the way I'd expected. Instead, he gave me the facts, his face grim. "They found the body about an hour ago. Her housekeeper found it. She lives in, but she'd been out since morning. It's her day off. She came back to pick something up. There was something broken in the hall, a vase, I guess, and she went through to check on her missus."

"To see if she was drunk?" I wasn't joking. He looked too serious.

"She didn't say that, but I guess, yeah," Elmer said. "Anyway, she went into the library and found her strangled."

Elmer's partner was looking at me very straight, weighing everything I said. I knew he was a novice at detective work, and I figured he was probably suspicious of me. At that stage in your career you're suspicious of everybody except your partner, but his look made me careful with my words.

"Strangled? Manually or with a ligament?"

Elmer cleared his throat. "Look, Reid, I don't believe this, but I have to tell you. She'd been strangled with a piece of cord which was broken. And in the corner of the room, under a china cabinet, we found a piece of metal."

"What kind of a piece? Had she been bludgeoned?"

"No." He composed himself carefully and then said, "It was a military dog tag. We've spent the afternoon checking it out, and we find it was a Marine Corps dog tag." My mouth must have fallen open because he nodded. "Yeah, this is the hard part. We found out that it was yours."

"Mine?" The news hit me like a punch in the gut. I'd been set up. "Mine? That explains it."

"Explains what?" His partner took over now that the news had been broken.

"My house at Murphy's Harbour was broken into some time overnight, I guess. I was back up there today and found it. Somebody broke in the back door and stole my dog tags."

"Yeah?" Elmer's partner spoke softly, the disbelieving voice of a copper who's seen it all. "What else'd they take?"

"Nothing. I reported the theft. George Horn, the guy who's minding the store up there, he printed the box I

189

kept the tags and some other stuff in. Got a good set of prints; I turned them over to Irv Goldman in Fifty-two Division about an hour ago."

"Very convenient," the partner said.

Elmer held up his hand. "Easy on, Joe. I know Reid better'n you. He didn't do this, I know it."

"I sure as hell didn't."

"Have you ever met this woman? Been to her house?" The partner was persistent.

"Yes, I was there last night. I went there because the check I'd been given to rescue her son had been stopped payment. I went to collect my money from her."

"Did she pay you?" Elmer asked. He was my friend, but he was a policeman as well. He wanted all the facts.

"No, the payment was twenty-five grand, and she told me to go and see her husband. I went over to his girlfriend's place, and you know what happened there."

Elmer went to the fridge, opened it, and took out a jug of orange juice. He waved it at his partner. "Want some? We don't keep booze in the house. I used to hammer the stuff, and Lou doesn't buy any now we're together."

His partner waved him off, and he took a glass from the cupboard and poured himself a drink. "You likely brought some beer with you, eh, Reid?"

"Yeah, it's in a cooler outside."

"Not for me," his partner said. He wasn't here to socialize. He was here to lock me up for the homicide, to get stars on his work even if it screwed up Elmer's romance with my sister. He wasn't going to kick back.

"Do I get the impression I'm a suspect?" I asked him.

"For Crissakes, Reid. I know you didn't do it. But we wouldn't be doing our jobs if we didn't talk to you. It was your dog tag, and you're connected with the family. The papers would hang you and us together if we don't clear this up."

"For the second time," I said, and sat down. "I've been through this kind of crap once before, Elmer. I don't

190

want any more suspicion. Check with Irv. He'll tell you about the prints."

"Yeah, I know." Elmer nursed his orange juice, cradling it in two hands. "I know you didn't do it. But the thing of it is, she was murdered last night, just after you'd been to see her. The housemaid gave us a description. Says you and the victim had an argument, you threw a glass at the wall and left. Then her boss got into the sauce, so she went up to her room and watched TV and was asleep by the time the news came on at ten."

"When was Mrs. Michaels killed?"

"The autopsy's still going on, but preliminary signs are that she died around two A.M. last night." He looked down at me, miserably. "Reid, I know this is bullshit, but do you have an alibi for last night?"

"Only for the time I was up at Prince Arthur Place. I went back to Fred's apartment after that and watched TV, went to bed."

"What time did you get there?" The partner was quick with the question. I looked up at him, seeing the glint in his eyes that meant he had me handcuffed and locked up already, the hell with me, the hell with Elmer.

"Around eleven. I phoned Fred, then watched TV. I caught the late news, including the local news around eleven-thirty."

The partner almost purred. "Then you had all night to slip back to the Michaels house, do what was done, and go home."

Elmer exploded. "Shut the fuck up. I'm telling you, I've known this guy longer than you've been out of Pampers."

"And you're bangin' his sister."

The line hung in the air like the silence between a lightning flash and the rumble of thunder, and in the silence I leaped to my feet and stuck a stiff finger on the end of his nose as if it were a bell push.

"Listen, snotrag. Any cracks out of you and I'll tear your head off and stuff it where the sun doesn't shine."

Elmer grabbed my arm. "Easy, Reid. He's just an asshole kid. My partner's on vacation. I'm stuck with this punk; ignore him."

The other detective was looking at me. The sneer had gone from his face, but it was superior as he spoke softly. "Pretty violent, aren't we, Mr. Bennett."

I sat down again. I didn't apologize. It would have done no good. Anyway, it wasn't his opinion that mattered. The way things looked, I was going to have to convince twelve of my peers that I had not strangled Norma Michaels.

Elmer drained his juice and turned to the sink to rinse the glass and gulp down a swallow of cold water. Then he set the glass down and turned back to me. "The thing is, Reid, there's more."

"More? Like what?"

"Well, when the death was reported to the husband, he told us he'd found some receipt you'd signed, a receipt for twenty-five grand, paid by the husband's girlfriend."

"I signed that in Michaels's office yesterday morning." I slapped my forehead with my palm. "I've been set up. He asked me to predate it to when his girlfriend was alive, said he wanted her name cleared, no mention made of the rubber check she gave me."

"But she was dead," the young cop said. I looked at him, seeing his future. He would have a long, safe career as a copper. He never deviated from the rules. He'd never get his ass in a sling over jumping to conclusions. Guilty people would get away, innocent people would be sent down, but he would be able to look himself in the eye every morning and know he had done his stinking job. In that flash of a glance I gave him, my own future swam before my eyes. Even if I didn't end up in jail, could I ever go back to police work?

"Yes, she was dead. I spent a lot of yesterday evening trying to kick start her heart."

"Damn, Reid. It was dumb to date that note that way," Elmer said. "The thing of it is, Michaels is saying that his girlfriend wanted his wife killed and that she paid you to do it."

"That money was to get his kid back from the Freedom for Hire people. Young George Horn helped me, and I gave him half this morning." Why does the truth sound like a tin trumpet?

"The thing is, he's made a case against you, and we have to investigate. I'm sorry." Elmer looked utterly miserable. He was going to have to explain all of this to Louise when he got off duty.

"You want me to go down to the station with you?"

"It'd save worrying Lou," he said.

"Okay, Elmer, I'll go tell her."

"You want me to come?" I could see the idea worried him. He was crazy about Louise. He'd have done anything to spare her any concern.

"Naah, relax a minute, I'll sort it out." I walked out into the garden. The barbecue was flaring, and Louise was shaking water out of a pop bottle to douse the flames. The burgers smelled good.

She looked up at me. She reminds me of my mother, and the concern in her face kicked me back through the years to some time I had come in late from fishing and Mom had worn the same expression. "What's going on?"

"This case I went up north on, it's taken another twist, and Elmer has asked me to help out for a while. I have to go with him."

She's nobody's fool. "If that was all of it, he wouldn't have looked like he does."

"You know how it is; he doesn't like involving family in his job. No policeman ever does."

"Are you going to arrest somebody?" Jack asked.

"Very soon," I told him. "Right now it's a game of cops and robbers, and I have to play."

He stretched up to his full four feet eight. "I'm going to be a detective when I grow up, like you and Elmer."

"Good idea," I said. "Listen, can you guys take care of Sam for me?"

"Sure." He dropped to his knees and fussed Sam, who was sitting as close to the barbecue as he could, looking hopeful. "Good boy, good old Sam."

Sam blinked and looked at me. I raised one finger to him, and he stiffened. "Stand up, Jack," I said, and he did, straight-backed as a soldier, alongside Sam. I pointed my finger at Sam. "Okay, Sam, go with Jack." It was my formula for handing over. From now until the process was reversed, he was Jack's dog and I was the stranger, pined for, maybe, like a lost friend, but not to be obeyed.

Jack turned immediately and ran to the corner of the yard, under the big oak tree that splits the fence. "Come on, Sam," he called, and Sam bounded away to him.

"I don't know how long this is going to take," I told Louise, "but make sure Sam gets walked and don't let the kids stuff him with burgers."

"You're making this sound serious," she said. "If it was just an investigation, you'd take Sam. What's going on, Reid?"

"I'll be in the office, and Sam's better off here. I'll see you tonight, but I'll ring before I come back. I'll probably be back when Elmer gets off work. See you then." I winked at her and tapped her on the arm lightly, then went back into the kitchen. Louise was going to follow me and speak to Elmer, but the barbecue flared again, and she stayed where she was, lifting off the burgers.

Elmer and his partner drove an unmarked police car so I didn't have to sit in the cage. In any case, Elmer insisted I sit in the front with him, sticking his partner in the back, where he sulked silently, arms folded, waiting for me to get mine.

The police station was busy. It was lunch hour for half the evening shift, and policemen in uniform were coming and going with lunch pails and boxes from the chicken place up the block. A few citizens were sitting around the front of the office, smoking and muttering and wishing they were somewhere else. Elmer led me past them, up to the detective inspector's office. "You remember Andy Burke? Used to be sergeant of detectives in Fifty-four Division," he told me. He was nervous, like a kid bringing his girlfriend home for the first time, wondering what the family would think. I guess I wasn't helping. I said nothing.

Burke was a big man in a light summer suit with a beer belly that hung way out over the big belt he was wearing. I guessed he had his .38 at the exact center of the back of it. He was sitting forward in his chair, so I was probably right. And he was giving somebody hell on the phone.

"You know better than that," he growled. "If we don't get a warrant, we're dead. We must've arrested that sleaze a dozen times; he knows the law better than you do. You gotta go by the book or he walks. Do it by the goddamn book or don't do it."

He hung up and looked up at me. "Hey, Bennett, right? Used to be in Fifty-two?"

I knew him only slightly, and it was odds on that he didn't remember me, but he was abreast of Elmer's investigation and knew I would be coming in. He stood up and shook hands, but perfunctorily, not wanting me to assume any familiarity. "Siddown. Want some coffee?"

"No, thanks, Inspector. Just want to get this mess cleared up and go home."

"Yeah." He swung his feet up on the desk. There was a smear of dead chewing gum on his left sole, and I couldn't see his face until he parted his feet, like curtains, and peered out. "Fill me in," he said.

195

"It's complicated, and it's messy, but I'll tell you right off the top that I didn't touch that woman."

"Of course," he said heartily. It would have cheered me more if I hadn't heard a lot of policemen say the same kind of thing to a lot of rounders.

"So are you planning to arrest me or what?"

He pulled a package of Old Port cigars out of his jacket pocket and lit up before answering. "You reckon we should?"

"I heard about the dog tag," I said.

He lit his cigar and waved the match out, making it a gesture of dismissal. "Yeah, how'd that thing get there?"

"It was stolen from my house sometime overnight, sometime after three o'clock yesterday, which is when I was last at my place."

Smoke poured up around his feet, which he had closed together again. "You report the theft?"

"Yes, to the cop who's filling in for me at Murphy's Harbour. We got a good latent off the box I kept it in. I turned that over to Irv Goldman in Fifty-two Division."

He glanced up at Elmer, who hadn't been invited to sit down. "Have you talked to Irv?"

"Will do," Elmer said, and left.

Burke parted his feet again and squinted at me through his cigar smoke. "Sounds phony as hell," he said. "I'm not saying you're lying, but you have to admit it sounds like bullshit. Somebody steals something from your house, kills this broad, and plants the evidence."

"I'm being set up." So far I was still on top of my anger, but I could feel it boiling up inside me. Pretty soon I would have the urge to shout, and then they would be confident I'd done what they thought. I decided to get all the skeletons out of the closet. "Pretty soon you'e going to hear another thing that sounds like evidence."

He swung his feet down and reached out to tap his cigar into the ashtray. I noticed it was filled with ash

196

but had no butts. Did he eat them along with the little plastic holder? "What more'm I gonna hear?"

"You'll hear that I was paid twenty-five grand by a woman who hated Norma Michaels's guts and stood to gain from her death."

His expression didn't change, so I knew I wasn't telling him anything fresh, but he took his cigar out of his mouth and waved it vaguely. "Fill me in," he said, "all the way in. Fact, tell you what, why don't I get a tape recorder in here and we get it all down."

"Feel free," I said, and sat back while he bellowed for a junior detective, who got the machine and set it up. Then Burke waved the man away and spoke, enunciating carefully for the sake of the machine.

"This tape is being made at the request of Detective Inspector Burke. Mr. Reid Bennett, chief of police, Murphy's Harbour, has volunteered to help us in our investigation of the Norma Michaels homicide. He is not under arrest, he has not been cautioned. This is for the record only." Then he nodded to me, and I told him and the machine the whole story, starting with my first meeting with the woman in the bar.

I'm a professional, and the statement didn't need any questions from him to keep it on track. When I'd brought it up-to-date, he asked a couple of details. Where was the son, Jason Michaels? I didn't know. Who did I think had broken into my house and stolen the dog tags?

That question made me frown and think for a moment. "I'm not sure. But it looks to me as if Michaels Senior set it up. He pulled that stunt on me with the receipt. It looks as if he has the most to gain from making me look guilty. I'm not sure what he's up to, but all the fingers point at him."

"You think he sent somebody up there to go through your house and come up with something to plant in his house, then went home and offed his old lady?"

197

"Makes more sense than anything else I can think of," I said.

Burke ground out his cigar butt on the edge of the ashtray, then dropped it into the wastebasket. "More sense than any alternative except one," he said.

He reached out and turned off the tape recorder and looked at me out of big brown eyes with deep blue bags under them that sagged down into the pouches of his face. "You've been a copper long enough to know that the guy we suspect the most is you."

SEVENTEEN

◆

I kept my temper. He was doing his job, nothing more. "Look, what you've got is circumstantial evidence. Two items. First, the receipt, which I wrote yesterday. Second, the dog tag. That's it. Period."

"I know," he said comfortably. "But that's more'n I get on ninety-nine percent of homicides. Why should I take your word for it?"

"Because we both know I didn't do this. That's why. That dog tag lives up in Murphy's Harbour, in a tin box in my house. Why would I have taken it out of there and come down to Toronto to strangle some woman with the cord?"

"Why not? Lots of guys are proud of their service, wear their tags all the time. The way it looks, you and her were down to your underwear, wrestling on the couch. She pisses you off. You strangle her and take off. You got problems with that?"

"I took those things off the day I got out of the service, and I've never had them on since. They're in a tin box with my goddamn medals, my father's medals from the big war, and some souvenirs of my mother. Ask anybody if they've ever seen me wear them."

"Like who would you suggest?" I got the feeling he didn't think I'd murdered Norma Michaels but wished I had. It would have made his work load a lot lighter. He might have been able to get home in time to watch the late movie with his wife. It would probably be the first time he'd made it in a couple of years.

"Like . . ." I paused. "Not that many people ever see me with my clothes off. But I guess George Horn has seen me swimming at my house up north. He's the deputy copper there, a law student from the U. of T. And then there's my girlfriend."

"You've got a girlfriend?" He cooed it disbelievingly. Just a ploy, trying to get me mad to see if I would give anything away.

"Did you think I kicked with the other foot, Inspector?"

He shrugged. "You've got the reputation of being kind of a loner," he said.

"What's this, psychographic-profile time? You've got me pegged as some kind of guy who keeps to himself until the full moon, then heads down to Rosedale and strangles some drunk housewife with my dog-tag cord?"

"How did you know she was drunk?" He stood up suddenly, looming over his desk.

"Because I called on her last night around seven. She hauled out the rye and tried to get me paralytic. I took half of the first one she poured and left. Ask the maid. She let me in, and she heard the noise when her boss threw the glass at the wall. But you know that already, don't you?"

"You telling me how to conduct an investigation, Bennett?" He shouted it, but I didn't flinch. Maybe it was an interrogation ploy of his; maybe he was teed off. I didn't know, or care much. "We've got hard evidence on you, Bennett. You can try to dismiss it, but you're tied to this family pretty close. Then we get two items of evidence that make it look as if you're the killer. How much more do I need?"

"Motive might be a start," I said, and he threw his hands up in the air explosively.

"Motive? Motive? I've got twenty-five thousand dollars' worth of motive." He shouted it, but he didn't look at me. He stood there sweating in his cheap suit and hated me and the dead woman and everything else that stood between him and his pension. But he didn't look me in the eye.

"Why don't you take a close look at my face?" I asked him, and he glanced at me in surprise. "Not because I'm Robert Redford. Take a look at the fact that I've got no goddamn eyebrows left on my head and these red patches aren't sunburn. They're the price I paid on this job for that twenty-five grand. I earned it by getting the Michaels kid away from a mob of killers. I got shot at and burned, but I made it without killing anybody. That's where your mysterious twenty-five grand comes into it."

He sat down, still not looking at me, and got out his cigar package. It was empty, and he crushed it and threw it into the waste can disgustedly. "All right. You're a goddamn hero. So what?"

"So why haven't you got the Michaels family in here? Why aren't you asking the father how come he set his own son, well, stepson, up with Freedom for Hire, hoping the kid would get killed? And ask him why his girlfriend then came around to me and asked me to get the kid back? And ask him how come Dunphy and Wallace knew where she lived? And why they went up there and drowned her in her own tub?"

"That's what you'd do, is it?" He sat down, sighing as if it had taken a major effort, opened the top right drawer of his desk, and took out a fresh pack of Old Ports.

"Yeah, that's what I'd do. And I'd also get hold of Jason Michaels and ask him where he got to after he waved bye-bye from the airport at North Bay."

He ripped the cellophane wrapper off his package, doing it slowly as if the action gave him real pleasure. "Good thinking, sir. Have you ever considered police work as a career?"

"Have you done it yet?"

"Yes, I've done it. And I've done every other goddamn thing you learned about in the Boy's Own Big Book of Detecting."

"And what did the guy say?"

Burke dug out his lighter first, then a cigar, and lit up before answering. "He told me to rub salt in my ass."

"Just like that?"

"No, it was much more polite. But he told me he had no information for me and sent me on my way."

"And you went? Just like that? Turned around and left? Or did you back away, bowing?"

Burke blew out a long, tired plume of smoke. "You're a pain. You know that?"

"Seems to be the popular opinion. Did you find the kid as well?"

"No." He looked at me out of his tired eyes, wondering, I guess, if I might be able to lighten his work load. He drew on his cigar and gave me the rest of the story. It wasn't very much.

"The pilot of the company jet says he landed at Buttonville, north of Toronto. His own car, that's the pilot's, was there but the kid skipped, didn't wait to ride into town with the pilot. He phoned for a cab and left."

"The cab must have come from Markham. Did your guys check?"

"Of course they did. Didn't help. The cab dropped the kid at the nearest subway stop, top end of Yonge Street in Toronto. He could have gone anywhere from there."

"Where does he live, anyway? I don't figure him for a homebody. Probably got a pad somewhere fancy."

"Not that fancy. He lives in the City Center, up behind Maple Leaf Gardens. Apartment eleven sixteen, west block. I've got a uniformed man over there waiting to see if he shows up."

"You know, he might have done this," I said carefully. "When I mentioned his mother, he sneered. He despised her for putting up with the husband."

"Sure. So he got up to your place, stole your dog tags, and left one at the scene. Right?"

I shrugged. "Yeah, I know, it's more organized than that. If he'd come in and found her drunk and got mad at her, he might have hit her on the head with a Ming vase or something, but he wouldn't have strangled her. That's not typical."

"How not typical?" Burke put his feet back on his desk, but he edged his chair away so he could look at me while he talked. He wasn't just listening now, he was working, watching every move I made.

"You've investigated more homicides than me, but the only stranglings I've ever seen have been sexual. One of them was a straight murder, the other was kinky. The strangler was just trying to crank up the other party's orgasm, only he got carried away."

Burke nodded. "Yeah, I had one like that once," he said, and I wondered why he was taking such a soft line. Was I off his suspect list, or was he trying to lull me? Then he dropped the other shoe.

"You were right about one thing."

"What was that?"

"Sex," he said, and sighed out a long blue column of smoke. "Yeah, this one was a sex killing. The broad was in a housecoat, nothing on under it."

"And she'd had recent sexual activity?"

He nodded. "Very recent. The forensic guys got a good semen sample?"

"What blood type?"

He grinned at me like a big Cheshire cat. "You figure I'm gonna say AB negative and you'll throw your hands up and say, 'See, I told you it wasn't me.' Right?"

"You're telling me it's O positive, the same as mine."

He nodded. "O positive. Same as yours."

"The same as half the goddamn population," I said angrily.

He waved me down. "Yeah, I know. But it's another piece of evidence."

"That plus two bucks'll buy you another five Old Ports."

He looked at me dreamily through the smoke and said, "You know, my kid, nineteen, he's in college. Ryerson, taking journalism. I found him smokin' up. He said, 'It's the pressure, Dad.'" He snorted. "Pressure. An' now you're on my case for smokin' cigars." He reached out and tapped the ash on top of the pile in the ashtray. "Advice I don't need, Bennett. I need a goddamn break."

It was my cue, and I took it. "You mean you'd like me to look around for you, see if I can come up with anything else?"

He swung his feet down and stood up, glowering at me around his cigar. "You know damn well I can't say that to you. You're not on the department, you're a suspect, for Crissakes. How can I ask you to go out and do my job for me just because I've got fourteen unsolved homicides, three accidental deaths, and a slew of missing persons to worry about an' only five guys assigned to me? I can't ask you to help."

I stood up. "Let me rephrase that. I have some uncompleted business to discuss with Jason Michaels. I was thinking of looking for him. If I should encounter him someplace, could I bring your dilemma to his attention?"

He grinned and took the cigar out of his mouth with his left hand, sticking out his right to me. "Very Christian," he said, and we shook. "Now piss off, will ya."

I ran into Elmer Svensen in the hall. He was hurrying back the way I'd just come. He checked his stride and held out one hand to me. "What happened?"

"Cross me off your worry list; the big man set me free. I'm looking for Jason Michaels. If I find him, I'll call you in."

He grinned, a quick, nervous flicker that died instantly. "Good. Louise would've had my guts for garters."

"Worry not. I'm out of here. See you at Louise's."

"If I ever get off work," he said gloomily, and turned away again.

I needed my car, so I took a cab back to Louise's house, catching her putting the kids to bed. Sam was in Jack's room, lying beside the bed. He stood up and wagged his tail when I tapped and came in. Louise was listening to Jack saying his prayers. He was at an age when he figured religion was redundant, but Louise still takes it seriously. For a while, as a little girl, she had almost decided to become a nun. I stood and waited until they were finished, Jack peering around at me as he gabbled through it. Then I said, "Hi, folks, I'm home."

"For keeps?" Louise asked. "I can make you some supper."

"A burger would be good, if you did one too many on the grill. Could you stick it in the microwave for me, please?"

"Tell me a story, Uncle Reid," Jack begged. "I was gonna watch the movie, but Mom won't let me."

"Good." I sided with authority. "TV is for losers. You should read more."

He pouted but didn't argue. He got the same line from his mother. "Listen. I'll start on one of your books, just one chapter, if you'll hand Sam back to me. You know how, right?"

"Okay." He sat up in bed. Louise winked at me and left. Jack called, "Here Sam," and Sam stood up, looking at me and wagging his tail. I could have taken him away, but I never do. It's part of his training to do as he's told without question. I don't want to break the pattern. Jack rubbed Sam's head and said, "Good boy. Go with Reid," and Sam broke away from his hand and fawned around me like a puppy.

I bent down and fussed him. For four years he's been about the only permanence I've had in my life, and we're bonded pretty tight. Jack looked on enviously. "He didn't play like that with me," he said. "He chased a ball and played, but not like that."

"He thinks he's my brother," I minimized. "Now, what's it going to be, the Hardy Boys or *The Wind in the Willows*?"

"Mom's always saying I oughta read that," he said, settling down under the covers, "but it's got a lot of big words in it."

"It's a hell of a story, though. You listen." I got the book, a worn old copy that my father had bought me when I was close to Jack's age. Like a lot of working-class Brits, he was a big reader, and he steered us onto good books at a time when most kids were depending on Bugs Bunny for intellectual stimulation.

A quarter of an hour later I left Jack reading chapter two on his own and came down for my burger. Louise had fixed a salad to go with it and served it on a crusty Italian roll. I dug in happily. "You want a beer with it?" she asked, reaching for the fridge door.

"No, thanks. I have to go out again. I'll take a glass of milk, please."

She poured it and sat down opposite me, waiting patiently until I'd finished eating before she asked, "What's going on, Reid? Elmer came here as grim as death. Now you're going out again. What's happening?"

"It's the murder of these two women, the one drowned in her tub and the other one last night. It's all to do with the Michaels family, the people who had me get their boy back from playing soldiers. I'm involved, so the police have asked me to help sort things out."

"And that's it? All of it?" She stood up and put my dishes in the sink. "You know, you make me mad, you guys. You and Elmer both. You're policemen, and you edit the facts down so far that there's nothing left over for your family."

I pushed my chair back and picked up the milk. "Think yourself lucky, Lou. We do a job that's dirty a lot of the time, misery and pain and ugliness, and we don't want you to get any of it on you. That's what makes it tough on police marriages. You're out all day dealing with filth, and when you come home, you want to escape from it. If you bring it home with you, it makes your family as miserable as you are, doing the job."

"And if you don't bring it home?" she asked softly. She's too intelligent for games. She wants facts, and she's strong enough to face them.

"Sometimes, if you feel you can't bring it home, it turns you to drinking too much or to other women, cheap women that you feel won't be hurt by contact with the seamy crap you have to put up with. What you want, need, I should say, is a woman who can welcome you home whatever mood you're in and not figure that you're mad at her when you don't want to talk."

She ran water into the sink and washed off the dishes. "Man must work, and woman must wait," she said.

I stood up and put my hand on her shoulder. "Come on, Lou. Don't tell me you and Elmer are having problems?"

"Not until tonight," she said. "He hasn't had a drink since we met. We've been out to cop parties where well-meaning friends shove doubles into his hand, and he never touches them. And he's loving and funny, and he adores the kids. No. No problems, until he walks in on duty and I realize that I only know half of him, the off-duty half."

"That's the real half," I said. "The tough part is something he puts on with his uniform or with the clothes he wears to the detective office. It's a hard shell you grow so the crud doesn't touch you. Don't worry. He isn't going to bring any of it home."

She dried the dishes and hung up the tea towel with a little flourish. "Okay, O wise one. It's just that the roses round the door are feeling a little wilted just now."

"I'm glad you found him. You needed one another. I just hope that Fred can be like you."

"You mean you're going to keep on being a copper?" She's like our mother, getting right to the heart of anything, no beating around the bush.

"My options are limited," I said. "I'm thirty-seven years old, and it's all I know."

"You could go back to the university, get a degree, and go to work at something different."

I laughed. "Can you see me in the ivied halls, surrounded by kids half my age? And can you see me in the job market, up against them when they've got twenty more years of service to offer a company?"

"It's an option," she said.

"Not one I can take up with any enthusiasm." I gave her shoulder a quick squeeze. "I may be home late. The best thing might be if I shacked up at Fred's apartment."

"No," she said firmly. "You come back here. The spare room is yours, you know that."

"Thanks, then. Try not to be too noisy when Elmer gets back."

She grabbed for the tea towel and flicked it at me. "Men," she said, but she was laughing.

I decided the best thing I could do was talk to the pilot of the Michaels company jet. From the way he'd greeted Jason at the airport, I figured they hung around together. Probably the pilot didn't drink or smoke dope or any other rich-boy vices that Jason Michaels might have, but maybe they tagged along, sharing the ambience and the girls who were drawn into the fast lane. So I drove up Yonge Street and east to Buttonville Airport.

It's a small place, mostly used by recreational fliers, and it closes at night except for local flights, circuits and bumps for people working on their licenses. By the time I got there, it was virtually deserted, but the landing lights were on along the runway, and the tower and the interior of the terminal were lit, so I went in and started playing detective.

The security man was impressed by my badge, but he was a summer replacement, while the regular man was on vacation, and didn't know anything about the Michaels jet. However, he did allow me to go up into the tower, and I went up and found a couple of guys, one of them sitting looking at the radar screen; the other one, at a radio.

The guy on the radar was busy, so I went to the other one and introduced myself as a copper. He shook hands abstractedly, then turned and gave somebody clearance to taxi.

Then he half turned from the radio and shoved his headphones up on one side so he could listen to me. "Yeah, Chief, what can I do for you?"

"I'm trying to get in touch with the pilot of the Michaels company jet. It's a Lear jet, and he landed here this afternoon. 'Fraid I don't know the guy's name."

"He in trouble?" The controller frowned. His forehead looked as if he did it a lot. It was permanently creased. He was fortyish and plump, an unhealthy plumpness that made me think his tension had turned him into a chronic nibbler. There were sandwich wrappings and a candy-bar wrapper in the garbage can beside his desk, so I was probably right.

"No, nothing like that. We have a mutual friend I wanted to get in touch with. I know the other guy better than the pilot. In fact, I don't even know the pilot's name."

The man frowned again and then popped a peppermint Life Saver as intently as if it were Valium. He was about to put it away but thought about it and waved it at me. I shook my head and smiled. He needed all the candy he could get. He shoved the cylinder back into his shirt pocket and said, "Well, we don't like talking about our pilots." He waved one hand and crunched his Life Saver and swallowed the pieces. "Especially to the law. You know how it is, one or two of them bring in the odd extra bottle on trips from the States." He thought about his words and added, "Not Gerry, mind, he's straight arrow. But you know how it is."

209

"This is strictly social. Does the plane live here? I mean, is he in and out regularly?"

"All the time. Generally short hops. But his outfit is big. They have holdings in the States, Mexico, all over. He goes everyplace you can think of." He was still unsure of me, but I didn't think anything I could say was going to change that, so I didn't try. I just beamed.

"His name is Gerry?"

"Yeah, Gerry Bowen. Not Boeing, Bowen." In his trade I guess it was a joke, and he grinned at it. I matched him. Uncle Tom taught us all a lesson.

"Do you have a phone number for him?"

"Sure, it'll be in the register. We keep a book on all the owners and pilots." He turned back to his radio and spoke crisply. "Roger one-seven-nine. Clear to taxi runway zero-three."

I waited, and he turned back to me and waved at a file cabinet. "Top drawer, red cover. Bring it over, would you, please."

I brought him the book, and he flipped through it. "Yeah, here we are, Gerry Bowen." He read me the phone number. It was a four-eight-nine number, an exchange in the north end of Toronto. "Could I get the address as well, please?"

He frowned again, thinking about it, then shook his head. "Sorry, I'm not supposed to tell anybody anything. I know you're a policeman an' all, but that's policy."

"No sweat. Thanks for the number." I nodded politely and wrote it down. "If Gerry comes in, tell him I was asking after him." That was camouflage. I knew he would tell the pilot, anyway. At least now it would look innocent. He wouldn't bother ringing the man right away and warning him.

"Yeah, will do." The radio took his attention again, and he carried on a quick conversation consisting mostly of numbers.

I turned to leave, and the other controller called out over his shoulder, "You wanna see him, better do it tonight. He filed a flight plan for Boston in the morning." He turned to see how I was taking the information. He was younger than the other man and more laid back, and I waved thanks.

"What time's he leaving?"

"Eleven A.M. Usually our guys file the day of the flight, but he said he'd be busy in the morning, so he did it early."

"Thanks for the news. I'll hustle my bustle." I nodded to him and left, making a note to be back there next morning if I came up blank on the night's work.

There was no guarantee I'd get anything from the pilot, especially over the phone, so I called Elmer Svensen. He was in his office, sounding tense. "Hi, Elmer, it's Reid. I'm trying to find the pilot of the Michaels jet. Do you have the backwards phone book handy?"

"Hold on." He was crisp, wound up tight over the case and its proximity to his private life. I stood and listened to the sounds of the detective office, male voices arguing and a typewriter making a cop's pace as somebody took a statement or wrestled with a report. Then Elmer came back, and I gave him the number.

"Yeah, Gerald Bowen, 32 Laager Crescent. That's two a's, not like the beer."

"A new one on me," I said. "Any idea of the cross streets?"

"Hold on, I'll check." Another pause and he came back on. "West off Yonge Street, north of Lawrence."

"Thanks, Elmer, I'll drop by."

"Think that's going to help?"

"I'm not sure. He was buddy-buddy with young Michaels. Maybe he knows where the kid is."

"Still doesn't get us anywhere," Elmer said gloomily.

"Maybe not, but we ought to talk to the kid. He's the only one we haven't heard from. The mother's dead, the girlfriend's dead, the father's clammed up. Maybe he knows something, and the little bastard owes me."

"Good luck," Elmer said. "Where'd you get the number?"

"Up at Buttonville Airport. They keep the Michaels company jet there. Oh, and while we're talking. He's due to fly out at eleven tomorrow, to Boston."

"Boston?" Elmer said. "And the father's clamming up? Likely going down to get some chowder." He laughed shortly at his joke.

"I guess, but he'll be gone like a wild goose in winter, so we'd better talk to him before then."

"And you're going to do it?" I could have told what his caseload looked like from the anxiety in his voice.

"Count on me, kid," I said. "See you later."

EIGHTEEN

◆

Bowen lived in the north end of Toronto, close to the
401, the main artery that shoots you around the worst of
the city traffic, except in rush hour, when the worst of
the city traffic congregates there. At other times, though,
he would be only fifteen minutes from the Buttonville
Airport should Michaels rub the lamp and order him to
appear.

His home was a renovated semidetached on a street
that had Audis and BMWs parked all down one side. I
found a place up the block from his door, left Sam in the
car, and walked. The house had an ornate brass knocker
that shone like gold, and I rapped it smartly, wondering
if he was ex-service and couldn't resist polishing any
brass he had on the property. After a thirty-second pause
the door opened and a small, pretty woman in her twen-
ties smiled at me without speaking. She looked Hispanic,
and I got the impression that maybe her silence was
caused by an ignorance of English. I smiled back and
said, "Good evening, is Mr. Bowen in?"

She smiled a little harder and said, *"Habla español?"*

I did, a little. I'd picked it up from Ramón Chavez in
my platoon. Most of what I knew was swearing, not
much use here. I shook my head and used up most of
my repeatable knowledge. *"Perdoneme, no hablo. Señor*

213

Bowen es aquí?" Sorry, I don't. Is Mr. Bowen here? There. From this point on it would be sign language.

She shook her head, still smiling, and said what must have been that he wasn't. I cocked my head and said, *"Yo su amigo,"* but she didn't bite; she just looked sad and stood her ground. We stood like that for a moment, and then I tried my second string. *"Parlez-vous français?"*

Bingo. She did. Not well, but better than my Spanish. So I spun her a quick little fairy story. I was a friend of Gerry's and had to leave town the next day. He'd asked me to look him up when I was in town. Would he be back that evening?

I still came up blank. He had gone. He was often away overnight. He was a pilot, as I knew, and he had to go whenever his boss sent him.

I knew that wasn't true. The company jet was on the ground until the morning, but I would have had to go and wait in the car for him except that my nose saved me. Faint but unmistakable on the warm evening air I smelled cigar smoke.

I phrased my next question carefully so she couldn't fob me off with half an answer. Was her visitor a friend of Mr. Bowen's? That made her blush and hesitate. She didn't want me reporting to good old Gerry that she was entertaining cigar smokers in his absence. She hedged, well, yes, he was, she admitted, and I took the opportunity. "In that case, perhaps he could tell me where to find him," I said, and edged past her and followed my nose into the kitchen, where the cigar smoke was coming from.

Her visitor was a compact man of about thirty, Hispanic. He was sitting with a can of beer in front of him, smoking his cigar and waiting for the woman to come back to her glass of red wine.

He looked up at me in surprise, wondering maybe if I was Gerry Bowen and going to get excited about his presence in my house.

The girl spoke rapidly to him in Spanish, and he dug out a smile of his own and stood up, offering his hand. I shook it and said in English, "Hi, name's Greg."

I was weighing him up. He had a scar on his face that looked as if it had been done with a knife. That's not unusual for a macho man from his culture, but his hair was cropped short, and there was a toughness to him that didn't fit with the city. He looked more like a soldier.

He shook my hand perfunctorily but didn't give his own name, so I played it like a tourist. "You a friend of Gerry's?"

He nodded but didn't say anything, so I pressed on, the big, clumsy WASP. "He said to look him up, and I'm just in town tonight. I wondered if you knew where he is?"

He spoke now. Probably the word he was easiest with. "No."

"Okay if I wait for him?" I didn't sit down. He was still standing, and he looked tough. I would have to be quick if he decided I belonged outside. He didn't answer, anyway. Instead, he spoke rapidly to the girl in Spanish, not taking his eyes off me.

"My friend says you should go," she told me in careful French.

"Not very friendly," I said. "This is Gerry's house. What's this guy doing here?"

She looked anguished. Women didn't repeat snotty remarks like that to men, even in translation. Not where she came from. "He is my friend," she said.

"And what does he do, this friend of yours? He looks like a soldier." She didn't answer immediately, and I repeated the last word in Spanish. *"Guerrilla."*

His anger flashed; I could tell from his tone, although his face didn't change expression. Not much would change it, I guessed, outside of glee as he watched somebody getting wasted.

215

The girl spoke now, riding over his last words. "You must go. Please," she said in French. "Mr. Bowen is not here."

"Thank you. I'll tell him how hospitable you've been," I said, and her anxiety increased again. She was illegal, I guessed, existing in this place at and probably for Gerry Bowen's pleasure. If he kicked her out, she would be back on the street looking for off-the-record work somewhere else. Or even back down south where most girls did not live in houses this nice.

I nodded to the man, then backed off a step, where he couldn't reach me with a sucker punch, and turned away. She came with me to the door. As I stepped out, she caught my sleeve between finger and thumb. "Please, don't say anything. This man is my friend. Mr. Bowen does not know." Her French was starting to slip, and she relapsed into rapid Spanish.

I winked at her. *"Di nada, señorita. Buenos noches."* There, that should put her mind at rest.

She waited anxiously at the door while I walked back to my car, then closed it. I got into my car and sat and patted Sam for a moment, thinking. Gerry Bowen was a flier. He got around. But why would he have a Hispanic girl working for him, or living with him, an educated girl who spoke French? And why would the same girl have connections with a guy who came across like a mercenary? None of it would have mattered if young Michaels hadn't been involved with Freedom for Hire. It made me wonder whether there was a deeper connection between the Michaels organization and the mercenaries. Was Michaels Senior involved in some force-of-arms takeover in Central America?

There was nothing to do but wonder and wait, so I waited. One by one the lights went off along the street. A few residents came home, one or two couples, laughing and relaxed after an evening on the town, and a couple of solitary men with briefcases, shutting their car doors

216

wearily and walking slowly to their houses. And then, at quarter to two, the Bowen door opened, and the man came out. He didn't look back. He turned at the curb and walked to the corner, moving at the leisurely pace of a man who had enjoyed his evening.

I started my car and drove after him, keeping far enough back and going slowly enough that I might have turned in from the far corner and been checking for house numbers. He didn't look back. Either a clear conscience or a complete lack of concern. Not a nervous citizen.

At the corner of Yonge Street he waited and after a minute or so caught a cab. I pulled out behind him and followed, down Yonge and across Eglinton, toward the cosmopolitan west end of the city.

He paid off the cab at a fleabag hotel called the Alameda. Maybe somebody Spanish had owned it once, and maybe that was why this guy was staying there. If he'd wanted anonymity, he had chosen well. I guessed that most of the patrons wouldn't be there much longer than it takes to warm up a pillow. I gave him a minute or so to go in, then sauntered after him.

A middle-aged man in a greasy suit was sitting behind the counter reading an Italian soccer magazine. He looked up at me suspicously. Most visitors at this time of night would be signed-in guests or couples.

"Yeah," he said.

"Hi. Looking for a guy. He just came in." I took out my wallet and extracted a ten. He watched it warily.

"No visiting in the rooms after midnight," he said.

"Except for broads." I did a big grin, and he cracked a smile of his own.

"Well, you know."

"Yeah, I know. What's his name, this man?"

He folded his newspaper. "I'm not supposed to tell names or nothin'." Not supposed to, as opposed to not allowed to.

"But if I was to drop this ten-spot on the floor and while you picked it up, I happened to check the book, what would I see?"

"Room three oh five," he said, and reached out for the ten.

I held on to it. "Name'd he give?"

He sighed and flicked through his card index. I reached over and took the box off him. Room 305 was occupied by Mr. J. Alvarez. The only home address given was Detroit.

"Thanks." I handed him the ten and then took out a second one. I was feeling flush with Michaels's reward money stashed in the bank. "I'm just going up to see him. Don't bother letting him know. I want it to be a surprise."

"Hey, listen." He suddenly got Italian on me, waving both hands. "I don' want no trouble."

"You're not getting any, are you? You're getting twenty bucks. Is he alone up there, or has anyone else dropped in?"

He licked his lips. "Well, there was one guy, fellah 'bout his size. He came in an hour or so back. Like it's a double room, we don' complain. Two guys, guy 'n' a broad. You know how it is."

"Intimately," I said. "Tell me, are the rooms either side of him taken?"

"Why you wanna know?" He was so worried now that he wasn't even looking at the second ten.

"Well, I've got a jug in the car, and we might just laugh it up a little."

He knew it was a scam, but he didn't mind. Booze he could live with. "Oh, 's okay," he said, and reached for the second bill.

I held on to it. "I'm just going to the door and get the jug. You get this when I come back in. Okay?"

He shrugged, palms up. "Sure, is fine."

I went to the door and whistled Sam. He squeezed

through the open car window and bounded up to me. I held the door for him, and he came in ahead of me. The desk clerk gave a little gasp of alarm. "Hey, you said a jug."

"You really should get your ears looked at." I tucked the ten into his top pocket and went up the stairs. He talked to himself in rapid Italian, but I didn't look back.

There wasn't any sound on the third floor. Not surprising at that time of night but encouraging. I guessed that most of the patrons wouldn't want police around, anyway. Unless I burned the place down, they would stay quietly in their rooms. There was light showing under the worn, old threshold of room 305, and I banged the door confidently.

After ten seconds of silence a man's voice called in accented English, " 'O's there?"

"Immigration. Open up." Sam stood at my left side, panting. I wondered if he would be quick enough if one of the men had a gun. Come on, Bennett. I cooled myself down with a quick breath. This is Toronto the Good. Guys don't have guns.

The door opened, and the man from Bowen's house peered out. I shoved the door wider and stepped in, telling Sam, "Come."

There was another man sitting on the bed, holding a glass. He looked like a countryman of my guy, and it looked like water in the glass, or tequila. The first guy said, "Gerrout."

"Not yet, Señor Alvarez. You sit down."

He wasn't going to until I told him, "This dog is trained to go for your balls. Sit down when you're told."

He sat, knees together.

"Good. Now, let me see your passport."

"Passport? What the fuck you doin'?"

"Passport," I repeated, and held my hand out.

He swore under his breath and squirmed his hand into his right pants pocket and came out with an American passport. The picture might have been him, but the name was Fernando Guzman.

"You've been telling lies to the hotel people, Fernando. Why would you do that?"

"My name is my business," he said. He was a little more confident now. His buddy was with him. They had arms somewhere, knives certainly, maybe something heavier. He would try to talk himself out of trouble, but failing that, he would act. I was glad I'd brought Sam with me. They looked like hard men.

"And what business is that, Fernando?"

"Jus' business," he said.

"And what's your boss's name? Would it be Green? Or Webster?" He started to relax, I could see it in the muscles of his face, and then I sprung the third name. "Or Dunphy?" And his muscles flickered.

He recovered, but not well. "Never heard of him."

"Never heard of Green or Webster? That I can buy. But Dunphy, now that's different. Where is he?"

"I don' know who you talkin' about." He shrugged and tried to loll, and I hissed at Sam. Sam snarled low in his throat, and Fernando sat up straight.

"I don't have time for this," I told him. "Give me Dunphy and I walk away. If you don't, I take you to the cops."

He spoke in Spanish, and his buddy set down the glass very deliberately on the night table. But he took too long leaning over the drawer, and as he tried to slip it open, I kicked it shut on his hand. He yowled, and Fernando sprang at me. I straight-armed him under the chin with the palm of my hand, sending him sprawling as I told Sam, "Fight," and he took over, driving Fernando back into a corner. Fernando was pressing himself back almost flat on the wall, babbling in Spanish, one hand cupped over his groin.

I shoved the second man aside, and he rolled onto the bed, nursing his hurt fingers. There was an automatic in the night table and I took it out and checked it. The safety was off, and I slipped the magazine out and looked. Loaded. I shoved it back into the butt and pointed it at Fernando, moving out of the possible range of the other man. "Easy, Sam," I said, and he stopped pressing and fell silent, watching Fernando carefully.

"Illegal firearms. That's bad, Fernando. We put guys in prison for having guns in Canada."

"Is not mine, is his." He jerked his chin toward his buddy.

"Sure, your gun is someplace else, I guess. Never mind, I'll find it. But first, where's Dunphy?"

He swore at me, flat and unemphatic. *Muy macho.*

"I'm going to ask you one more time. Then I'm going to start breaking you up," I said. It's not my style. I'm a copper and I go by the rules. Usually. But this time I was in real trouble. Dunphy was behind the killing of Alison Beatty and probably behind the killing of Mrs. Michaels. And that meant he was behind the attempt to frame me for the murder. My only chance of a clean sheet was finding Dunphy. The police couldn't help. I had broken the law already. They would have to let this man go and charge me with unlawful entry, assault, God knew what.

"Where is Dunphy?" I said slowly, and I saw the fear coming alive in his eyes. He was tough in combat but not one-on-one with a gun and dog against him. I smiled and slammed him across the face with my left hand. He fell sideways and sat on the ground, holding his face, not looking at me.

"Get up," I said quietly, and when he didn't move, I hissed at Sam, and he growled and bared his teeth. Fernando kicked at him desperately, and Sam grabbed him by the ankle and held him as he yelled, keeping just enough pressure on the ankle that he couldn't get it free.

"Easy, Sam," I said in the same tone, and he fell back a pace. Then I said, "On your feet," and Fernando got up slowly, pressing himself back against the wall. "Next time I hit you with the gun and you have no teeth," I said. Just talk, but he bought it. It wasn't me he was scared of; it was Sam. And Sam gave him an excuse to opt out of his machismo. His partner would vouch for Sam's ferocity. He was able to talk without fear of being scorned later.

"Dunphy 'as gone nort'." Fear had thickened his accent.

"Where north?" I asked, and in that moment his partner jumped at me. I didn't even have time to command Sam. I straight-armed him in midair with my left hand, but in that moment Fernando bolted. Sam was standing, whining, waiting for a command, and I called, "Track," as I struggled with the second man. He was wiry and hard, and I was holding the gun which I didn't want to use, handicapped. He cracked me a good punch in the left temple, and then I got him in a bear hug and head smashed him across the nose. He fell, and I left him and ran out of the door after Fernando.

He was on the floor at the end of the hall, Sam tugging at his arm. I was dazed from the punch I'd taken and from using my head as a battering ram, but I stuck the gun in Fernando's face and told him, "Freeze."

He froze, and I told Sam, "Easy," and he let go and stepped back a pace. I could hear voices in a couple of the rooms and knew I had to be fast. The guy downstairs had heard the ruckus, and he might just chicken out and call the police. I was in enough trouble.

"Where is Dunphy? No crap. Where is he?"

"He 'as gone nort'," Fernando hissed. "Gone nort' to find that guy."

"Which guy?" I jabbed him in the chest with the muzzle of the automatic, not hard but crisply.

He pulled his hands up over his face. "That guy 'o shot his frien'." He struggled for the word and lapsed into Spanish. *El indio.*

I shoved him again with the gun and stepped over him, calling Sam after me. Behind me a door opened, and a man's voice said, "Fer Crissakes, keep it down out there. I'm tryin'a sleep."

"On your feet," I said, and Fernando stood up, backing away from Sam. "Downstairs," I told him, "and don't try to run or the dog will get you."

The desk clerk was standing at the bottom of the stairs, bobbing from foot to foot nervously. "Wha's happening?" he asked in a voice that told me he didn't really want to know.

"Nothing, thanks. Me an' my buddy're goin' for a drink at my place. G'night." I had slipped the automatic into my pants pocket, and I beamed at him. Apart from the anger on Fernando's face, there was nothing to disprove what I'd said.

I walked Fernando to a phone booth a couple of blocks over and told Sam, "Keep," while I went in and called Murphy's Harbour police station. I figured George would have patched the phone through to his house, or to the police car via the radio. It rang eighteen times, and I hung up reluctantly. He must be out in the car, checking properties for signs of break-ins. Maybe he was out of the car looking at the back door of the liquor store or the bank. Or maybe he was sitting behind the wheel with a bullet through his head.

I got my quarter back and called Elmer Svensen's office. He was there, sounding weary but still working. "Elmer, Reid. Got something for you."

"Good news, I hope. I'm getting no place," he said.

"Yeah, picked up a guy who knows Dunphy. He's seen him since he got back from the north."

"Where are you?"

"On Cynthia Street, close to the corner of Grange."

"Be right there," he said.

"Good, but before you do, ring the Parry Sound OPP. Tell them Dunphy is back up in the Murphy's Harbour area. My friend here says that he's gone north to kill George Horn. I can't raise the kid on the phone. Have them check the station and make their presence known, lots of flashing lights, and have someone try to raise George on the station phone. You got the number?"

"Gimme," he said, and I did. "Right. Stay put; there in ten minutes."

I hung up and went outside the call box to stand side by side with Fernando, looking as if we were just shooting the breeze, in case some citizen came by and phoned the local police and I had to do things by the book.

For the same reason, I didn't bother interrogating him. If he had argued with me, somebody might have heard and called the heat. Nobody did. I heard a couple of cars way down the block on Dufferin Street, one of the city's arteries, moving slowly, bakers or produce people at groceries, heading in for an early start on their day's work or guys coming back from successful dates. Then I heard a speeding car, and a minute later Elmer Svensen and his partner pulled up at the curb.

Elmer got out and took two quick steps up to me. "This him?"

"Yeah, Fernando Guzman, Florida. I think he's involved with the Freedom for Hire people. He tells me that Dunphy's gone north."

"Where'd you dig him up?"

"Step over here a minute and I'll tell you." I repeated, "Keep," to Sam, and he sat on his haunches, staring at Guzman calmly.

Elmer and his partner walked off a few steps with me, and I said, "I found him at the pilot's house, the company pilot for the Michaels outfit. Followed him to the Alameda Hotel. There's another guy with him, likely gone by now. They had a gun, and I got Sam to take this one out and bring him down here. So far there's nothing on him that you want to touch with a ten-foot pole. It's all been pretty shaky procedure. But if I walk away and then call Sam off, you can talk to him like you just found him here. You may get something. You may not, but it'll all be kosher."

224

"Thanks, Reid." Elmer slapped my bicep lightly. "Where you heading now, home?"

"No, I'm going up to the Harbour to help George Horn find Dunphy. Tell Lou something so she won't worry when I don't show up. I figure Sam can dig the guy out if he's hiding around the station or wherever."

"Okay." Elmer nodded. "I've called the OPP, and I've got a kid at the station calling the Harbour every three minutes until we raise your deputy."

"No response yet?" I was starting to worry seriously. George was not the kind of man to leave the phone unanswered.

"No, I just checked before we got out of the car. Nothing." That was Elmer's partner, and he was on my side now. I guess Elmer had told his fortune for him, along with something of my pedigree.

"Okay, good luck with this guy."

I turned and jogged to the corner. From there I turned and looked back. Sam was dividing his attention now, guarding Fernando but also keeping the two detectives away. He was snarling at them, but when I whistled, he bounded away toward me. I saw Elmer and his partner step forward to Guzman; then Sam was beside me, and I jogged back to my car and put him in and headed north, taking the automatic out of my pocket and laying it on the seat beside me.

NINETEEN

♦

I flew up the highway, pushing my car as hard as it would go, ignoring every speed limit and overtaking the few vehicles on the road as if they were standing still. At a few minutes to five I was wheeling into the side road that leads down to Murphy's Harbour. It was still dark, but the birds were awake, and when I pulled in to the station and sat, I could hear the morning chorus.

There were lights on inside the station, although the police car was not parked outside. That was normal. I generally leave the lights on while I'm out on patrol. The only question was, why was George Horn still away? Had he taken the scout car to his home? I moved carefully. Without opening the door or killing the motor, I wound down the passenger side window and told Sam, "Seek." He squeezed out and ran in circles around the station, moving deeper and deeper into the bush that surrounded us. He even crossed the road and went up over the rocks on the far side, nose to the ground, searching for signs of anybody who might be hiding.

It was a kamikaze mission for him, and I hated doing it, but without his help I could have stepped out into an ambush, and once they had shot me, they would shoot him out of revenge and caution. This way we both had a chance.

After three minutes or so he came back into view, and I whistled him in. There was nobody within two hundred yards of us. From any farther than that they would not have had a clear shot. I cut the motor and ran to the back door of the station. It was locked, but I let myself in and checked around quickly. The place was tidy but empty. No clues to where George had gone.

I had to find him, and I thought for a few seconds about my firepower. Then I unlocked the shotgun. It was loaded with SSG, heavy buckshot that would give me a kill over thirty yards. I thought about that for a few seconds, then unloaded it and stuck in a couple of rifled slugs. They're a one-piece projectile, accurate up to maybe seventy-five yards and heavy enough to knock down a bear. Then I added three more SSG shells and stuck a couple of extras into the pocket of my light jacket. If I had to return fire, I could do it. I figured the shotgun would be a better street weapon than the rifle. And if all else failed, I still had the automatic I'd taken off Guzman.

My next move was to phone the OPP and see if they had managed to raise George. The constable at the other end was young and pushy. "Naah, no idea where he's gotten to. We've had our guys make a couple of drive-throughs. They haven't seen anything." I could almost hear him chewing gum, relaxed, wondering why we were in a lather over something he didn't understand.

"Listen, in case you didn't get the whole message, we're looking for two very tough characters, Dunphy and Wallace. They're trained soldiers wanted for suspicion of a couple of homicides. They're dangerous."

"Yeah, I heard," he said. "Why in hell'd a couple heavies like that be wandering around Murphy's Harbour beats me."

"They're out to kill my deputy, George Horn, that's why. Get the guys back on patrol here. If you can't do it yourself, let me talk to the person in charge."

He became a bit more respectful at that. "Yeah, well, I'm on my own, Chief. The sergeant went off at four. I'll call the guys back and send them over."

"Good. Have them show a lot of presence. I want their lights flashing, the works. We're talking about dangerous people."

"Will do," he said, and I hung up.

My next move was to call George's home. His mother answered and told me that George had been out all night. I didn't alarm her but asked her to give him the message that the colonel was in the area and to call me when he got home. She rang off, and I stood for a moment wondering what George was up to. He didn't have a girlfriend in town, not one that I had heard about. He must still be on patrol. And that could mean he was dead. There was nothing to do but search for him and hope.

I had Guzman's automatic stuck into my belt, and I went back out and into my car, bringing Sam and the shotgun with me. It was still dark, but the predawn chill told me that the sun was coming up soon. I left the windows down and drove off slowly, all through my little town.

This was the last week in August, tourist season still. Because of that the bait shop was already open, ready to cater to early-morning fishermen. I went in and found Jacques Perrault checking the minnows in his tank. He frowned when he saw me. "Hey, Chief. I thought you was on 'oliday with your lady."

"She's out west working. I'm trying to locate young George. Has he been by?"

Jacques shook his head. "No. I was open 'alf an hour already, 'aven't seen him."

"If he comes by, could you give him a message, please?"

"Sure t'ing. Shoot." He reached for a pencil and scribbled as I spoke.

"Tell him that Dunphy's here. He's to go to the OPP office at Shawinagan and wait there until I call."

228

"Got it." He knew that George and I had been involved in an adventure up north, but I guessed he didn't watch much TV. He didn't have any reaction to Dunphy's name.

I nodded thanks and went back to the car. It was gray light now, when the trees behind the town start to loom as individual points, like small mountains, and you're aware of having the world to yourself. It's a favorite time of mine, but this morning I didn't savor it. Where was George?

The scout car wasn't anywhere in town. I drove around all the main buildings, checking the backs of them, even getting out to check the garbage dumpster behind the liquor store where they were making renovations. I had a feeling that Dunphy might have taken pleasure in leaving George's body there and taking off in the scout car. Or, on the other hand, he might have stuck George in the car and driven it into the water somewhere. Unless George had been alert or somewhere else instead of here. But where?

It figured that the OPP car would have driven around my bailiwick once, so that meant they would have seen the scout car had it been abandoned by the road. Which meant that I should look deeper, checking all the places George might have driven into, the off-road areas we normally checked at night. There were dozens of them, but it had to be done.

I left the town behind me and headed north up the heavily wooded road that runs behind most of the lakeside houses along this shore. Some of them are visible from the road, but others are hidden behind the trees, and I pulled into one driveway after another, checking for the scout car. By now it was completely light, and I cut the headlights and drove quietly, hoping not to alert Dunphy if he was waiting somewhere. It seemed unlikely. If he wanted to nail George, he would be waiting at the station, hidden on the hill across the road, but Sam had

229

already checked there and come up empty. Most of the cottages had cars outside them, and one had lights on in the house. I saw the owner at the kitchen window and got out and asked if he'd seen anything of George. The guy was an aging Brit with the racial stereotypes he'd picked up in English boys' books and never changed. "Goofin' off on you, is he? You can't trust Indians," he said amiably.

"This one you can. He saved my ass," I said.

I must have come across irritable, because he immediately backtracked. "Ah, well. I don't know this particular guy. Some of them's okay, I s'pose."

"Thanks for the help," I said, and backed out, leaving him wondering how such a bleeding heart had managed to become chief of police.

It took me half an hour to get up as far as the northern lock, but I didn't cross at the bridge there. Instead, I kept on north, stopping at the town dump to drive in and around the side of it over the flat field that had been the site of one of my most notable battles against some bikers. But the car wasn't there.

And then, a hundred yards farther on, I saw a car parked at the entrance to a cottage. The cottage itself lay down the slope toward the lake, fifty yards in behind a stand of spruce. I didn't stop but drove by at the same speed, glancing at the car. It was a 1987 model, and I didn't recognize it. I know by sight the cars of most of our longtime residents, but maybe these people, their name was Bull, I remembered, had visitors in from the city. Or maybe this was the car Dunphy had come north in.

I stopped my own car a hundred yards down the road and got out silently, carrying the shotgun. Sam was behind me half a pace, and I kept him there. If it was Dunphy, he would shoot Sam on sight, and I figured I could find him myself before that happened.

I reached down and patted Sam, then gave a quick jerk on his choke chain. That's his command for silence and attention, and he stood up very straight when I let go of the chain. I saw his nose moving as he sniffed the air. He would bristle if he sensed anything.

Now I left the road and took to the trees, moving as if I were on patrol. It was full daylight by this time, and I could see where I was stepping, avoiding sticks underfoot, moving in total silence through the trees.

The house had a driveway running down the north side of it, ending in a graveled area big enough to turn a car around in. As I edged through some birch trees, fifty yards from it I saw a car there. The police car.

I stood behind a tree and looked at it carefully for almost a minute. It was facing me, as if George had driven in and prepared to back up and drive out. The windows were all wound up as far as I could tell, and there were no bullet holes visible in them. That much was good. He hadn't been bushwhacked in the car. But where was he?

I glanced down at Sam. He was still on duty, sniffing the air alertly but not bristling. The wind wasn't making it easy for us; it was out of the north, behind me, carrying away any scents he might pick up on the air. I stayed where I was, scanning every bush, every tree as far as I could see, out beyond the house on its west side. To the right, the lake side of the house, the ground dipped away to water level, but I didn't think Dunphy would be down there. As a soldier, he would take the high ground. I could see nothing, but I was uneasy. The scout car could have been here for hours. George wouldn't have left it all this time.

Finally I stepped out from behind my tree and moved on, as carefully as if this were a patrol in enemy territory, stepping from tree to tree, shielding myself from the house.

I was twenty yards closer when I heard the click of a lock, and I froze. Then the side door of the house opened, and George stepped out casually. He had a smile on his face, and behind him I saw pale blue nylon and then the pink face of the daughter of the house, Eleanor. I grinned and relaxed. So that was how George spent his nights. Good for him. Eleanor was a pretty girl, a medical student at Queen's, I'd heard. I watched as George kissed her and then stepped out toward the car, deciding I would backtrack and josh him later. I didn't want to embarrass him or his girl.

Then a ruffed grouse exploded out of the bush in a whir of wings up close to the road on the far side of the drive from where I was standing. I looked up sharply, seeing the bird and following its trajectory back down to the ground, and there, crouching with a rifle in his hands, was a man.

I roared, "George, down," and the man whirled and fired at me, but I'd rattled him, and the triple burst of bullets was yards off the mark.

I fired back, missing him, tearing a chunk from the side of a tree inches above his head. If he'd been a soldier, he would have stayed put and fired before diving away, but he wasn't. He dived and rolled before firing again, and once more he was wide of the mark, but this time my return shot hit him. He flew backward, his rifle tumbling away out of his hands. Then he lay still. I pulled tighter behind my tree, heart racing, checking left and right for other men. If this was Dunphy or Wallace, he would have backup, and now that they had a man down, the other would stay in hiding, waiting for our first mistake.

George was on the ground, squirming toward the scout car. The girl was in the open doorway, screaming helplessly. I shouted to her, "Get indoors," and then ran toward the downed man, crouching and jinking as I ran.

I stopped ten paces from him. His gun was lying four feet beyond him, and he was still, his left side a pulpy mess of blood.

I checked around and then told Sam, "Seek," and he ran up the slope toward the road, nose to the ground. I watched him go. He was following the man's track back to the car, I guessed, but then I heard an engine start, and the car roared away. There was a second man, and he'd gone.

I stood long enough to hear which way it turned on the road, back down toward the town. Then I ran down to the scout car, whistling for Sam. He bounded after me, and I tugged at the door as George stood up. "It's locked," he said.

"Gimme the key. There's a man down in the bush. Call the emergency people. Tell them we need a chopper, if they can get one; he's hurt bad. Take this gun and watch yourself."

He gave me the key, and I tossed him Guzman's gun, then unlocked the car and whistled Sam inside. As soon as he was in, I jumped behind the wheel, backed up, and roared up the driveway, bouncing almost to the ceiling on the ruts.

The car was gone from the driveway, but there was a trace of dust in the air where it had headed south, and I raced after it, reaching for the microphone. I called the station, but there was no answer. Damn. We had only one channel on the radio. We needed two, a second straight through to the OPP, but we didn't have it. The world was deaf to my emergency.

The road winds behind all the cottages, and I didn't see the car again until I got almost to the bridge. It was across it, turning south on the road on the other side. I squealed into the turn, grazing the side of the car against the abutment, and pelted after him. Automatically I flicked on the emergency switch, and the siren cut in, sawing the morning quiet to shreds as I rocked down the road behind him.

The other driver was good, and the car he was in was small and maneuverable. I didn't catch sight of him again all the way down the west road and out to the highway. I stopped at the intersection and checked the

233

dust on the road for wheel tracks, but they didn't tell me anything, so I moved instinctively, turning down the highway toward Toronto, hammering as fast as my big six would take me, siren screaming. There is a good straight patch a mile down the road. You can see for three-quarters of a mile, but I didn't see the car on it, so I wheeled into a gas station on the side of the road. It was still closed, but the owner was out unlocking his pumps. He looked up in astonishment as I slammed to a stop beside him.

"Did a red compact go by a minute ago, speeding?" I shouted.

He was stupefied and slow. Then he said, "No, nothin' like that. Just a couple trucks."

"Thanks. Can I use your phone? I'm the police chief, Murphy's Harbour."

"Help yourself." He waved me on but bustled after me, mouth open. Not many of his days started this excitingly.

I dialed the OPP. A new man was on duty, crisp and efficient.

"Bennett, Murphy's Harbour. I'm looking for a red compact, could be a Mazda, license REN 111. It must be heading north from our side road. The guy in it is armed and dangerous. Approach with caution."

He repeated the number and said, "Right, I'll get it on the air, but we've got only one car out, the shift's just changing."

"Ask the sergeant to turn the guys out right away, and alert the rest of your people, could you, please?"

"Sure. Hold on." He turned away from the phone and after thirty seconds was back on. "This connected with the shooting down at the Harbour? We just got a call from your deputy there."

"Yes, that man's hurt bad. He could be dead. But send an investigator if you can. He's tied in with two homicides that happened in Toronto, Beatty and Michaels, two women."

"Shit. What's he doing up here getting shot?" Even hardened policemen have the curiosity of washerwomen.

"Let me talk to the guy in charge, please. I'll fill him in."

Another pause and I was talking to their inspector. His name is Anderson. He's an officious bastard. I've had trouble with him in the past, but now he was cool and efficient."

"Chief Bennett? What's happening?"

"It's those men Dunphy and Wallace, Inspector. They're involved with the Freedom for Hire hassle I had a couple of days back in Quebec. They're wanted for a number of offenses and suspected of two homicides in Toronto. One of them swore he would kill the kid who helped me, George Horn. He was waiting for him, only I beat him to it. He's got a rifle slug in him."

"Was that necessary?".

"Better him than George Horn," I said firmly. "He had an army automatic rifle, and he was there to kill."

"I hope for your sake you're right," he said. "You certainly overreact to threats."

"We'll see. For now, see if you can get an investigator to the scene to check the guy's rifle and if possible to take a statement. I'm not sure he'll be in time."

"A rifle slug?" Anderson repeated. "That'd stop a train."

"It stopped him," I said. "I'm going back to the scene now, if your men come to the Bull house, half a mile north of the north lock, east side of the lake, I'll leave my car on the road, a blue Chev."

"I'll come myself," he said.

I hung up and stood for a moment gathering my thoughts. There was nothing more to do here. The only other people to be alerted were the Toronto detectives. I picked up the phone again and phoned Metro Toronto homicide office, getting through to Inspector Burke.

"Bennett here. I found a guy with a gun in the Harbour. I put him down and chased another in a red compact, REN 111. Could be a rental. He hasn't come south, so

235

he could still be in this area, maybe contacting a plane for a return to Toronto."

"Is it one of the suspects?" Burke sounded slow. He hadn't had much more sleep than I had, which was none.

"Didn't stop to check. My deputy's up there at the Bull house. The guy's name is George Horn. The daughter's there; maybe she'll answer the phone and put George on. He's a smart kid. This guy was waiting for him."

"Waiting where?"

"In the bush. Horn's got something going with the girl there. He was inside. The guy had an automatic rifle, military model. He was going to kill Horn for what he did up north, getting me away from them."

Burke didn't answer for a moment. I guessed he was puffing at the first of the day's Old Ports. Finally, he said, "What the hell, it's a nice day for a drive in the country. I'll come up and talk to the guy. Is he gonna make it?"

"I'm not sure. I took off after the car. Like I said, it didn't come south. He could be flying back to the Metro area or out of the country. All we can do is look for his car."

"Nice work," he said. "Just hope the bastard'll hang in till we can take a statement."

"Did you get anything more from the guy I handed to Elmer last night?"

He paused again and then spoke carefully. "Sergeant Svensen had occasion to talk to a visitor from the United States last night. But unfortunately he didn't give us anything useful to our investigation into the homicide of Mrs. Michaels."

"Pity," I said. "I'll be up at the Bull house, or if they've cleared the guy away by then, I'll be at the police station in Murphy's Harbour."

"I will see you there, Chief. Thank you for your assistance on this matter."

I hung up, wondering how long the department had been monitoring the phone calls from the homicide office. I couldn't think of any other reason for Burke's formality.

The gas station guy was anxious for more information, but I thanked him for his help and told him to call me if he saw the wanted car. Then I drove back to the scene of the shooting.

George was still there with his girl, who had changed into blue jeans and a sweater. She was calmer now, kneeling beside the wounded man, trying to stop the bleeding with a blood-soaked sheet. I could see that much from twenty yards off as I walked down through the trees.

George turned when he saw me. "He's bad, Reid, bleeding like a stuck pig. You got him in the gut."

"You haven't touched the rifle?"

"No, it's where it fell." He pointed. "Something else you should know as well."

"What's that? You recognize this guy?" I was still walking toward the man on the ground, but the girl was between me and his face. I wasn't prepared for George's news.

"Yeah, I recognize him. It's Jason Michaels."

TWENTY

◆

"Jason Michaels?" I couldn't believe it. "You sure?"

"See for yourself." He stepped aside, and I ran the last few steps and looked at the man's face. It was Michaels, all right, gray faced. All the boredom and arrogance gone now. A sorry casualty, like a hundred others I'd seen, like I'd been myself, twice.

George was nervous. "This is bad, Reid. His old man's rich. This means trouble."

"Trouble, hell. He started this. He was lying in wait for you, going to drop you, and the girl as well, probably. If I hadn't been here, you'd be dead. Don't waste any pity on him."

"His old man's rich," George said helplessly. "We're going to need a lawyer real bad."

"Not as bad as he needs a doctor. Did you call for the chopper?"

"They said it was on its way." George was nervous; he wanted to say more, probably to ask me not to mention the girl when the statement came out.

I bent close to Jason's ear, speaking slowly. "Can you hear me, Jason?" He didn't answer, but a muscle twitched in his face. I took it for assent and went on. "Did Wallace send you?"

He didn't answer, but his eyelids flickered, and I could

tell there was still somebody in there. "The helicopter's coming. You'll be in hospital in a few minutes. You're going to be okay."

Now his eyes opened for a moment, and he whispered. I bent and caught the word. "Dunphy," he said.

"Then you're clear," I lied. "He's the guy who'll go down. Just hold on." I moved the sheet aside and looked at his wound. It was bad, but it could have been worse. The slug had almost missed him, catching him within an inch of his side, tearing him open but missing most of the internal organs. The hydrostatic shock of the impact was his worst enemy. It had slammed everything in his body with enormous internal force. Heart, brain, everything, was jolted. That and the loss of blood would kill him if this were the boonies, but with help he would recover.

I stood up, and the girl replaced the sheet, pressing gently but firmly. She was calm, used to the sight of blood in operating theaters, I guessed. She would be a good doctor. George was looking up and behind him, and I raised my eyes and listened and heard the faint whup-whup-whup of a helicopter approaching from down the lake. "Go flag him down," I told George, and he ran down the driveway and out onto the dock.

The girl looked up "He's luckier than he looks," she said. "He's torn up, but you missed the spleen. His intestines are going to need putting back together, and there's the risk of peritonitis, but that's all. An inch higher and he would have bled to death before we could get him to a hospital for a splenectomy."

"Thank the Lord for that. I didn't want to kill him, just to drop him. And thanks for the first aid."

Behind me I could hear the helicopter lowering itself to the dock. Then the engine note slowed, and within seconds two men came up past the house with a litter. One of them was in plain clothes. The other one was an ambulance attendant. They ran to the downed man, and the attendant stuck a needle in his arm and held up a bottle of plasma.

"Help me get him on the stretcher," he said, and he raised the bottle while the other man and I lifted Jason, cradling him under the waist, trying to prevent any more strain on his wound.

I took one end of the litter, and George took the other while the attendant walked beside us, holding up the bottle of plasma. We walked carefully over the rough ground and onto the driveway. Jason groaned as we moved, a good sign. As long as he could feel, he was reacting, fighting for life. I didn't want his death on my conscience, but I was glad he was on the litter and not George Horn, probably with a sheet over his face.

I spoke to the other man as we walked. "His name is Jason Michaels. He was with the mercenary force, Freedom for Hire. George here and I got him out. Now he was back trying to kill George."

"That all you got?" the man grunted. His jacket was smeared with blood, and he was angry at the mess. Blood was something only other people got on them.

"Got a tape recorder with you?" I asked him.

"Yeah, in my pocket."

"Get everything down," I said. "He's ready to talk."

We had reached the dock, and as the detective turned to look at me, I could see contempt in his face.

"You're a bastard, Bennett," he said.

I didn't answer. Excuses wouldn't help. "Just get the statement. George, go with this officer, witness Jason's statement, and give them the story. I'm waiting here for the OPP investigation team."

"Right." We crouched automatically under the downdraft of the chopper and shoved the litter inside. The ambulance man stepped up, still holding the plasma bottle. Then the detective and George got in, and I backed away and stood watching as the pilot lifted off and swung away north, ignoring the line of the lake now, heading straight for the hospital.

I walked slowly back up the drive. Eleanor was standing at the top beside the house, rinsing the blood off her hands, rinsing and rinsing as if the action would wipe out all that had happened here. She looked up dully as I approached. "What was that man trying to do, Chief?"

"George told you where he went the last few days, did he?"

"Not much." She straightened up, shaking the water from her hands. "He said you and he had been north, been through a forest fire and brought a man out. That's all."

"There's more. The man who was shooting at him, the one I hit, that's the guy we brought out."

She looked at me and shook her head, confused. Then she did the practical thing, opened the back door and nodded an invitation. "Come on in. I'll make some coffee."

I came after her, and she went into the kitchen. She ran the water and washed her hands one last time, with soap, then dried them on a towel that hung on the back of the door. I watched her, missing Fred. This girl was younger, shorter, but she had the same air of good sense to her. I got the feeling she didn't rattle easily. Another good trait for a doctor. "This is getting heavy," she said. She gave her hands a little jerk, angrily, and hung up the towel. "I like George. But I don't want my parents getting the news this way. They'll freak out. They still figure him for the Indian kid on the gas pump at the marina."

"He's a hell of a lot more than that," I said. "You can be proud to be his friend."

She ran water into the pot. "Friend is fine," she said, turning the tap off with another angry gesture. "But you don't know my father. He's WASP through and through."

"Tell you what." I was improvising. "He doesn't have to know all of it. Just say you heard a noise when you woke up and you saw a man with a gun and called the station. George was here. I was here. That's enough. He'll believe that."

"Will you back me up?" she asked, looking at me levelly.

"To him, yes."

"Fine." She grinned now. "This whole thing is so unbelievable he won't know what's true and what's not." She put the coffeepot on the stove and turned on the gas. It lit with a quiet pop, and she leaned against the stove. "Funny," she said. "That guy out there was an inch from being killed and all I can think about is what my father is going to say."

"Welcome to the world." I grinned with her. "That's what matters. You did your best for him. Now it's time to do the best for yourself."

"You've been through this before, haven't you?" she said.

"Over and over," I told her. "It happens."

She was about to speak again when I heard Sam bark outside and then the crunch of wheels on the gravel. I looked out the window and saw two cars pull up. One of them was a black-and-white OPP cruiser; the other, a similar model, only with no insignia.

Inspector Anderson got out of the first. He looked grim, his normal expression. He's an ambitious man, always on the lookout for a new rung on the ladder to promotion. But I smiled when the doors opened on the second car. Two detectives got out, laughing at some private joke. I knew them well, Werner and Kennedy, a couple of professionals who had worked with me the month before on a major case. I knew I'd get an honest hearing from them.

I went out and told Sam, "Easy," then walked forward to meet the men. "You didn't waste any time."

"Is the victim still here?" Anderson asked.

"No, the chopper lifted him out a couple of minutes back. He's okay, he'll recover."

Werner and Kennedy ambled down and shook hands. Werner was grinning. He's a typical old-style copper, a little overweight and amiable even when the world is falling apart all around him. He said, "Couldn't wait for duck season to open, eh? Had to get the old shotgun offa the wall and nail whatever was moving."

"This was more sporting. Ducks don't shoot back," I said.

Kennedy was a bit more serious. He nodded politely to Eleanor Bull, who had followed me outside, then asked, "You got his gun someplace?"

"Nobody's touched it since he dropped it. This way." I led the three of them up to the rifle, and they crouched and looked at it. "Never seen one like that," Kennedy said. "Looks automatic."

"It's a military assault rifle, looks like the new British Enfield bullpup," I said. "It's the weapon the Freedom for Hire people were training with up north."

Werner turned to Eleanor, who had followed us up. "Hi, I'm Sergeant Kennedy," he said. "And you're?"

"Eleanor Bull. I was here when it happened," she said.

"And what did happen?" Anderson was anxious to get into the act, and he cut off Werner's question.

"The other policemen, George Horn, he was outside my door, and then I heard three bangs ratatat, then one different bang, then three more and another one, and I came out and saw the man on the ground."

"Three shots first," Anderson mused aloud, turning and looking at me as if he expected me to go red.

"He fired when he saw me," I said. "And I fired back."

"Warning shot, eh, Reid?" Kennedy suggested, and I nodded. It wasn't quite true. I'd have nailed him first crack if I'd been more careful with my aim.

"This man was crouching, waiting for a clear shot at

George. I shouted, and he fired at me. I fired back. You can see the scar on this tree." I pointed, and all three of them examined the gash on the trunk of the cottonwood Michaels had been using for shelter. "Then he dived away and turned and fired off another burst at me. That's when I hit him."

"There's a moral to this story," Werner said. "And the moral is, don't screw around with an ex-marine."

Kennedy turned to the girl and asked, "Would you have an old wire coat hanger in the house, please?"

"Sure." She looked puzzled. "You want one?"

"Please," he said. "I want to pick this thing up."

Eleanor went back to the house, and Anderson turned to me, barking out questions in a voice that told me he didn't put too much value on the truth of my answers. Kennedy was slightly behind him, and he rolled his eyes toward heaven as Anderson bored in. I went over what had happened a couple of times, giving the same answers every time until anyone except Anderson would have known I was telling it straight. Then Werner asked, "This guy Michaels, isn't he the one you got away from this army outfit?"

"Yeah, that's the part I don't understand. He deserted them. Now he's back using one of their guns, backed up by a guy in a car who took off on his own. It seems on the face of it as if he was trying to make amends for leaving them in the bush, undergoing some kind of test."

"Sounds pretty farfetched to me," Anderson said, and sniffed like a Methodist preacher condemning bingo games.

"Got any better ideas, Inspector?" Werner asked innocently.

"There has to be one," Anderson snapped.

"Yeah, well, where did the kid get ahold of one o' these things? You can't buy one over-the-counter." Werner pointed to the rifle, and Anderson shrugged.

"Maybe he's a gun collector. Sounds like a personal feud to me. I don't think we have to go looking for any deep significance."

Eleanor came back out with a hanger, and Kennedy bent it into a hook and picked up the gun. "Thanks," he said casually. "Now if you'd be kind enough to let us take down a statement, I'll be happy to let you get on with your day," he said.

He went down to the house with Eleanor, and Werner put the rifle into an evidence bag, and then we all searched for the spent rounds. We found all six of Jason's and my two. Werner picked them all up with the end of the coat hanger and put them in two separate bags, one for the automatic shells, one for the shotgun. Then he and Anderson took my statement.

I made it complete, starting with the information I'd got from Guzman in Toronto the night before and giving them the gun I'd taken from him. Anderson grabbed that with great enthusiasm.

"An illegal weapon," he said. "Why didn't you turn this in when you spoke to the Metro police?"

"Because I expected to find somebody up here trying to kill George and I wasn't going to come after him bare-handed," I said easily. "Here, the gun hasn't been fired."

"But you already had the shotgun," Anderson persisted. He was one of those guys who perspire when they think hard, and his face was glistening, his eyes narrowed with intensity. Persistence personified.

Werner headed him off. "Not in Toronto he didn't," he said. "If you'd of been coming back to face a guy with a gun, you'd of hung on to the automatic as well, wouldn't you."

"It's against regulations," Anderson said.

"And trying to nail a policeman with an assault rifle is against the law," I said. "It was my decision, and I took it. Now you can keep the gun."

245

"It will go in my report," Anderson said, trying to make it sound like a threat.

"I'd be disappointed if it didn't," I told him. I was suddenly weary. No sleep plus a firefight plus Anderson's bitchiness had finished up all of my reserves. All I wanted was to head home and sleep for a week. The best I could hope for was one hour before Burke and the homicide guys arrived from Toronto, but even that thought was a comfort.

"Listen, I'm through. I'm going down to my place the other side of the lock on this road. If you want me, come and knock, but if you don't have to, let me sleep."

"Which house?" Anderson wanted to know.

"It'll be the one with the Murphy's Harbour police cruiser parked in the yard," I said, and Werner guffawed.

"That'll narrow it down," he said. "So go crash."

"Most policemen would stay on duty until the job was finished," Anderson said, his eyes glinting.

"Look at it this way, Inspector. You get an attempted homicide pinch all to yourself. Should look good on your record." I nodded at them all and went back to the cruiser.

George had left the shotgun propped against the wall of the house, and I stuck it in the back of the scout car and called Sam into the front seat. As I was starting the motor, Eleanor and Kennedy came out of the house, and the girl called out, "Coffee's ready, want a cup?"

"No, thanks, Eleanor, I'm bushed. I'm heading home for some shut-eye. Get your dad to call me when you've spoken to him and I'll tell him what happened."

She was young enough to blush. "Thanks, Chief," she said.

I waved without speaking, and Kennedy nodded; then I backed out and drove slowly up to the road and headed home.

As I drove, I remembered that I hadn't called Fred as I'd promised the night before. At the time we'd arranged, I was in the homicide office, talking to Burke. I checked my watch. It was quarter to eight, quarter to six Saskatchewan time. I would call her when I got in and try to catch her before she started her day. She'd said she was up early, but maybe not this early, unless she was involved in some sunrise-on-the-prairies sequence. I grinned at the thought. Dawn wasn't Fred's best time. She preferred to get up around seven-thirty and yawn over coffee for half an hour if she had the chance.

I was thinking of her and smiling as I rounded the corner in the road that leads down to my modest little place, and I almost gasped when I saw her Honda sitting in the drive. It couldn't be. She was on the prairies, and her car was underground in the parking lot of her apartment building. I squealed the scout car to a stop, reading the license over. Yes, it was hers. And then I saw her. She was getting into a boat at the end of the little dock behind my house, looking around fearfully but doing it because there was a man at the motor and he had a gun on her. It was Wallace, and he looked at me and fired off a quick shot, then threw the boat into gear and pulled away, with Fred tumbling into the center of the boat.

I grabbed the shotgun and dived out of the car, with Sam after me, but it was too late. Wallace was crouching low, ten yards from the dock, too far for even Sam to leap at him. He fired again, a quick snap shot that whistled high over my head, and I raised the gun, then lowered it. The cloud of buckshot it would throw would include Fred. I was powerless.

He sat up higher now and laughed. But then I saw my fishing rod leaning against the post at the end of the dock. It was set up with good five-kilogram breaking strain line and a heavy red-and-white spoon with a triple hook on it. My only chance. Wallace fired again as I grabbed the rod and cast it, concentrating on getting it across the boat ahead of him, a hard cast on a moving target. He fired again, but as he did, the line whistled

247

past his face, and I set the hook, snagging him in the side of the head hard enough to break the line.

He screamed with pain and hurtled backward into the water, clawing at his face. Fred sat up in the boat and shrieked as it spun around in a circle, following the direction Wallace had forced the motor into as he fell.

The motor was slowing, but even so, the boat came full circle and hit Wallace square in the head. "Grab the motor," I shouted, and Fred stumbled back the length of the boat and took the control.

"Great. Bring it in," I called, and she turned for the shore, leaving Wallace sinking in the lake.

She came in clumsily, and the boat hit the dock with a bang that stalled the motor. I scrambled aboard, with Sam leaping in after me. Fred clung to me, sobbing. "Oh, God, Reid, what's going on? Who is he?"

I kissed her quickly and patted her shoulder. "It's over, honey. It's all over. Just sit down a moment and we'll pull him in."

She sat down on the seat ahead of me, and I restarted the motor, then reached out and squeezed her hand. "I'll explain in a minute. I want to get him before he drowns. He's a murder suspect."

She rubbed her eyes and then looked around. "He's gone," she said flatly. "He's drowned."

"It's only six feet deep there; we'll find him," I said, and ticked the motor forward, staring over the side. "I have to bring him up. What happened, anyway?"

She's a woman in a million. No panic, no stumbling over words. She took a breath to steady herself and told me, "The movie collapsed, no funding. Somebody who'd promised didn't come through. Anyway, I flew home late last night. Checked with Louise and then decided you would be up here, fishing. So I got up early, thought I'd surprise you."

"You did," I said. "You scared the hell out of me. This guy's bad. Where was he?"

248

"He was standing by the house when I got here. I didn't like the look of him, so I didn't get out. I just called out, 'Is anybody home?' "

"Then what?" I reached out and took her hand again, my heart still pounding from the shock of seeing Wallace threatening her. She squeezed my hand tight.

"Well, he said, 'I'm looking for Reid. We were in the service together,' something like that. And I told him I was sorry, I couldn't help him. Then he said something like, 'Hey, haven't I seen your picture in the paper?' "

She gulped suddenly. "Reid, I was so dumb. I should have said, 'No, you must be mistaken,' but I said, 'Possibly, I'm an actress.' "

"And he knew who you were?" Right at that moment I wanted to leave Wallace underwater forever.

"I guess." She tried a little laugh. It came out harsh. "So he pulled the gun and grabbed me through the window and said, 'You're coming with me.' "

"And he took you to the boat?" I was trying to work out why a professional like Wallace would have risked being seen instead of heading for the house, where he could have ambushed me.

"He tried to take me to the house, only I threw the keys away into the water. Then he hit me and said, 'Okay, we'll do it the hard way.' He was just getting me into the boat when you arrived, and you know the rest."

"You thought to ditch the keys. You're incredible. Marry me," I said impulsively, and she gasped, then laughed.

"You serious?"

"Absolutely. I've never met a woman like you, not ever."

"You're pretty remarkable yourself," she said. "And as I'm between jobs at the moment, I'll say yes."

"Between jobs? I thought this was a six-week thing." I didn't want to talk about her career. I wanted to find Wallace, dead or alive, but Fred was more important than he was, so I listened to her answer as we moved slowly ahead, staring into the water.

"Like I said, the funding fell through. I flew home last night and thought I'd come up here and catch you still in bed. I got up at four-thirty for this," she said. Then she pointed, shouting. "There. There he is."

I eased the boat forward and cut the motor. Wallace was floating facedown, close to the bottom of the water. I reached for the anchor and lowered it over, next to him, then hoisted gently, catching the fluke under his arm and pulling him to the surface.

Fred reached down and caught him by the back of the jacket. I pulled in the anchor and joined her, pulling Wallace up vertical in the water. "Sit as far on the other side as you can," I said.

Fred did it without speaking, and I hoisted Wallace up face first and lowered him into the boat. He was unconscious, bleeding from a bad gash on the back of his head. Then I saw what the Daredevle spoon had done, and I winced. It was hooked deep into his cheek, so hard that the whole right side of his face was twisted out of shape.

"Is he alive?" Fred asked anxiously.

"I'm not sure. Let's get him ashore and get working on him."

I took over the motor again and drove us back to shore, not bothering to dock but pulling right up to the beach and lifting Wallace out. I laid him face down and pushed his back a couple of times, getting water out of his mouth. Then I rolled him faceup and checked the pulse in his throat. It was still going, so I concentrated on mouth-to-mouth. Fred crouched next to me, and her familiar light perfume was in my nostrils as I worked.

"What can I do, call an ambulance, what?" she demanded.

"Better," I said between breaths. "Take the cruiser and drive north to the Bull house; it's north of the bridge. There's a couple of OPP cars there. Put the siren on and drive slowly. Somebody will come out if you miss the house; it's seven or eight past the bridge. They'll radio, it's quicker."

"Right." She stood up and ran for the cruiser, backing it quickly and spurting away to the road.

I worked for another minute before I heard the siren start. Then it stopped a few seconds later, and I concentrated on Wallace. He started to breathe on his own, but he didn't open his eyes. He was badly hurt, and I swore as I stood up and rested for a moment. Dunphy was still out there somewhere, and Wallace was the only lead to him we had.

TWENTY-ONE

♦

The three cars came screaming into my driveway, the OPP cars first, then our own scout car with Fred in it. All the doors seemed to slam at once, and all three men came running toward me. Fred took her time. I guessed she was still shaken.

I stood up, and Anderson ran past me to stare down at Wallace.

"Jesus Christ, look what you did!" he said, pointing at the fishing spoon.

Werner laughed. "Fishin' as well as huntin'. Quite a morning, Reid."

"The boat hit him in the head," I said. If this case hadn't involved Fred, I would have gone along with Werner's joke, but I wasn't finding anything funny.

Kennedy knelt and fingered the gash on the back of Wallace's head. "Pretty solid thump he took," he said. He thumbed back Wallace's eyelids and stared at his pupils. "No difference in the size of the pupils, though. Maybe he's going to come around soon."

"Did you call the ambulance?"

"On its way. I guess we should get the son of a bitch inside," Werner said. "Keep him warm."

"Right. But in the meantime, he's left a car somewhere, maybe at the Marina. This is one of their boats.

Someone should check there. You might find Dunphy waiting for this guy. And close off both ends of the Harbour. We'll need four cars. One each on the highway, one each on the side roads north of the lake. He might try to duck out the back way."

"I'll get on it," Kennedy said. He turned to Fred. "One more time doing our jobs for us, huh? This guy don't marry you, he's crazier'n I thought."

"I'm going to," I said. "You're invited. Now let's get this guy inside."

Werner and Kennedy scooped up Wallace while I picked up the shotgun and opened the house door. They carried him in and laid him on the couch. Fred went upstairs and brought down a couple of blankets and a clean towel to go under his head. Then the other three took off. Anderson lingered on the step to get the last word in. "There'll have to be a full inquiry."

"See you there. Now go check if you can find Dunphy. You know what he looks like?"

He didn't bother answering that one, just turned away, rigid and righteous.

Fred stood looking down at Wallace. "Will he make it?"

"I think so. It takes more than a bump on the head to finish off a Georgia cracker as tough as this guy. Look at his right hand. Fingers missing, but he was still holding the motor with it, firing with his left."

She bent and lifted his right hand out of the blankets. "Lord, that's right," she said. "You know, I didn't even notice the bandage when he grabbed me. But he was holding a gun as well. It must have been hard for him."

"Tough," I repeated. "Don't worry about him."

She stood, lowered Wallace's injured hand, and faced me. "Honestly, Reid, I don't know how much of this I can handle."

I put my arms around her, and after a moment she softened, and we kissed very gently.

"But you will marry me?" I asked.

"Yes," she said, and we kissed again.

Behind us Sam whined. Fred let go of me and turned to him. "Don't worry. You're part of the deal." She laughed shakily and bent down to fuss him.

I knelt down and did the same thing, rubbing the scorched hairs on the back of his neck. "You're a part of a family, old son." I told him. "No more me and you against the world."

Fred was looking down at me, and she suddenly gave a little gasp. "You're burned," she said. "I thought you looked different, but so much was going on I didn't think about it. You're burned. Your eyebrows have gone."

"They'll grow back. I'll be my usual gruesome self in a couple of weeks, in plenty of time for the wedding," I promised. And then Wallace groaned.

We turned and saw his eyes fluttering open. He lay for a moment, and then his hands came up to the hooks in his cheek, and he whimpered.

I crouched beside him. "The ambulance is on its way. You'll be fine. They'll get those hooks out in no time."

He swore and closed his eyes.

Fred said, "Shall I make something, coffee, tea?"

"Tea, please." I grinned at her, trying to distract her from Wallace's pain. "My old man was a Limey. He made me a morning tea drinker."

Wallace groaned again, and I turned back and found he was touching the back of his skull. He took his hand away and looked at the blood on his fingers and swore again.

"The boat came around in a circle and clobbered you," I told him.

"I was in the water?" His mouth was distorted by the pull of the hooks in his cheek, and his voice was strained.

"You could've drowned."

He tried to grin but grimaced with pain and said, "You're gonna be sorry you pulled me in, cowboy."

"In the meantime, I'll still go to bat for you if you tell me where Dunphy is?"

254

He looked at me without speaking and then closed his eyes. I waited, and when he didn't speak, I gave him a prod with my finger. "Last chance for any kind of break, Wallace. If we don't get Dunphy, you're going away.

He spoke now, whispering sardonically out of his twisted mouth. "When I get out, you're dead."

I didn't bother getting into his verbal shoving match. He was beaten, all the ways there are. If brave talk was a consolation, he was welcome to it. There aren't many other comforts in jail.

Fred came to the door and made a little cup-and-saucer drinking gesture, not speaking. I nodded, and she turned back to the kitchen.

"You want a hot drink?" I asked Wallace.

"Got any bourbon?"

"You're in shock," I said, and he grunted out a laugh.

"An' I'm gonna be inside. No bourbon there. 'T kinda guy are you?"

"Canadian," I said. "I've got some good rye."

"Just so's it's eighty proof."

Liquor is the wrong thing to give an injured man, but I knew he was right. There would be no booze for him for the next few years, and besides, it might induce him to talk to me. I went out to the kitchen, leaving Sam on watch, and poured an ounce and a half of Black Velvet.

Fred frowned. "I didn't know you were a morning drinker."

"This is for Wallace. His last chance for a drink. He's going inside."

"You know that's no good for him?" We both knew it wasn't, but she's too strong to bother arguing with me. She just laid out the facts.

"It may not be, but it may be good for the investigation."

She shook her head doubtfully. "He's a bad person, but you shouldn't do anything to harm him any more."

"I know," I said, and took the drink back to him.

He looked at the glass and licked his lips, then grimaced with pain from his cheek.

"Pretty cheap ain'cha? What's this, an ounce?"

"That's fine for a start. They're going to want to do tests when they get you into hospital. Booze won't help."

He accepted the glass with both hands, holding it in his left and steadying it with his right as he tilted it gently into his mouth and lay with the whisky unswallowed for half a minute. Then he sank it and sighed. " 'F I tell you where Dunphy is, do I get seconds?"

"How will I know you're telling the truth?"

"You won't." His voice was harsh again. "Listen, don't jerk me around. This is my last drink for a while, anyways. Dunphy's in Toronto."

"Tell me where and let me make a call and I'll give you a double," I promised.

Now he opened his eyes and held the glass out to me. "Drink first."

I didn't take the glass, and he lowered it to his chest. "Okay, it's your liquor. He's in the big hotel near the museum. You know it?"

"What name is he registered under?"

He groaned. "I don' know. Jus' make the call and bring me that drink."

I picked up the telephone from the little occasional table next to my chair and dialed the homicide office in Toronto. My lucky day. Elmer Svensen was in.

"Hi, Elmer. Reid. Dunphy is registered at the Park Plaza under a phony name."

"Hold on." I heard him turn aside and issue a couple of crisp orders; then he came back on. "Good work. I've got some guys heading over there. Who tipped you off?"

"Mr. Wallace," I said, and then I had to give him a quick summary of the morning's efforts, edited down so that Wallace wouldn't get bitter.

"He singin'?" Elmer asked disbelievingly.

"In return for certain considerations, Mr. Wallace is assisting me in my inquiries," I said. It sounded like something out of Agatha Christie, but I needed Wallace working for me.

"I'll follow this up. Call me if there's anything new. The cadet here will pass messages."

"Go get him," I said, and hung up.

Wallace turned his head toward me, the red-and-white spoon dangling like some pagan ornament from his cheek. "Drink," he said.

"Right there."

I poured him a solid double and took it back. This time he tried to sit up but fell back, swearing feebly. "Head feels like it's fallin' off," he said. He sipped the drink and swallowed, lingering over it pleasurably.

I waited for about a minute and then asked him, "What's the tie-in between your outfit and young Michaels?"

He opened his eyes and blinked at me slowly. "I can't say for sure. Him an' Dunphy was thick when I joined up with 'em. Way I figure it, the kid's old man had made some kinda deal with Dunphy. Wanted the kid toughened up, off'cer material, Dunphy called it."

He sipped and then spoke again. "In the boonies, training, the kid was a candy ass. Couldn't run, couldn't hump, couldn't shoot. I could see he's the kind would fall apart when the killing starts."

"That's why you were on his case? I heard some of it when I was hiding up there."

"Boot camp I was s'pposed t' be running. 'Stead of that it was a goddamn kindiegarten. Yeah, I got on his case. Tried to give him some balls."

"What happened when I turned up? Did he tell you?"

Wallace tightened his left hand around his glass. "Yeah." He smiled, then winced with pain. "I had him doin' push-ups, an' he couldn't finish. So then he broke down, bawled like a baby. I told him to smarten up, his mommie wasn't gonna get him out of this. And he said she was. Just angry, like a little kid. So I worked on him a little, an' Dunphy wanted to turn the guys out to find you, only I didn't go for it. I figured you'd come in from the end of the lake. Went down there on my own and found your pack and waited."

He scowled and finished his drink. "Would've had you dead to rights only for that goddamn Indian."

"You brought the kid up here with you to find George?"

"Yeah." He extended his left hand wearily and let the glass drop to the floor. "The kid was feelin' bad about my hand an' all. So I said we should get back up here an' put things straight."

"And he came?" I had a dozen questions. How had they got in touch with Jason? Why had he gone along with them? Why had his father's girlfriend tried to get him out if the father wanted him in Freedom for Hire? And why did the father want him in the outfit, anyway? And had Wallace committed the two murders?

I came at the questions obliquely. "One of your Mexicans told me Dunphy had come north. That's why I headed up here. Why would he have said that?"

"Fuckin' spicks," Wallace said. "Should'n'a said nothin'."

And that was it. He closed his eyes, and when I tried to talk to him, he growled. "I'm tellin' you nothing. Pretty soon you'll have to tell me what I'm charged with an' read me my rights an' get me a lawyer. Until then, you've had all you're gettin'."

"I'll get around to all of that when you're in the hospital," I promised. "Right now, rest, but don't go to sleep. You have to stay awake."

He opened his eyes again and sneered. "I've been hit before," he said. "In the Tet offensive. Got blown up, shot, hit with mine fragments. I know about wounds."

It was an opening, and I took it. "I was there, too. Were you infantry?"

258

It didn't work. He looked at me for about thirty seconds and then rolled his head away from me and said nothing.

Fred brought in the tea, and I told Sam, "Keep," and went back to the kitchen with her.

"Did he tell you anything? I mean, like why he was trying to take me away in that boat?"

"Revenge," I said, and the ugliness of the thought burned me. "He wanted to get at me, not you. If it hadn't been for me, none of this would have happened."

She sat and drank her tea, not looking at me, and I raised one hand helplessly. "I'm so sorry about this, Fred. I've been alone for a long time, and I didn't expect what I do would affect anybody else. I've got to get out of this line of work."

She set her cup down and said, "Not for my sake, Reid. But how much longer can you keep on being lucky? When will somebody like him hurt you? Maybe kill you."

"It isn't like this very often," I said.

She pursed her lips and stared me down. "I've heard you say that before," she reminded me. I sat helplessly, returning her look as gently as I could.

"I'm sorry, babe, it's the only way I know to earn a living."

Then she got up and came over and put her arms around me. "I love you, Reid. I don't want some policeman knocking on my door telling me that somebody like that man in there has hurt you."

I held her tight, patting her back with my fingers. It was good. I hadn't realized how much I wanted someone like her close to me.

I kissed her hair, and slowly she turned her face, and we kissed properly. And then I heard the rushing of wheels on the gravel outside. We let go of one another and stood up and looked out the window. An ambulance was pulling in with an OPP cruiser behind it.

Fred opened the door, and I beckoned the guys inside. The ambulance men were carrying the stretcher, and when Wallace saw it, he snarled. "I can walk, dammit. You call this a wound?"

The ambulance driver was thirtyish and macho, chewing gum as he spoke. "It's your ass," he said.

Wallace swung his feet down off the couch and tried to stand. He buckled, and the second ambulance man tried to help him, but Wallace shoved him away. "I'll do it."

The supervisor looked at the hooks in his cheek. "Got yourself good," he said cheerfully. "Third time this week I've had guys with hooks in." Wallace ignored him and stood up.

The assistant hovered behind him as he walked out to the ambulance, and I briefed the OPP man. "His name's Wallace. He's charged with abduction, attempted murder. He hasn't been cautioned, and he's tough. Go with him and stay on your toes. He's bad news."

The constable was young. Most of his experience so far had been picking up pieces of people after highway accidents. He whistled in surprise. "Who'd he try to murder?"

"Me. Fired a couple of shots at me from a handgun. He was in the act of abducting this lady at gunpoint, and I turned up."

The guy swung toward Fred like a flower turning to the sun. "When did this happen, miss?"

"Minutes ago," she said. "Shouldn't you be out there with him? He's dangerous."

He wanted to impress her, so he started to unbutton his shirt pocket to take out his book. I reached out and held his wrist. "Your detectives have already seen him. Just caution the guy and watch him. We're making a statement later to Sergeant Kennedy or Sergeant Werner."

He recovered and said, "Yeah, sure," then to Fred, "You sure you're all right?"

"Perfectly. Thank you." She paid him off with a gorgeous smile, and he backed out of the doorway, beaming.

Fred stood next to me, and I put my arm around her as we watched the young cop climb into the back of the ambulance and sit facing Wallace, who had given up now that his gesture had been made and was lying on the stretcher. The assistant slammed the back door, and the ambulance left. Fred turned to me. "You didn't finish your tea," she said.

"Sounds good." I gave her a squeeze and then let her walk ahead of me into the kitchen. She threw out my part cup and refilled it from the pot.

"What now?" she asked as she handed it to me. She said it briskly, but I was sad to see how her usual buoyancy had been punctured. I felt guilty and angry at Wallace.

"I'm going to phone Toronto and tell Elmer Svensen all the details; then I guess we should go over to the hospital at Parry Sound and make statements. Then it's over and we can go on with our holiday."

"Promise?" she asked solemnly, and I nodded.

"Promise. I don't care if the police station burns down, we're going to take off on a trip, anywhere you want to go."

"Anywhere except Saskatchewan." She laughed. "I've never seen so much damn sky in my whole life. Not a tree, not a building, just flat land and sky forever."

I patted the couch beside me, and she came and sat, carrying her own teacup. "So what happened? One minute I'm talking to you and everything's fine, the next thing they've folded. What fell apart?"

"It was the producer's fault. He was so damn anxious to get the film under way that he took somebody's word that the extra money was going to come in."

"A verbal promise isn't worth the paper it's printed on," I reminded her, and she laughed.

"Yeah, I've heard that before. It's a Goldwynism, right?"

"Accurate, by the sound of it." I reached out my left hand and took hers, and she gave me a squeeze. "I'm sorry about what happened. I didn't think you were anywhere close."

"Forget it," she said. "It's good to be back despite the welcoming committee."

She was relaxing again, and I watched her with pride, as if I'd been responsible for it. She's a woman in a thousand, an actress who didn't bother dramatizing an event most people would dwell on forever. She would have made a hell of a good policewoman.

We sipped our tea companionably for a moment, and then the phone rang, shattering the mood. I set down my cup and took the phone. It was Elmer Svensen.

"Reid, glad I caught you. Is Wallace still there?"

"No, the ambulance just took him away, up to Parry Sound Hospital."

"Damn." Svensen clicked his tongue against his teeth. "I want to ask him some questions."

"He likely wouldn't answer. He clammed up tight after he told me about Dunphy. Any luck finding him?"

"No. A guy answering his general description was registered at the Plaza under another name, Brady. Yeah, that's it. Anyway, he checked out this morning. Paid in American dollars. I've got a couple of uniforms up there, but I don't expect to see him again."

"Wallace probably knew he'd gone. Listen, one big piece of news. The kid's father, Michaels, he's tied into Dunphy some way. You should talk to him."

"Tied in how?" Svensen asked, and he listened carefully while I gave him what Wallace had told me, about the training and turning the son into "officer material."

"I think I'll get someone checking the old man's business," Svensen said. "It's hard to get a handle on it. The original company is a mining outfit, but he's changed. The Mountie I checked with says he's into 'a bit of this, bit of that' kind of stuff. Nothing we can pin down, but

262

the Mountie thinks he might be involved with arms dealing."

"That makes sense. It would explain the Mexicans hanging around, Guatemalans, whatever."

"Did you think they could be Cubans?" Svensen asked.

I whistled. "No, I didn't. But they acted tough enough to be trained men, and the Cubans train their guys well."

"Complicated, isn't it?" Elmer said, and I nodded automatically. "I'm putting a couple of guys out at Buttonville Airport, at the Michaels company jet. Maybe the guy is going to head out from there, maybe even take Dunphy with him."

"Be smart to have some Emergency Task Force backup," I said. "Dunphy is tough, and he's a pro. If he gets ugly, a couple of shiny-faced detectives won't stand a chance."

"I'll take it up with the inspector," Svensen said. "Are you going to the hospital?"

"Yeah, we'll have to make statements. I can talk to Wallace if you want. What did you want to know?"

"The usual, I guess," Svensen said. "Where he was the night those two women were killed. Where he and Dunphy were headed so we can get the boys at the other end to pick up Dunphy. And see if you can get the OPP to get clearance for a blood typing in case it was him did that rape."

"I'll do my best, but he's cagey, and he won't want to tell me much. I stuck two hooks of a Daredevle spoon in his cheek."

"Should've been his ass," Svensen said cheerfully. "Anyways, just so you stopped him, I don't care how. Listen, Burke is coming up there. Turn Wallace over to him. He's good at interrogations. Won't harm a hair on him, just wear the bastard down."

"Good. As soon as I've turned him over, I'm heading out with Fred." I didn't bother telling him about Fred's involvement. He had enough on his mind right now.

"She back? Good news. Now you can have a real vacation," Svensen said. "Talk to you later," and he hung up.

Fred was looking at me, smiling. "Did you mean it, about taking off somewhere? Someplace they can't find you?"

"Promise," I said. "Somewhere quiet where we can start planning to make an honest woman of you."

She laughed. "Damn, and I was just getting used to living in sin."

"This is sinful?" I asked her, and kissed her.

"Must be," she murmured. "It isn't illegal or fattening."

I laughed and helped her up. "Let's go, lady. One more hour of talk and we're free as a breeze."

"You've told me that before," she said. "Let's hope you're right for once."

TWENTY-TWO

◆

We had a pleasant ride to Parry Sound. The highway runs close to the shore of Georgian Bay, passing over inlets and little lakes where early-morning fishermen were sitting in boats spinning for the big smallmouth bass that often surprise you this time of year. Hawks were starting to gather for their flight south, sitting on the phone wires beside the road, and the cottonwoods and birches were edging from green to gold.

Fred didn't say a lot. She sat back and enjoyed the view, reaching across every now and then to squeeze my hand. Sam lay on the back seat with his head down. I didn't turn to check, but I got the feeling he was watching us, a little jealous, maybe.

We reached the town, which was filled with cheerful summer tourists with sun hats and shiny noses.

The hospital is close to the center of town. It's small but modern, a low red brick building that reminds you of a city apartment. Knowing the way nurses feel about germs, I left Sam on the back seat of the scout car, winding the window way down for his comfort. Then Fred and I went up the steps and checked with the admitting nurse.

She was brisk, but she recognized me and grinned. "You here for our two-star patients, Chief?"

265

"Yes, please. We have to talk to the OPP detectives. Where are they?"

"They're over in emergency with the second man who came in. The doctor is taking those hooks out."

"How about the other kid? The one who was shot. How's he doing?"

"Just out of surgery. He was lucky apparently. Nothing serious was hit."

"Good." I smiled at her. "We'll go see the detectives."

We found Werner talking to a pretty black nurse who was laughing at some comment he'd made. When he saw us, he said to her, "If you could rustle up two more cups, these people look thirsty."

"I'll try," she said, and asked us, "How do you take your coffee?"

We told her, and she nodded and clicked off through a swinging door. Werner said, "Hi. The doctor kicked me out. Wan'ed to kick us both out until we gave him that guy's pedigree."

"What's he say about the injuries?"

"Says the bump on the head is superficial. They haven't X-rayed him yet, but the doctor doesn't think the skull's damaged. He just wants to get your handiwork off before they take a look."

"May be painful," I said. "The hooks had gone into the cheekbone, I think."

"Could be worse," Werner said.

"Yes." Fred was narrowing her eyes with concern. "It could have been his eye."

"No. Worse 'n that." Werner grinned. "Could've been me."

We laughed, Fred a little shamefacedly. "You have no heart," she told Werner, and he laughed again.

"Wore it out years ago in this job."

"The kid's out of surgery. The desk nurse said he's doing all right. Have you got anybody up there with him?"

Werner frowned. "No, just the uniformed guy. Left

266

him outside the operating theater. Told him to wait with the kid till I got back. He won't take a statement or anything. You wanna talk to Michaels?"

"It might be best. I shot him, but he knows me. He might open up a little quicker."

"Okay, we'll both go up." He ducked into the treatment room for a moment and then came back. "Gonna miss our coffee if we leave now," he said, then asked Fred, "Would you mind? The nurse'll tell you where we are. Could you bring it up, please?"

"No problem," Fred said. "It's not in my contract, but this is an emergency."

"Attagirl." Werner winked at her and then nodded me toward the door at the end of the hall. "He's on the third floor somewhere."

We went out to the elevator and waited a minute or so before one stopped for us. It held an orderly with an elderly woman in a wheelchair. The old woman tutted with annoyance as we got on. "Hurry up. Hurry up," she said, and the orderly looked at us and rolled his eyes.

We rode up two floors and got out, and the old woman tutted again. "I'll never get back to bed," she said.

Werner grinned at me as the doors closed. "Who in hell's waiting in bed for her? Burt Reynolds?"

"Has to be exciting, whoever he is," I said. I was winding down, happy that this case was almost over. Soon I would be free and Fred and I could head off somewhere unknown. Not Toronto, I hoped, although I would let her choose. Maybe we could drive west, around the top of the lake and on, north of Superior, somewhere really private.

We saw a uniformed man sitting outside a closed door. He was chewing gum and looking bored, but he stood up when he saw Werner.

"How's he doing?" Werner asked him.

"Fine, I guess," the constable said carelessly. "He's only been back half an hour and he's already had visitors."

"Visitors? Who?" Werner's playfulness had fallen away in an instant. "I thought I told you to watch him. They still here?"

The constable swallowed hastily. "No, the guy was just there a couple minutes. Said he was with the Mounties."

Werner was opening the door as I asked the officer, "Did you see any identification?"

"Well, no," the kid said. He was looking younger and more foolish by the second. "But he looked like a Mountie, fortyish, mustache, brisk way of talking."

"English?" I almost shouted the question, and the kid was too shocked to answer. "Was he English? A Limey?"

"Well, yeah." He had gone white. "Isn't he a Mountie?"

Werner suddenly reappeared at the door of the room and shouted, "Nurse! Nurse! Emergency."

I ducked past him into the room as he stood and bellowed. Jason Michaels was lying in the hospital bed with a red stain spreading through the front of his hospital robe. The sheet that Werner had jerked away was soaked in blood. I sprang forward and felt for the pulse in his throat. Nothing. The kid was dead.

I ran out of the room, grabbing the OPP man. "Give me your gun."

"What?" He whipped his pale face away from Werner. "My gun?"

"Now," Werner said. "That's an order."

The kid unholstered his pistol and handed it to me, fumbling it. I unsnapped the chamber and checked the load, then ran toward the exit. Werner was running the other way, toward the nurse's station by the elevators. I slammed the door open and leaped down the stairs four at a time. At the first floor I ran to the emergency treatment room. Fred was standing outside it with the nurse, taking a tray of coffee cups from her. She flashed a startled look at me when she saw the gun, and the nurse gave a small scream.

"Stay with Kennedy," I told Fred, and threw the door open. Kennedy was inside with the doctor, who looked around angrily at my entrance.

"Who the hell?" he started, but I cut him off, talking to Kennedy.

"Dunphy's been here, killed the kid. He may come for this guy. Shoot him on sight. I'll check outside."

"Right." He reached to the back of his belt and pulled his own gun, and Wallace laughed. "I got an alibi," he called.

Fred was outside the door, and I caught her arm and shoved her into the treatment room. "Stay put until I come for you; stay with Kennedy."

She opened her mouth to speak, but I shoved her, and she went, looking over her shoulder as I ran to the front of the hospital. The same nurse was on duty, and she looked up in surprise, then gasped when she saw the gun. "What's going on?"

"Did a fair guy, five nine, forties, mustache, come out of here?"

"No." She shook her head. "Not out or in. Haven't seen anybody like that."

"If you see him, don't try to stop him. Get on the PA and say, 'Dunphy's at the front door.' But don't let him see you do it. Okay?"

"If you say." She frowned at me and opened her mouth to ask more questions, but I was gone, out the door and around the building, looking for other exits. I whistled Sam as I ran, and in moments he was loping with me as I pounded toward a shipping door in the side of the building.

There was a linen supply truck there, and a hospital worker in a tan cotton coat was checking the load. He stared at the gun openmouthed. I gave him Dunphy's description, and, when he shook his head, gave him the same instruction I'd given the nurse. "Say Dunphy's at the west-side shipping door. Got that?"

"Yeah, sure." I left him chattering to the truck driver nervously and ran on, around to the back of the hospital, where a door opened into the parking lot. A car was pulling away, fast, leaning into the curve as it squealed around the corner and into the driveway that led to the street. I could see two men in the front seat, one of them turning to look back at me as I ran. Fair hair. That was all I could see at the forty yards' distance, but I sank to one knee and braced both hands for three quick shots at the rear of the car. I missed the tires, but I heard my bullets clang on metal. Maybe I'd found the gas tank at least.

My own car was parked at the front, and as I ran for it, I was able to see the other car whisk into a left turn and head out of town. But by the time I was in the car, they were out of sight.

I flew after them, Sam crouching beside me on the seat, bracing himself against the jolting of the drive. It was guesswork. They could have turned off on a dozen side streets, pulled into a driveway, and gone on their way when I'd passed, but I didn't think so. When you're running that hard, you use speed, not guile.

I tried the radio on the scout car. Unless George was back at work, there would be no answer, but it was the only chance I had of scaring up help.

An older voice answered, and I recognized Jim Horn, George's father. He's slow and methodical like most Indians, but he followed my instructions and patched me through to the OPP. Within seconds I was talking to the desk man at the local detachment.

"Reid Bennett, in pursuit of a red Mustang, license XXZ 790, south on Tracy Street, Parry Sound. I think he's heading for Highway 69. Fugitive is Dunphy, wanted for murder of a patient at the Parry Sound Hospital. I've lost sight of him, and he could be on the highway at this time."

"Gotcha." The desk man wasn't fluent in radio jargon, but he knew his job. He relayed the message to his own radio, then came back on for more details. I gave him what I had—the car had bullet holes in the rear, two men in it, armed and dangerous. Then I was at the highway and barreling south, hoping I was doing the right thing.

There were slow-moving vehicles in front of me, but I whipped the siren on, and they pulled over onto the paved shoulder, letting me by until I was out front, facing a mile-long downgrade, and at the far end of it I caught the flash of a red car.

I told the OPP and pushed my foot even harder on the gas pedal, but it was already flat to the floor, and I was hammering at 140 kilometers an hour, about as fast as the car would go. I swore and kept pressing, then lost the red car as it crested a slight rise in front of me.

I was there in seconds, facing another long pull downhill, but this time there was no car. And then I saw the turnoff on my right, leading down to the lake. I slammed into second gear, screeching the motor into a whine of protest but slowing enough to make the turn without rolling.

The road was unmade, and a cloud of dust still hung in the air. I plowed through it, praying that no innocent driver was coming the other way, hoping he would hear my siren if he was and would have enough brains to pull over out of my way. There were sudden twists and turns as the road went around big obstacles, and I had to stay in second and hammer the brakes for the curves, pushing the car and my driving skills to the limit. And then I broke through the trees and found the water ahead.

The red car was stopped at the water's edge, and the two men were at the end of a dock where a third man with a motorboat was waiting. Out beyond them I could see a floatplane bobbing gently on the roll of the water. The men glanced back but kept running, and I drove in to the very end of the dock and jumped out with my gun in my hand.

One of the men jumped into the boat, but the other crouched, and I saw the gun in his hand as I fired twice. I missed and dived and rolled sideways as his return fire clattered over my head. Four shots, close together. An automatic. It meant he had another four or five shots against the one I had left.

He was still crouching, both hands clutching his pistol, and it was a game of nerves as I lay and aimed at him, taking endless moments to calm myself and make the last bullet count.

Our shots must have crossed in midair. But I had the advantage. Lying flat, I was a smaller target. Mine hit him high in the chest, toppling him backward in the same instant a flurry of broken stone flicked into my face and ricochets whined over my head.

I jumped up, pointing my empty gun at the second man, but I was too late. He was already tugging at the pull cord of the motor. "Hold it right there," I shouted, and ran forward, stopping to grab the wounded man's automatic. I shouted, "Track," at Sam, and he bounded past me and leaped into the boat, grabbing the man.

The other man in the boat threw his hands up as I shouted, but the first one shoved him over the side of the boat and then turned to struggle with Sam, who was plucking at him, not quite fighting, trying to wrestle him off balance. He had a pistol in his left hand, and I shouted, "Fight."

Sam grabbed his gun hand, but he took the pistol with his other, too fast even for Sam to get hold of it, and snapped off a shot at me.

It hit me in the left shoulder, a familiar dull shock that numbed me and spilled me backward, dropping the automatic. Then Sam grabbed his gun hand, and he yelled in anger and lost his balance, going backward, over the side of the boat.

It was more than Sam could handle. He tried to hang on, but he was fighting an expert. It was Dunphy. I could see his bushy short hair as he came up, grabbing for air. Sam was still holding his arm, but he couldn't win. Dunphy could hold his arm under long enough to slow him, and he was working with his other hand, twisting Sam's choke chain. He would drown Sam. I sat up on the dock and painfully picked up the automatic with my good hand. As Dunphy surfaced, I shot him.

He sank, and in a moment Sam's head bobbed up. I called him, and he paddled quickly ashore and shook himself, then ran up beside me on the dock.

The other man was floundering in the water, swimming uncertainly toward the aircraft. I fired one more shot, into the water ahead of him, and it went skipping over the gentle waves toward his aircraft. "Swim back in or you're dead," I called.

Shouting was too much effort, but he got the message. He turned and swam back, and I recognized Jason's father.

"Grab Dunphy," I told him harshly. "He's in the water there." And I pointed with the muzzle of the automatic.

He did it, sputtering and kicking with the effort. I laid the gun down and patted Sam with my good hand. "Good boy," I told him. "Good Sam." He wagged his tail happily and then whined when he smelled my blood.

I opened a button on my shirt and stuck my left hand into it, having to lift it with my right. Then I sat and waited until Michaels waded ashore, dragging Dunphy. "Lay him on the dock," I told him, and I waited until he'd done it.

He straightened up, looking at me craftily. "Listen, I can make you a rich man," he said, but he licked his lips in fear. I hated him.

"Sit down and shut up," I told him.

273

He did it, still looking at me anxiously, but I got up and walked up to him, keeping back far enough so he wouldn't try anything. "Sam. Keep," I said, and Sam crouched in front of him, his eyes on Michaels's face.

I was getting weaker, but I made it to the car and turned off the siren, which was still sawing the air. Then I switched on the radio and called, and thank God, George Horn answered.

"George, Mayday. Three men down, including me. At the water, on a turnoff seven kilometers south of the Parry Sound exit."

"Right. Stay on the air." He left the radio, and I sat there, sinking into a daze. Then he came back on. "How bad you hit?"

"Shoulder," I said. "High. Collarbone, I think."

"Hold tight; they'll be there in a few minutes. Want me up there?"

It was almost beyond my power to answer, but I said, "No," and then added, "Thanks," and dropped the microphone.

TWENTY-THREE

◆

The chopper came minutes later. I'd passed out, but Sam's barking woke me, and I saw a policeman trying to talk to Michaels. I called weakly, and Sam came, the policeman hurrying after him over the sloping beach.

"You're hit," he told me.

"Cuff that guy to the wheel of this car and take the keys out."

He ran back for Michaels and brought him over to the car. Michaels was arguing until he saw me, then he shut up.

The officer put him into the car. Behind him I could see the ambulance attendant checking the other men on the dock. He soon moved from the first one I'd hit and concentrated on Dunphy. Good. He would make it. I guessed the other guy was gone.

I struggled out of the car and put Sam outside, telling him, "Easy." He looked at me and whined. He knew I was hurt. Then the policeman waved at the ambulance guy, and he came running up the beach toward me. That was when I let go.

The rest of the afternoon was like a replay of 'Nam. I remember being put into the chopper and then nothing more until I woke up to find Fred hanging over me, looking scared.

When I opened my eyes, she bent down and kissed me, on the forehead, as if she were my mother. "Hi," she said.

"Hi, yourself," I said, and then started throwing up.

Later she laughed about it. "I hope you're not getting allergic to me."

"Anesthetic. I'm sorry," I said. She was sitting next to me, holding my right hand. My left was in a sling, and I was bandaged up over the shoulder. "Will I play the violin again?"

"Never," she said, and added, "I hope," and laughed.

I squeezed her hand. "I'll be out tomorrow and we'll take a trip," I promised.

"A week," she said. "And then we sure as hell do take a trip."

I drifted off again, and when I woke up again, it was light outside. Fred was still sitting beside my bed, and Elmer Svensen and Inspector Burke were standing at the foot.

"Hi," I said. "Is there a drink here?"

"Just this stuff," Burke said, picking up a metal jug from the night table. "Hope it's not a urine specimen."

He gave me a paper cupful, and I said, "How's everything going?"

"Good." Burke nodded briskly. "Untangled the whole mess while you were nappin'.

"And?"

Burke almost purred. "Poetic justice. You know, living by the sword et cetera. Michaels was cooking up a big arms contract for some banana republic. Only he wanted to play both ends against the middle. He was going to hijack his own shipment, using his own private army, Dunphy's crowd, an' sell the same guns twice."

"Where'd the kid come in?" I was puzzled. "Surely a scam like that would be at arm's length. He wouldn't want his own kid involved."